A Be

AFTER THE FIRE

A captivating historical mystery set on Shakespeare's stage

JOHN PILKINGTON

JOFFE BOOKS

Revised edition 2020
Joffe Books, London
www.joffebooks.com

First published in Great Britain 2010

ISBN 978-1-78931- 314-7

PROLOGUE

PORT ROYAL, JAMAICA, 1670

The English captain stood on the quayside, sweating in the furious heat, and looked the traveller up and down. When he finally spoke he made no attempt to disguise his opinion of the sunburned, shabbily dressed man who stood before him.

'Yes, I'm bound for Bristol,' he grunted. 'I carry sugar and molasses. We're full to the gunnels, but there's a berth if you can pay for it. And I mean in good English money!'

The traveller smiled thinly. He had come a long way, and he was too tired to become angry, which was fortunate. His anger, once unleashed, was potent and deadly, but it was locked away in a part of his mind he rarely visited, and then only when the occasion demanded it. In the four years since he had been transported to the Indies he had learned not to waste his anger, but to nurture it and to value it. It was a powerful ally, one that had kept him alive.

'Will this serve?' He fumbled in his clothing and brought out a worn leather purse. As he loosened the drawstring, coins glinted in the harsh sunlight: not only gold guineas but French pistoles, Dutch guilders and other currencies that even the English captain barely recognized.

The captain showed his surprise. But if he had a mind to ask how this fellow came by such a hoard, he kept his mouth shut. There was enough there to buy a passage for the Lieutenant-Governor himself, and servants to boot. He merely nodded and glanced at the sun, which was mercifully beginning to sink.

'Loading's about finished,' he said. 'We sail at first light. I'll send a boy for your baggage.' He swung his gaze back to the sunburned man, who was stowing his purse away.

'There's no need,' the other answered. 'This is all I have.' He indicated a sailcloth bag at his feet, bound with leather straps. The captain glanced at it, gave a shrug, then turned on his heel and headed for the gangway.

The traveller watched him walk up the plank on to his ship. It was a large vessel, an old man-of-war converted to carry slaves from the west coast of Africa. Having crossed the ocean and shed its human cargo, the ship's hold had then been stripped to carry raw goods back to Bristol: the last leg of the 'Triangular Trade' that was making some Englishmen very rich.

If anyone in the busy port had noticed, they would have seen a hard expression on the traveller's features. For it was on a similar vessel to this that he had arrived at Port Royal in chains, half-starved and racked with scurvy. Had he been inclined to tell his story from that time onwards, few would have believed it. The animal struggle of the first months in blistering heat, enduring repeated lashings and vile food; the desperate escape that he and the boy had hatched, which took them to Surinam where the Dutch would have killed him, save for . . .

He drew a breath, gazing at the colourful crowd who thronged the quayside. This was the point where he usually left off remembering. But this evening, with the final leg of his return before him, he allowed himself to think upon it.

In his mind's eye he saw the wretched boy on his knees, pleading with their Dutch captors for mercy; small good it did him, for they spoke no English. And now, as if detached

from the scene, he saw himself: the innocent party, explaining in his fluent Dutch how he had been forced into escaping with this wicked young fellow, who was guilty of many crimes, while he was entirely innocent. He, a man of good family, had been falsely accused in the first place — merely for being in the wrong place at the wrong time! And he told how, during the Great Fire which had consumed London, he had been taken by the watchmen for a looter. Why, there was such panic in those terrible few days, he was lucky not to have been accused of starting the Fire himself, as others had been! But then, wasn't that just like the English, all bluster and shouting, and no common sense? And he had joked with the Dutchmen, winning them over with his story until in the end they believed his account. And he had stood in the boiling heat of the fort at New Amsterdam and watched the boy being dragged away, shrieking curses at him.

He pushed the memory aside. What did it matter now? He had survived in the New World, he had even prospered. In Port of Spain he had shed his disguise along with his Dutch accent and become an Englishman again, a traveller who had seen enough of the colonies and was eager to return home. He smiled to himself, watching the surly captain moving about the deck of his ship, barking orders. It had amused him to see the fellow form a low opinion of his prospective passenger, before the sight of a purse full of gold wiped the smirk from his features. Had the captain known what else the man carried, let alone what he meant to do with it, his shock might have been greater.

As if to reassure himself, the traveller bent down, loosened one of the straps about his bag and slid a hand inside. His fingers probed under layers of clothing before closing about a little earthenware jar, its lid sealed tightly with gummed linen. He felt its hardness and its coldness, and a tiny point of light appeared in his eyes as he gazed out across the harbour, to the sparkling sea beyond.

The contents of the jar had cost him an hour of hard wrangling with a Portuguese trader he had met in a stinking bordello on the edge of the jungle, back in Surinam. That much was evident to any casual observer, who might have seen two men haggling over their mugs of watered rum before striking a bargain. What no one saw was what followed later on a lonely forest path, after the transaction had been completed: the Portuguese sinking to the ground, coughing blood, his hands clawing feebly at the legs of his assailant. The other man had stepped back unhurriedly, wiped his stiletto on the leaves of a tree, and slipped it into its sheath.

He had waited until the Portuguese choked out his last breath, then stooped to retrieve the money he had handed over from the fellow's pocket. Then he had seized him by the heels and dragged him into the undergrowth, where the jungle creatures would find him. After that he had turned away and walked back to the settlement, to begin his homeward journey.

And now, standing on the quayside, his features creased in another smile, for at last his journey's end was in sight. A few weeks crossing the ocean, and he would be on English soil again. He imagined the cool rain of autumn, and the welcoming door of a tavern. He would order 'lamb's wool' — hot, spiced ale with roasted apples; he could almost taste it.

And there was something else he tasted, but that was a different kind of sensation. That particular appetite required other means of gratification, which would have to wait. But then, he was in no hurry; for he had the means now to do all that he wished.

CHAPTER ONE

Mr Joseph Rigg was dying; and he was very good at it.

So Mistress Betsy Brand thought, as she stood smiling in the wings. As Banquo in the company's new production of *Macbeth*, Mr Rigg was showing off his skills to full effect. The handsome actor with the smouldering eyes, much admired by ladies of fashion, staggered back as the Three Murderers bore down upon him.

'Let it come down!' shouted First Murderer. He brandished his dagger, and a gasp went up from the pit.

'Oh, treachery!' Rigg cried. As the dagger sank into his chest, he called to the cringing figure of his young son.

'Fly, good Fleance — fly, fly, fly! Thou mayst revenge—'

The boy backed away, hands raised in horror, then turned and fled into the wings. As he passed by Betsy he stuck his tongue out at her. Betsy pulled a face back, then returned to watching Mr Rigg, who fell to the boards clutching his chest. A gout of fake blood spurted across the stage, drawing another gasp from the packed theatre.

'O slave . . .' his voice faltering, Rigg stretched an imploring hand towards the audience. Then he groaned, and let it fall. As his body went limp, a huge sigh went up.

'Shame!' a gallant shouted from one of the side boxes, prompting a snort of laughter from his friends. But from the pit came a chorus of hisses, followed by loud applause. Eyes still on the corpse, the crowd paid little mind to the words of first, second and third murderers who now closed the scene. As the trio made their exit, a murmur of approval rose: Rigg had stolen the show again.

Backstage, all was bustle. At a blast of the stage manager's whistle scene-men hurried to their stations, and the two halves of a new backdrop were slid into place along their grooves. 'The Palace of Forres!' The voice of Downes the prompter rang out, and quickly the scene was set for the banquet, when Banquo's ghost would make his appearance to terrify Macbeth.

Betsy turned to make her way back to the Women's Shift. It was the opening performance at the Dorset Gardens Theatre, of Mr Betterton's revival of the Scottish play, and the response was good. There would be a second house and a third, at least. She nodded to the actors in the next scene as they gathered for their entrance. Then a figure in a splendid crimson gown pushed her way through, blocking Betsy's path.

'Mistress Brand — how well you look as a witch!'

Aveline Hale, in the role of Lady Macbeth, wore a broad smile; but her eyes failed to match it. Mistress Hale despised the theatre. Like many another pretty young woman with no fortune of her own, she made little secret of the fact that she was on the stage merely for as long as it took to attract a rich man, preferably with a title. After all, who could forget that young Nelly Gwyn, the King's favourite mistress, had started as an orange-wench in the theatre, and was now set up in her own smart rooms in St James's Park?

'Cods,' Betsy muttered to herself. Her own well-shaped body was concealed under a heavy black cloak, her blonde hair beneath a matted horsehair wig. Her white make-up had been overpainted with streaks of grey, and patches of black drugget served as missing teeth. She was First Witch, the most important role she had yet been given, after two years with the Duke's Company. And she had no intention of making a poor fist of it.

There was a stir, and Mistress Hale turned aside as did the others, to make way for Mr Thomas Betterton himself. For who else would play Macbeth?

He was in his mid-thirties now, the greatest actor in England and leader of the company; handsome and dignified, and free of the vanity so many players exhibited. Betsy Brand's heart always warmed when she saw him, as it had from the very first time she set foot in the old Duke's Theatre. That was back in the converted tennis court in Lincoln's Inn Fields, when Thomas and his wife had taken pains to put the nervous young actress at her ease. She smiled at her mentor, who nodded in return before his gaze swept the assembled company. 'Well, my friends,' he said. 'Shall we to the banquet?'

From the auditorium, the theatre orchestra struck up with a flourish. Betterton took the arm of Mistress Hale, and stepped out on stage to a roar of approval.

Betsy made her way through the cluttered scene-room. One of the ex-soldiers who served as a doorman was standing nearby, having a quick smoke. When he saw Betsy he threw her a lecherous grin, before snuffing his pipe out. Betsy walked to the stairs that led to the Women's Shift. Her next entrance came after the long banquet scene, and she had time to spare. She was about to climb the steps when someone spoke softly to her from behind.

'Mistress Brand . . . always a pleasure.'

Betsy turned, to find a pair of cold blue eyes gazing into hers. 'Mr Tripp,' she forced a smile. 'How do you do?'

The eyes belonged to a stocky man in a golden-brown periwig and a tabby suit edged with lace. Samuel Tripp the playwright had been haunting the theatre for the past week, badgering Mr Betterton to read his new play. He made Betsy an ironic bow.

'I do very well.' His eyes did not leave hers. 'And allow me to say I deplore the way your talents are being wasted in a witch's part. You should've had Lady MacDuff, at the least.'

The compliment meant little to Betsy, for she knew the man too well. 'But I relish the role, Mister Tripp,' she answered. 'And my good friend Mistress Rowe plays Lady MacDuff admirably.'

Tripp's mouth curled slightly. 'Rowe has but a modest talent compared with yours,' he replied. Betsy saw the glint in his eye, then started as his arm shot out to grasp her by the waist. 'Let me wait upon you after the performance,' he murmured, bringing his face close to hers. 'I'll buy you a supper at Lockett's, and after we'll—'

'Another time perhaps.' Betsy reached round her back, gripped the man's hand and removed it with a strength that took him by surprise. Then she stepped backwards and fixed him with a wry look. 'I'm not one of your Moorfields jilts, Mister Tripp,' she snapped. 'I'm an actress.'

The other gave a little yelp of laughter. 'Why, so you are!' he agreed. 'And as buxom and pretty as any in London! Now leave off this show of modesty, and admit you find me a handsome fellow!'

'Oh, flap-sauce!' Betsy's chest rose, and those who knew her better would have advised the playmaker to tread warily. 'I'm not your plaything.'

'Indeed she is not!'

The voice that rang out from a short distance away was as familiar to Tripp as it was to Betsy. They both turned to see the figure of Joseph Rigg, the front of his linen shirt still stained with blood, standing at the top of the steps to the Men's Shift.

Tripp drew a breath and took a step backwards. 'My dear Rigg! A splendid death scene, if I may—'

'You may,' Rigg interrupted in a droll voice. 'Yet I dislike the way you manhandle Mistress Brand. Good witches are so hard to come by.'

Relaxing, Betsy curtsied to Rigg as graciously as her voluminous cloak would allow. She was not unused to such treatment. Samuel Tripp was but one of many who had

earned the nickname 'blowflies of the tiring-room', and who regarded all actresses as fair game.

Tripp favoured Rigg with a thin smile. 'As indeed are good supporting players, sir,' he answered. 'Surely it's time you stepped out from Betterton's shadow, and demanded a bigger role for yourself?'

Rigg, who was known to possess a formidable temper, met the man's expression with his famous smouldering eyes. But the door to the Women's Shift flew open, and a female voice called: 'Betsy! Where've you been? I need you to help pin me.'

The diminutive figure of Jane Rowe appeared half-dressed at the top of the steps. From the stage, Betterton's voice rose, ranting at the appearance of Banquo's ghost. The spectre was played by a hireling who doubled for Mister Rigg.

The tension was broken. With a smirk at Betsy, Tripp turned and walked out by the nearest door, which led to the side boxes. Betsy glanced up at Rigg, but the player was already half-inside the Men's Shift. 'Where's the boy?' he called. 'I'm for a glass of claret.' The door slammed.

Betsy climbed the steps. 'What was that about?' Jane asked. 'Did Tripp put his paws up your cloak?' But with a shrug, Betsy dismissed the matter. She and Jane had joined the Duke's Company at the same time. Two nervous young actresses, somewhat abashed at the brazenness of the world they had stepped into, they had agreed to look out for each other from the start. Seasoned performers that they now were, they still did so, though their backgrounds could scarcely have been more different: Betsy was from a good family who disapproved of her choice of profession, while Jane was the daughter of a butcher who was grateful for the fifteen shillings she brought into the household, almost every week.

Female voices spilled from the open door of the Women's Shift. As Betsy and Jane entered, an older woman, a hireling who was playing Third Witch, looked round. 'Mistress, can you help me keep this headgear from falling over my eyes?'

As Betsy helped the woman secure her hat, Jane brought her a small mug. 'Take some Hungary water,' she said. 'You'll need a restorative before you cast your spells.'

The door opened and the youngest member of the company, Louise Hawker the tiring-maid, entered, looking flustered.

'Louise!' Jane threw the girl a pained look. 'You promised to mend Lady MacDuff's gown, yet it's still torn. Now there's no time to do anything but pin it.'

Louise blinked. She was a frightened little creature, not made for the hurly-burly of backstage life. Yet she was a good seamstress and a hard worker, who had even won the grudging respect of Aveline Hale. Just now, however, she looked not merely nervous, but fearful.

'Your pardon, mistress,' she answered. 'I'll do it at once. I got distracted.'

'Whatever's the matter?' Betsy asked, still attending to Third Witch. 'You look as if you've seen Banquo's ghost!'

'Well, perhaps you'll not wonder at it, when you hear what I've just heard,' Louise replied. 'There's bad news from Covent Garden. Remember Long Ned, the African? He's dead!'

A silence fell, so that Betterton's voice could be heard all the way from the stage: '*Behold, look! How say you?*'

'Dead!' Jane looked shocked, as did the others. Everyone knew Long Ned, the handsome ex-slave from the Indies, who worked as an attendant in the men's bagnio — the public bathhouse. Ned had formerly helped out at the old Duke's Theatre as a scene-man, and, if truth be told, had earned something of a reputation as one who was sought out by certain wealthy ladies for purposes of private pleasure.

'How did you learn of it?' Betsy asked.

'Mister Prout and Mister Hill were at the bagnio when it happened,' Louise answered. 'They've just come in. They say Ned dropped right to the floor, without warning. Within minutes he could neither move nor speak — then he was dead!'

There were more reactions, but most of them were muted. James Prout, the company's dancing-master, was a regular customer at the bathhouse. Julius Hill was an actor who had recently joined the Duke's Company, taking small roles. Since he was playing the doctor in *Macbeth* he was not needed until late in the play, so would have passed the early part of the afternoon at his leisure. Neither man was given to spreading empty rumours, and hence the report must be true.

'Well, Long Ned will certainly be a loss to the bagnio — and an even greater one to some of our sex!' a young actress observed in a shrill voice. There were one or two sniggers, but Jane Rowe frowned at the woman.

'That he will, mistress,' she said. 'But some of us valued him as a friend. He had his failings, what man doesn't? Yet he was kind and gentle, which are rare enough qualities in Covent Garden!'

The young actress pouted and turned away. But other heads were nodding. Jane moved off to finish her dressing, while Louise Hawker took a pincushion and set to work on Lady MacDuff's gown. Gradually, normal hubbub resumed. The news of Long Ned's death, Betsy thought, would provide entertainment about Covent Garden and the western suburbs for a day or two, then fade as quickly as the memories of her performance as First Witch. Such was the nature of the world she inhabited. And though she loved acting, there were times when she wondered whether there might be some less fickle activity that would suit her. She sighed, and thought upon her opening lines for the next scene.

Meanwhile from the stage, Macbeth's voice floated up: *They say blood will have blood . . .*

An hour later, the Duke's Company took their bows to enthusiastic applause and left the stage. At once the scene-room was filled with a milling crowd of actors, hirelings, and the hangers-on who always gathered at this time. Outside in the pit, the orchestra played a cheerful finale. Betterton, Mistress Hale and the other leading players received the praise of their fellows with good grace, then went to their rooms. Now the gossip flowed, and it was soon apparent which topic was on people's lips: the demise of Long Ned at the bathhouse. And as witnesses to the event, James Prout, the gangling dancing-master, and the supporting player Julius Hill, were soon the centre of a small circle of listeners, including Betsy.

'I swear, the fellow dropped like a stone!' Prout said, savouring his role as purveyor of fresh gossip. 'I was barely a dozen feet away from him, in the tepidarium. I saw him pass by with a pail, heading for the steamroom — fit as a fiddle he looked, as always — then, *voilà*! The poor man drops to his knees, shaking like a leaf. Hardly uttered a sound, I swear! See now . . .' the dancing-master turned to Hill. 'Julius will tell you, for he was closer than I. Is it not so, my friend?'

Hill was still in his costume, and looked uncomfortable. An unassuming man, with few of the airs and graces affected by other players of limited ability, he merely nodded. Then seeing some elaboration was expected, he cleared his throat.

'Whatever befell the man — some strange condition or sickness, perhaps — it was indeed sudden,' he said. Then seeing one or two anxious faces, for the dreadful plague of 1665 was yet a recent memory, he added: 'Yet none that we need fear, I'm sure. By good fortune there was a physician nearby who examined the man, and found no token.' He shrugged. 'I can only think that Ned had some weakness of the heart . . . perhaps he had overexerted himself of late.'

That brought one or two smiles. And clearly disliking the role of narrator, Hill looked pointedly at James Prout. 'Very likely,' the dancing-master agreed. 'Whatever befell poor Ned must remain a mystery.' He shook his head. 'Such a sweet fellow . . . always so obliging.'

He glanced round, but there were fewer listeners now. The company was beginning to disperse, as people drifted away to change. William Daggett the stage manager appeared, fearsome with his bristling moustache, and scene-men went off to their tasks. The orchestra had finished, and musicians were clambering up the stairs, talking loudly.

Betsy stood watching the noisy, colourful pageant, the happy release of tension that always followed a successful performance. The death of a former hired man, even a popular one like Ned, would not dampen the company's spirits. She was on the point of following Jane, who had already gone up to the Women's Shift, when her eye fell upon a man standing by a side door. One of the scene-men, a burly, taciturn fellow named Thomas Cleeve, was staring at the retreating back of James Prout . . . and her eyes narrowed. It may have been merely the poor light of the backstage area, but to her mind Cleeve looked not merely affected by the news: he looked frightened. His face was pale, and as Betsy watched he put a hand to his forehead and rubbed it. Then, sensing someone was watching him, he met Betsy's eye, and at once hurried out.

Betsy turned, only to see Samuel Tripp, who had appeared from nowhere and was smiling at her. Throwing the playmaker a withering look, she began to climb the steps again.

* * *

Betsy and Jane Rowe left the theatre together, by the lane that led through the ruins of Salisbury Court towards Fleet Street. The rebuilding of London was proceeding apace, and many new houses had already risen from the ashes of the Great Fire. But here outside the walls, the picture was somewhat different. During those terrible few days, not so long ago, the flames had leaped the city's west wall and consumed the old precinct of Whitefriars, as far as the Temple. And yet, Betsy mused, fortune was an odd jade: for she and her fellow actors had benefited from the sweeping away of the old buildings. In the intervening years, Mr Christopher Wren himself had designed the Duke of York's fine new theatre by the Thames, in the gardens of burned-out Dorset House. The Dorset Gardens Theatre, as most called it, was best approached from the river, where its white portico and pillars loomed over the better-off theatregoers who arrived by boat. But that was not Betsy's route: like most of the actors, she took her chances in the noisy, muddy streets, threading her way to her home on the edge of the ruins, in what was now known as Fire's Reach Court.

'Harlots! Foul painted jades! The Lord will strike ye down dead, as he has your dark-skinned friend!'

Neither Betsy nor Jane had noticed the wild-eyed man who stood in the street, raising his fist to the cloudy autumn sky. In the other hand he clutched a tattered Bible. The fellow wore threadbare clothes of twenty years back: black doublet and breeches, grey worsted stockings and an old crowned hat. As both women turned, he pointed a trembling finger at them.

'The bellows are burned, the lead is consumed by the fire! For the wicked are not plucked away: reprobate silver shall men call them, because the Lord has rejected them!'

'Mr Palmer,' Betsy smiled, 'have you been here all afternoon? It looks like rain again.'

Praise-God Palmer glared. 'Let it pour, woman — I'll not flinch from the Lord's work! Repent while ye may, and forsake this house of wickedness!'

But Jane Rowe drew her bertha about her shoulders and glared back; she had no time for Palmer or his rantings. 'Take yourself off, you dirty black crow,' she retorted. 'We're two honest women who earn our bread as well as any—'

'Honest women?' the man echoed. 'Ye who show yourselves in undress like the harlots of the town? Shame on ye! The Fire was God's judgement. Did He not burn this warren to the ground? Yet ye flaunt His will by building a new theatre upon it, a house of bawdy and devilment!'

'It's the Duke of York's theatre, Mr Palmer,' Betsy answered, as Jane tugged her sleeve. 'Perhaps you should direct your anger towards Whitehall . . .'

'You mock me!' The ranter took a step forward, but Betsy did not move; she knew the fellow's wrath never went beyond verbal assault. In her years on the stage she had

grown used to his presence outside one or other of the two royal theatres, the King's Playhouse or the Duke's. Whatever the season, Palmer would assail those who went in or out, deriding them for their sins, taking their jibes and threats without flinching. More than once he had been set upon by drunken rakes, and once by a couple of bad-tempered actors who blamed him for the poor house. Yet next day he was back, bruised but undeterred, shouting his scriptures with renewed energy.

'Come on, Betsy dear.' Jane was walking off towards Fleet Street. Beyond the rebuilt St Bride's, carts clattered over the Fleet bridge. Betsy was about to follow when a thought struck her.

'You're mighty quick with the news, Mr Palmer,' she said. 'Who told you Long Ned was dead?'

Palmer stared at her, then broke into a smile that was more like a grimace. 'Black crow, am I? Then mayhap I soared above Covent Garden and spied his miserable end for myself!'

'Miserable end?' Betsy echoed. 'Why do you say such?'

But Palmer's thoughts ran their own course, which few could have fathomed. He drew back, raising his Bible as if to ward her off. 'Question me not, woman, for ye have strayed from the path, and your mind is as a dark fog! Get ye into yon church, fall upon your knees and beg forgiveness — only then can ye hope to find salvation!' He paused, then: 'As for the wretch ye called Long Ned, he has paid for his sins. The Lord has struck him down like a wand. Let others take heed of it!'

'Betsy!' Jane called from the end of the lane. Betsy raised a hand to her then looked round, but Praise-God Palmer was striding off. She watched him until he rounded the corner of the theatre and disappeared.

Something in what he had said nagged at her; but try as she might, she could not think what it was.

CHAPTER TWO

The two women parted company in Fleet Street. Jane would cross the bridge and go into the city by Ludgate, to her father's house near the Butchers' Hall. Betsy turned westwards, picking her way through the press of folk on foot and on horseback, who threatened to splash her with mud. She crossed the street, avoiding a hackney coach which rolled by, and reached the corner of Fetter Lane. The spire of St Dunstan's-in-the-west loomed overhead, one of the few churches that had escaped destruction. Next door, the Fire Court sat every day at Clifford's Inn, settling the myriad disputes which had arisen over property, boundaries and the like. In a short time, London had passed through the terrors of fire and pestilence; was it any wonder that men like Praise-God Palmer saw the hand of a vengeful God in it?

She turned into Fetter Lane, then walked to the corner of Fire's Reach Court. Here was the limit of the Fire, where the old timber-framed houses stood crowded together, a remnant of the suburbs of Tudor London, and a time before the present King Charles's grandfather, James Stuart, had ridden down from Scotland to claim his throne. Not so far back after all, Betsy mused: the Duke's Company still performed the plays of that age . . . which set her thinking about *Macbeth.*

By now she had reached the door of her own lodgings, and lifted the latch.

It was evening, and the sight of a scuffed leather bag in the hallway told her that Doctor Thomas Catlin was home. Her expression softened as she looked down at it: the most precious thing her landlord owned. Indeed, apart from this tumbledown old house, it was almost the only thing he owned.

Then, Tom Catlin was a rare man: a physician who had stayed in London during the plague, and not fled like most of them. He had paid a cruel price for his courage: his young wife had died of the infection. His response had been to move out of the city and to work even harder, often for little payment. And though the plague was but a memory now he still drove himself in the same manner, and as a consequence was permanently short of money. When the actress daughter of his old friend William Brand had approached him seeking lodgings close to the Duke's Theatre, he had obliged her by fitting up the best upstairs chamber. As for Betsy, she had found in her landlord a true and firm ally; and when the Duke's Company moved away from Lincoln's Inn Fields, she had kept her lodgings at Catlin's. What she had not expected was that her feelings for Tom would grow from friendship to something stronger — though she had never admitted it to him. That, she was certain, would be the ruin of a good relationship.

She opened the parlour door and went in. A good fire burned in the grate, and Tom, in his shirt sleeves and russet waistcoat, was at his desk. As she entered he looked up and raised his eyebrows.

'I see there's no need to ask how *Macbeth* was received. A good house?'

'You need not fear, Doctor,' Betsy answered with a smile. 'I'll be able to pay this month's rent!'

Catlin nodded sagely. 'That's well,' he muttered, picking up a fistful of papers. 'Do you mark these bills? I may decide to flee one of these nights and take to the Bermudas, before my creditors lose all patience!'

Betsy kept a straight face. 'You mean the Bermudas off the Strand?' she asked, naming the lawless little community about Maiden Lane, which claimed old rights of sanctuary. 'You'd not be the first gentleman to seek refuge there. But if you mean the Bermudas across the seas . . .' She struck a ridiculous pose, and made her voice crack with grief. '. . . Heaven forbid, for I would never see you again! What then would I do?'

Stifling a smile, Catlin grunted and tossed the papers across his cluttered desk. 'You'd be in clover, that's what,' he answered. 'Fill the house with actors, who'd wreck the place and drink what's left of my cellar dry.' He picked up a mug from the desk, and frowned into it. 'Talking of which . . .'

At that moment the door flew open and a tall, scarecrow-like woman lurched in. Catlin ignored the interruption, but Betsy raised her brows.

'Peg — whatever's the matter?'

Peg Brazier, Catlin's twenty-year-old cook, servant and maid-of-all-work, threw her a scathing look. Her red hair stuck out from the edges of her cap, while her eyes fixed upon her employer. 'There's a butcher's man been at the door wanting his account settled,' she snapped. 'What was I to tell him? Answer that!'

Tom tilted his mug and peered at the emptiness within. 'What did you tell him?' he asked.

'I lied, what d'you think?' Peg retorted. 'But he'll be back, and unless you've a hoard of guineas I don't know about under the floor, next time he'll bring a beadle with him!'

Betsy held up a hand. 'Fear not,' she said. 'For I owe a month's rent — and I can pay it.'

'But how long will your few shillings last, mistress?' Peg asked, with a toss of her head. 'Until you're out of work again?'

'We'll have supper,' Tom Catlin said, turning to Peg and putting on his voice of authority. 'If my memory serves, there's a pair of roasted pigeons—'

'There's boiled leg of mutton and a bowl of anchovies,' Peg told him. 'After that, the larder's bare!'

'Then be so good as to serve them up, *Miss* Brazier,' Tom growled. The title generally applied to a whore or a kept woman, one of many insults the two of them had honed in their years of barbed discourse. But Peg, magnificently indignant in her workaday frock with sleeves rolled, rose above it.

'Would Master care for a jug of Navarre to go with it?' she demanded, as if the new French wine were within the reach of Catlin's pocket. But before he could reply, Betsy spoke up.

'My purse can't stretch to Navarre, Peg, but if you'd care to send out for a pint of Malmsey . . .'

Peg blinked and caught Catlin's eye, looking less like a servant now, and more like his daughter. Tom Catlin and his wife had not been blessed with children. Instead, they had taken Peg off the streets at the age of ten, before she could be sold into prostitution. And though she seldom had a kind word for the doctor, her loyalty to him was set in stone.

'Lord — what's the occasion? Has someone proposed marriage?' Peg asked. Then she reddened. 'Your pardon,' she muttered, suddenly flustered. 'I've gone too far again.' And with that she turned and fled.

Betsy and Catlin's eyes met, and both burst out laughing.

* * *

Later that evening, having dined on boiled mutton and anchovies, Betsy and her landlord talked for longer than usual. The reason for that emerged during supper, when Betsy learned that not only did Tom know of the death of Long Ned, but he was the physician who had been called to attend him.

'I was across Russell Street, at Will's,' he told her. 'A boy from the bagnio came running, said someone was poorly. But by the time I got there, there was naught I could do. Some sort of paralysis had set in, which in the end seemed to stop the fellow's lungs from working. He died of asphyxia.' Tom wiped his mouth on a napkin, and leaned back in his chair. 'An odd business,' he said. 'A fit, healthy young fellow expiring like that . . . very odd indeed.'

'You think there's more to it than the onset of some fever?' Betsy asked, with growing interest.

'There was no fever. Nor did the man complain of any ache or pain, in fact he barely uttered a sound. Just stiffened from head to foot, staring at nothing.' Tom's frown deepened. 'It occurred to me he might have been poisoned, except that I know of no toxin that would have such an effect. And when I made enquiry of the proprietor, he said Ned hadn't taken anything since breakfast save a little ale, and others had drunk from the same jug.'

Suddenly, Betsy recalled the words of Praise-God Palmer, who seemed to have learned of the death so quickly, despite the fact that he never went near the bathhouse. He naturally regarded such a place, which was frequented not only by whores but also by young men for similar hire, as another on his list of houses of sin and devilment. She told Catlin of the exchange outside the theatre, which prompted a shrug.

'News travels fast from Covent Garden, does it not?' he murmured. He lifted his cup of Malmsey and drained it. 'I confess I'm uneasy about this death.' He met Betsy's eye. 'You knew the man, didn't you? Would you say he was the sort who made enemies?'

'He may well have done,' Betsy answered. 'For despite his gentle nature, it was no secret what services he performed for certain wealthy patrons . . . of both sexes.' When Tom said nothing, she went on: 'But why do you ask? Surely you don't think he was murdered?'

'Well, it's hard to see how, since there wasn't a mark upon him. But then I didn't examine him very closely. Perhaps I should have done.'

The two of them sat in silence, mulling the matter over. Then recognizing the distant look in Tom's eye, Betsy rose from her chair. 'Time I went to my bed,' she said with a smile. 'There's a part in a new play, that of a grand lady, that Betterton would have me reflect upon.'

Coming out of his reverie, Tom Catlin rose from the table in turn. 'What play is that?'

'It's a comedy called *The Virtuous Bawd*,' Betsy told him, 'by that fop-doodle Samuel Tripp.'

Tom knew well enough what Betsy thought of Tripp, and was swift to divert her from that topic. 'Then I'll wish you goodnight,' he said quickly, and picked up *The London Gazette*.

* * *

The next day's events, however, would drive all thoughts of Tripp from Betsy's mind. For though the second performance of *Macbeth* had packed the house like the first, it would soon become talked of for reasons which the Duke's Company would prefer to forget.

There was no doubt now that the play was a success. And if at times Mr Betterton's version of it strayed from Mr Shakespeare's, as far as the Dorset Gardens crowd was concerned that was all to the good. The added scenes, along with the music, turned a dark play into something closer to an opera, giving the cast ample opportunity to show off their singing and dancing. Each act closed to thunderous applause, and by the time Act Five ended, the air of satisfaction backstage had turned to one of jubilation. It was clear the play would run for longer than the customary three nights. And what was more, wags in the company joked, since the man had been dead for over half a century, there need be no benefit night for the author!

The cast took their bows to cheers and shouts of approval, even from the rakes in the galleries, before crowding into the scene-room. This time, instead of going off to their closets, Betterton and other leading players stayed to join in the general celebration. Hangers-on were even more in evidence than yesterday, along with a sprinkling of actors from the rival King's Company, eager to share in the spoils. Glasses of a passable claret soon appeared, along with a keg of ale for the scene-men. To the wry amusement of Betsy and Jane, even Aveline Hale was in expansive humour, the reason for which soon became clear.

'Mr Betterton!' she cried, elbowing her way through the chattering throng. 'Is it true what I've heard . . . that we are to play before the King?'

The company's leader turned to her. 'More than likely, madam,' he answered. 'His Majesty has made it known that he wishes to see the play. I await his pleasure.'

Mistress Hale's smile widened in delight, prompting droll looks from some of her fellow actors. The doormen and scene-men, puffing on their pipes, grinned and clinked mugs. But if anything, the news was welcomed even more by the supporting actresses, and not merely because any of them might attract the attention of King Charles or one of his friends: should Aveline Hale make her catch, she would be gone from the Duke's Theatre, leaving room for others to advance themselves.

'It's an ill wind, I suppose,' Jane Rowe observed cheerfully, taking a pull from her cup. 'And if an orange-wench can bear the King's bastards, why not a butcher's daughter from Cheap?'

'You'd hate being anyone's kept woman,' Betsy said dryly. 'As would I . . . even the King's.'

'In time, perhaps,' Jane answered with a sly look. 'But I'd make the best of it while it lasted.' She lowered her voice. 'Now then, look who's about to try his luck.'

Betsy followed her gaze to see that Joshua Small, the chief scene-man, had left his fellows and was making his way towards them.

'Don't go!' Jane hissed under her breath. While Small's feelings for her were obvious to everyone, Jane had already made it plain to him that his attentions were unwanted. There was only one man Mistress Rowe cared about, and he was in the Fleet Prison for debt. But her other would-be suitor, a handsome enough fellow, was not one to give up easily. As he drew close, Jane spoke to Betsy out of the side of her mouth.

'Small by name, small of brain,' she muttered. 'Why don't he leave me be?'

Then both of them started. From a short distance away had come a thud, followed by a commotion. Heads were craned, as everyone tried to discern the cause. Quickly the crowd shifted, as a circle widened in the corner nearest the door to the forestage. Actors, hirelings, hangers-on, all were now taken aback at sight of the burly scene-man, Thomas Cleeve, lying sprawled on his back with a frightened look in his eyes. There was a moment of confusion before some stepped forward. The first was William Daggett, the stage manager, who called loudly to everyone to stand back.

'Give him air!' he cried, and dropped to one knee beside the supine figure, who seemed to be shaking. Most did step back — in fact, for reasons of their own, several people chose this moment to move away. Betsy, on the edge of the circle, saw that James Prout was one of them. Some of the actors, including Joseph Rigg and Aveline Hale, also decided this was a good moment to head for the tiring-rooms. Others stood about, wondering if some altercation had broken out between the scene-men, or whether the fellow was merely drunk. But now Thomas Betterton arrived and bent down beside Daggett, peering at the fallen man.

'Cleeve, are you badly hurt?' He asked. When the fellow merely mumbled incoherently, Betterton turned to his stage manager. 'What happened?'

Daggett shook his head. 'I don't know, sir.' He glanced up quickly, searching the crowd. Joshua Small was pushing his way forward to stand beside white-haired Silas Gunn, the oldest of the scene-men, a loyal servant of Betterton's for over a decade. Both men looked down at Cleeve, non-plussed by the event.

'Did any of you see what happened?' Daggett asked. Small shook his head, while Silas Gunn spread his hands.

'Nothing happened, master,' he answered in a bewildered voice. 'One moment he's taking a drink, then he jerks a bit, drops his mug and keels over. No reason for it that I could see.'

'Well, he can't seem to move,' Daggett said worriedly. 'One of you'd best go and fetch a physician.'

Then it was that Betsy Brand, staring down at Cleeve, recalled the man from the previous day, apparently shaken by the news of Long Ned's death. And in a moment, she knew somehow that what was happening to the scene-man was identical to what had happened to Ned. Quickly she stepped forward.

'Send a boy to Doctor Catlin's house in Fire's Reach Court,' she said. 'If he's home, he'll come at once.'

Betterton and Daggett looked at her, but knowing her neither would question her judgement. Betterton nodded to Joshua Small, who hurried off.

'Tom!' The stage manager brought his face close to Cleeve's. 'It's Will Daggett . . . can you hear me?'

The scene-man was trembling. It was clear that something was terribly wrong with him, but none could guess the cause. Suddenly he whimpered. 'My toes . . . I can't feel 'em!'

A murmur went up from the watchers, as portly John Downes the prompter appeared. Kneeling down on the other side of Cleeve, he held a mug to his lips. 'Take a mouthful, Tom,' he said. 'It's good Nantes—'

But Cleeve's only response was a groan. His arms and legs were twitching uncontrollably. 'I'm sinking,' he said, and threw a terrified look at Betterton. 'For the love of God, sir, can't you help me?'

The great actor, humble in the face of the man's desperation, gritted his teeth. 'In heaven's name, is there nothing to be done?' he asked Daggett.

'It's beyond me, sir,' the man muttered. 'I can only think he broke his back when he fell, or his neck.'

At that Cleeve rolled his eyes to meet Daggett's. 'Aye . . . the neck,' he said in a whisper. And now the company watched in dismay, as all at once the man stopped moving.

'His legs are stiff,' Downes exclaimed. 'His arms, too!'

Not knowing what else to do, Daggett slapped Cleeve's cheeks. 'Tom!' He shouted, and shook the man by the shoulders. 'Hold on, lad, the doctor's on his way.'

But Cleeve did not seem to hear. His eyes no longer saw: the pupils were dilated, fixed on nothing. And as one, the watchers — from Louise the tiring-maid to the few actors who, like Betsy and Jane, yet remained — grew still, sensing the presence of death. As they gazed, Cleeve's breathing slowed until it was too faint to detect, so that Daggett had to press his ear to the man's chest. Then he sat up, and turned to Betterton with a grim expression. A silence fell.

The great actor bowed his head, and others followed suit. Downes the prompter got stiffly to his feet, looking shaken. One of the women sniffed. And to everyone's surprise, a tear fell from gruff Will Daggett's eye, and rolled down to his bristling moustache.

Twenty minutes later Doctor Tom Catlin hurried into the theatre, only to learn that for the second time in as many days, there was nothing he could do.

* * *

It was a subdued company who gathered in the empty auditorium a while later, to hear Betterton utter a few consoling words. Some had already left; for if truth be told, Tom Cleeve had not been liked by many. He was a close-mouthed fellow who seldom smiled, and was known to become pugnacious when drunk. Yet the death of any man was a loss, and the way in which he had met his end was a shock. The doormen and scene-men, standing in a solemn group, seemed stunned by the event. Finally, after dismissing the remainder of the company, Betterton turned to Tom Catlin, who still stood by.

'Doctor, will you aid us? Can you make arrangements to have the body removed?'

'I can.' Catlin hesitated. 'Is there a family?'

'I believe so — wife and children both,' Betterton answered, and his brows knitted. 'It would also set my mind at rest, to know precisely why Cleeve died.'

'I've given you my opinion, Mr Betterton,' Catlin said quietly. 'The man died from an asphyxia.'

'But how?' The other countered. 'What brought it on?'

'I'm not a surgeon.' Catlin shrugged. 'Perhaps someone more skilled than I should examine the corpse.'

'Yet you are a friend,' Betterton said, and turned to Betsy, who stood near. 'At least you are Mistress Brand's friend, and she has always spoken highly of you.'

Catlin made no reply, but glanced at Betsy, who had been burning to speak. She seized her chance.

'Mr Betterton, there's something you should know,' she said. And quickly she told of Cleeve's behaviour the day before, adding that the way he had died seemed very like the way Long Ned had met his end at the bagnio.

Betterton looked taken aback, but the doctor was nodding. 'It's most odd,' he agreed. 'I was the one called to the *hammam* when the man collapsed. He fell over quite suddenly, as Cleeve did, for no apparent cause. From what I've learned, his symptoms were similar.'

'What are you implying, sir?' Betterton asked sharply. 'That there's some pestilence abroad?'

'I think not,' Catlin replied. 'Yet the more I turn the matter about, the more I believe something is amiss.' He hesitated. 'Were the two victims known to one another?'

'They may have been.' Betterton was frowning. 'I dislike the way this moves, Doctor. Are you suggesting a more sinister explanation?'

'I don't know what to suggest, but I'll find out what I can.' Catlin turned to go, adding over his shoulder: 'I'll seek leave to examine the body, and speak with you again.'

But as he went he caught Betsy's eye, and a look of understanding passed between them. And somehow she too knew that there was a link between these deaths, though its cause was hidden. She also sensed that it was important, and that it must be uncovered; and more, Mistress Betsy Brand wanted to be the one to uncover it.

CHAPTER THREE

The next morning Betsy was woken by Peg coming into her room with water for washing and a bowl of curds for her breakfast. She remained long enough to tell her that the doctor had left the house already and that she was off to market, before stalking out.

Betsy sat up, as the memory of yesterday's events flooded back. After a while she rose and began to dress, thinking of Betterton's last words as she took leave of him outside the theatre. He had been walking to the Duke's stairs to take a boat when Julius Hill hurried up to ask whether the company would play the next afternoon, as usual.

'Indeed we shall!' Betterton had told the actor brusquely. 'The best thing this company can do is to give an even better performance tomorrow than we did today!' Then he had turned away from Hill, to gaze at the grey waters of the Thames. 'In any case,' he added, 'the King himself may pay us a visit. We must remain on our mettle.'

So to everyone's relief, *Macbeth* would take to the stage for the third time; and little trace would remain of Tom Cleeve, whose body was taken away to his parish of St John's in Clerkenwell. Joshua Small, with a speed that surprised some, had already approached Will Daggett to suggest a replacement scene-man: his own younger brother.

It's an ill wind indeed, Betsy thought. In fact the only alteration in her routine was that Betterton had sent a link-boy with a message the previous night, asking her to come to the theatre in the morning. This was unusual, since no rehearsal had been called. So with curiosity aroused, she arrived at the Duke's an hour later, to find a small group gathered in the scene-room.

Betterton was there, along with William Daggett, Downes the prompter and James Prout the dancing-master. There was someone else: a fat, unsmiling man in a brown coat and heavy boots. Then Betsy remembered: he was Gould, the dour constable of Farringdon Ward Without. It seemed the law was now taking an interest in Cleeve's death.

'Mistress Brand!' Betterton greeted her. 'I have a request to make of you.' Taking her arm, he drew her aside. 'It's a somewhat delicate matter: I would like you to visit Tom Cleeve's widow in Clerkenwell, on behalf of the company.' And when Betsy showed her surprise, he added: 'No doubt she is in distress, as she's likely in dire need. I'm desirous to send someone of tact and discretion.'

'Perhaps a gift of money would be of best use to the woman,' Betsy observed.

'Indeed, and she shall have it.' Betterton put a hand in the side pocket of his black coat, and brought out a purse.

'Give her this with my blessing. I'll send a man with you, for protection. It's' — he hesitated — 'the district she lives in, is not one to be visited by a woman on her own.'

Betsy knew as well as anyone did that like many of the suburbs, Clerkenwell was a notorious haunt of prostitutes. But it occurred to her that in visiting Cleeve's widow, she might learn something that had a bearing on his death. And indeed, Betterton's next words showed that he had anticipated that.

'Furthermore,' he said, lowering his voice, 'if there's anything you can find out that might help put an end to the rumours that are already springing up, I'd be grateful.'

'What rumours are those?' Betsy asked.

'That there's been foul play, carried out by someone with a grudge against the Duke's Company.' Betterton was frowning. 'It's well known that Ned Gowden, to give him his proper name, was once employed by me, as Tom Cleeve was. It's probably nothing to be alarmed about, but . . .' he shrugged. 'As you know, there are some at the King's Theatre who resent any success we have. Of course, I would not accuse Killigrew or any of his actors of anything unlawful. But they're not above spreading falsehoods . . .' he trailed off, then brightened. 'I almost forgot. Doctor Catlin sent word to me a short while back: he's got permission to look over Cleeve's body. Perhaps he can discern something.' He glanced towards the constable, who was watching them. 'Now, I have matters to attend to. Will you do what I ask?'

With a nod, Betsy took the purse. And a short while later she was making her way through the narrow, crowded lanes north of Holborn, to emerge in Cowcross Street, Clerkenwell.

The man Betterton had sent with her as protector was the old scene-man, Silas Gunn. Betsy was relieved: she had half-expected it to be Joshua Small, who would have seized the opportunity to speak of Jane Rowe with her closest friend. Silas, by contrast, said little until the two of them entered Turnmill Street. Here, even at this hour, the trulls plied their trade; and now the old man startled Betsy by taking her arm.

'There's no need to panic, Silas,' she told him, breaking into a smile. 'I knew some of these women when they worked the streets near the old theatre. Unless, that is, you wish to pose as my *rum cull*?'

Silas blinked. Though his workaday world was the same as Betsy's, his manners were those of a bygone age, before the Civil War, when the word 'actress' had not yet been heard in England; when rumours of the first King Charles's French queen, Henrietta Maria, performing in a court masque had scandalized London society. With a look of embarrassment, he withdrew his arm and said: 'I pray you, Mistress Brand, nought was further from my thoughts!'

But Betsy's smile widened, and taking the old man's arm again, she drew him close. 'It was a joke,' she told him. 'And in truth, there's none at the Duke's I would rather have as my escort than you!'

The old man opened his mouth, then closed it. He did not speak again until the two of them had walked the length of the noisy, refuse-strewn street, past open doors where painted jilts lounged. Some laughed at the sight of Betsy Brand in her good sea-green cloak, leading an old man by the arm. But though one or two made lewd remarks, others recognized Betsy and greeted her. By the time they turned out of the lane, Silas was shaking his head.

'Lord, Mistress,' he muttered, 'I'll never hear the last, if word of this gets out!'

'I quite understand,' Betsy said, keeping her face straight. They had stopped at the entrance to a dim, narrow alleyway. 'Now, if this is Cooper's Court, I think we're here.'

Gunn nodded. ''Tis Cooper's. And according to Josh Small, Cleeve's house is the farthest one.'

The two of them walked to a door at the end of the closed alley and knocked. For answer, there came the howling of a child, before the door creaked open and a blowsy, sallow-faced woman in a faded taffeta dress appeared. For a moment she and Betsy stared at one another, before recognition dawned on both.

'Hannah?' Betsy's eyes widened. 'Is it you?'

'Betsy Brand.' The other woman gazed at her, then lowered her eyes. 'You'd best come in.'

* * *

They stood in Hannah's small, dingy kitchen while chaos reigned about them. In one corner, a pair of tiny barefoot boys fought over a broken chair-leg, shrieking insults at each other; in another, a baby in a soiled smock howled at the top of its voice. What furniture there was sagged with age, though so little light came through the dirty window it was hard to see anything very clearly, which was perhaps a blessing. Sensing with relief that his presence was not required, Silas Gunn told Betsy he would wait outside. As the door closed behind him, Hannah Cleeve gestured with a listless movement towards the only serviceable chair. As Betsy sat down, Hannah picked up the wailing baby with one hand, loosened the top of her dress with the other and put the child to the breast. Whereupon Betsy explained her reason for coming, and brought out the money Betterton had given her.

She had not expected Hannah to show gratitude, but the woman did not even look relieved. She took the purse, hefted it in her free hand and shoved it in a pocket. Then she raised her eyes to meet Betsy's.

'So . . . you've worked with Tom these past weeks, and you never knew I was his wife?' she said in a hard voice.

The room stank appallingly, but Betsy could bear it. What shocked her was the change in Hannah's appearance. She had known her two years ago as Hannah Beck, one of the prettier trulls who worked the Rose Tavern, by the King's Playhouse in Brydges Street. The Hannah she knew was loud-voiced and lively, as eager for a bawdy song as she was for a mug of mulled sack with the actors. Now . . .

'I didn't know, Hannah,' Betsy told her. 'Tom never spoke of you. In fact, now I think upon it, he never spoke about anything much.'

Hannah sniffed. The dark patches under her eyes spoke of a lack of sleep, while a yellowed bruise on one cheek told a more sinister tale.

'I had to get him staggering drunk to do it,' she said, and gave a grim smile. 'Fetch him to the altar, I mean. See, I was carrying his child.' She jerked her head towards the boys in the corner, who were still fighting. 'What I didn't know was, there'd be two of 'em.'

Betsy glanced at the boys: it was obvious now that they were twins. She smiled and indicated the baby. 'And now, there are three.'

Hannah's face clouded. 'She's not Tom's,' she muttered. 'I still work the lanes now and then . . . half of what that buffle-headed sot earned at the playhouse, he spent in the tavern!'

A weariness seemed to come over the woman, whereupon Betsy got to her feet. 'You sit,' she said. 'Perhaps I should go.'

Hannah did not argue, but sank down on the chair. The baby lifted its head, and quickly she put it to the other breast.

'I'm glad of the money,' she said after a moment. 'Only I'd be obliged if you told no one of it. As far as folk round here know I'm penniless. That way, Tom'll get a parish burial.'

Betsy nodded — then, quite suddenly, Hannah began to talk.

'I don't run into many theatre folk now,' she said. 'When I think back it seems they were good times, when the Duke's was in Portugal Row by the Fields, and Nelly Gwyn was at the King's. Now I hear she's got her own house, even her own servants. Did you know that?'

'I did,' Betsy answered.

'They told me there was a bit of a party,' Hannah went on. 'And Tom fell, cracked his skull.' She grimaced. 'Was he soused?'

'I really can't say,' Betsy said after a moment. 'The room was crowded . . . I didn't see him fall.'

'But you saw him die.'

Hannah's tone was sharp. Betsy returned her gaze and nodded. 'It was quick. I'm sure he didn't feel much pain.'

But Hannah dismissed that impatiently. 'What I'm asking you, Betsy, is this: is there something they're not telling me?'

'Why should there be?'

'Because for the past week — maybe longer — Tom was scared witless, that's why!'

Betsy felt her pulse quicken. 'Scared of what?'

'Of who, more like,' Hannah said. 'That's what I'd like to know. Some rook or biter he'd cheated, or owed money to — I don't know what lay behind it, and I don't care. But if he died by another's hand there's men I can call upon, would slit the devil's throat if I asked them to!'

'Whatever Tom died of, it wasn't by any means I could see,' Betsy told her. 'He was among his fellows when he keeled over. There were plenty who witnessed it.'

'Well, it seems mighty strange to me,' Hannah said. 'Of late, 'twas like he was looking over his shoulder — when he wasn't sousing himself. Jumpy as a hare, too. The night before he died he was gibbering like a bedlam fool. I couldn't get a scrap of sense out of him. He even talked about doing a flit, to the Bermudas.'

The baby shifted on her lap, and Hannah glanced down. 'It wouldn't be the first time he'd fetched up in that warren,' she muttered. 'He had a foggy past behind him, did Tom Cleeve.' Looking up at Betsy, she added: 'Did you know 'twas me got him that place at the Duke's new theatre? First honest job he'd had in years!'

Betsy shook her head.

'Aye, even if I had to lift my skirts for free, to seal the bargain,' Hannah said in a harsh voice. 'But it paid off: at least we had a wage coming in . . . and now, this!'

She was a bitter woman. But Betsy would not summon words of comfort, for she knew how empty they would seem. In any case, it seemed Hannah had more to say.

'So you take my meaning, mistress,' she went on. 'If you hear of anyone who was dogging Tom, I'd be obliged if you'd send word to me.'

In her mind, Betsy had a clear picture of Tom Cleeve, standing by the scene-room door staring after James Prout, and looking badly shaken by the news of Long Ned's death.

'I'll help you any way I can, Hannah,' she said thoughtfully. 'Yet you make me curious: you say Tom seemed terror-stricken, the day before he died?'

Hannah gave a nod. 'It's no use asking why, for I don't know. Whatever he was blathering about made no sense.'

'What was he blathering about?'

'Ned Gowden,' Hannah replied, and frowned. 'You remember Long Ned?' When Betsy gave a nod, she added: 'That's why I knew 'twas all gibber, for he hadn't set eyes on that cove in years.'

'Then they knew each other?' Betsy asked.

'Knew each other? They were thick as thieves at one time,' Hannah told her. 'And thieving's the right word: what those two got up to don't bear thinking about!'

Clearly Hannah had not yet heard of Long Ned's death. Then it was hardly a surprise, stuck here as she was with her children. Fashionable Covent Garden may have been only a mile away, but it seemed like another country. Betsy decided to break the news.

'Long Ned died,' she said.

Hannah jerked as if she had been struck. 'When?'

'Two days ago, in the bathhouse in Covent Garden. He was working there.'

The other stared at her. 'I like not the sound of it,' she said, becoming agitated. 'I thought 'twas nothing, Tom babbling about Ned, I mean. He spoke of the Fire, too; but who doesn't talk of that, or dream of it?'

The baby had finished feeding and rolled her head sleepily. Hannah got heavily to her feet, carried the child to a corner of the room and laid her down. The twins had stopped fighting, and were looking at her expectantly.

'I better feed these, too,' she said.

Betsy moved towards the door. She had much to think upon; but when she turned to make her farewell, Hannah was gazing levelly at her. 'I thank you for coming here,' she said. 'And if there's more to tell, I'd be glad to hear it . . . I mean, from you.' She paused. 'You're one of the few I'd trust.'

With a smile, and a last look around the grim little room, Betsy opened the door and went out.

Silas Gunn was standing outside, puffing on his blackened pipe. 'You women've had a fine old talk,' he mumbled. 'You didn't forget to give her the money, did you?'

But Betsy walked off down the alleyway as if she had not heard. Somewhat crestfallen, the old man stumbled after her.

* * *

It was almost midday, and there was only an hour before the start of today's performance, but Betsy did not go directly to the theatre. Instead, she took leave of her escort by Holborn Bridge, telling him she had forgotten something. Silas nodded and trudged off down Shoe Lane, whereupon Betsy hurried along Holborn, passed through Holborn Bar and within minutes was in Fire's Reach Court. But when she opened Tom Catlin's door, there was no bag in the hallway.

Peg appeared from the kitchen. 'You've missed him,' she said. 'He's been in and out . . . told me he was going to the theatre.' She frowned. 'Is it right, what I heard? One of your lot fell down, stone dead?' Then seeing Betsy already turning to go out, she called: 'It's not something contagious, is it?'

* * *

By the time Betsy reached the Duke's there was no time to look for Tom. The theatre was filling up, the orchestra tuning their instruments. The stage was aglow, its great candle-hoops lit and hoisted to the roof. Backstage, scene-men stood by to raise the festoon curtain, while hirelings milled about in costume. There was a new face among the scenemen, and Betsy guessed that this was Joshua Small's brother. She was hurrying towards the Women's Shift when a voice hailed her. She turned to see William Daggett fixing her with one of his fearsome stares.

'I was going to fine you for lateness, Mistress,' he said. 'Only Mr Betterton says you were on an errand for him.'

'Will you tell him I would speak with him after the performance?' Betsy asked. And without waiting, she began to climb the steps. But a figure emerged from the Men's Shift, and once again she met the eyes of Mr Samuel Tripp.

'Mistress Brand . . . I sought you earlier, but you must have been detained,' he began. 'I'm desirous to speak of your role in *The Virtuous Bawd*.'

Betsy frowned: she had not given Tripp's play a thought. 'Later, sir,' she answered. 'I'm in haste,' and before he could speak she disappeared inside the Women's Shift.

After that, all other matters were driven from her mind as she began preparing once again to play First Witch.

* * *

Act One was a triumph, as was Act Two. To the delight of the packed house, the witches howled and danced, Macbeth strutted, Lady Macbeth plotted and King Duncan was murdered. Act Three began, and now it was Banquo's turn. In cloak and wig, perspiring under her witch's make-up, Betsy stood in the wings with Jane. She had not intended to watch Mr Joseph Rigg expire again, partly because Samuel Tripp was lurking backstage, looking as if the Duke's were performing one of his works instead of Mr Shakespeare's. But the Women's Shift was crowded this afternoon, since Aveline Hale had decided to favour the others with her presence. The rumour that the King himself might come to the play persisted, even though there had been no sign of His Majesty. Hence there was more excitement than usual in the house. Betsy and Jane sensed it as they watched the Three Murderers make their entrance, daggers at the ready.

The murderers were an oddly matched trio, on stage and off. First Murderer was played by a brash young actor named George Beale, famously ambitious, who felt the role was beneath him and lost no opportunity in telling people of it. But then, at least he was a regular company member who could count on a weekly wage. Second and Third Murderer were hirelings, who had to take whatever work they could get: one of them tall and bony, the other a squat little fellow. As a consequence, their appearance on stage always occasioned laughter, until Mr Rigg's fine performance as Banquo quelled it. It was no secret that George Beale hated appearing with the other two men, whom he considered inferior creatures.

But today the atmosphere was electric, as once again First Murderer cried 'Let it come down!' and raised his dagger. Again the tiresome boy playing Fleance ran off stage, pulling faces; again the murderers performed their grisly task, and once more Banquo staggered, clutching at his chest. Blood spurted, the audience sighed, and the stricken man cried out. This time, however, perhaps to achieve a more dramatic effect, Rigg lurched towards the pit before falling to his knees and stretching out a trembling hand. Then the celebrated actor groaned and collapsed, his hand falling limply to the boards.

There was a moment's silence before applause rang out, louder even than yesterday. First, Second and Third Murderer had to shout to be heard. George Beale spoke his closing line — 'Well let's away, and say how much is done!' — and the three men hurried off, to some good-natured booing from the side boxes. Then as they entered the wings, Betsy heard the tall hireling say to his fellow:

'The devil . . . Rigg forgot to say *O slave*!'

It was true, though few had noticed; but it hardly seemed to matter, for Rigg had stolen the show again with his death scene. Betsy and Jane exchanged glances, whereupon there was a stir from behind. Both looked round to see Joshua Small, gazing out to the stage with a frown. 'The dunderhead,' he muttered. 'He's gone and fallen in front of the curtain line!'

They looked, and saw for themselves. Seemingly carried away with his performance — did he think the King might be watching, after all? — Rigg was not lying in his usual spot, but several feet forward, on the forestage. Had this been rehearsed, scene-men would have been standing by to bear his body away, so maintaining the illusion of death. But it was not rehearsed, and no one was ready. With a curse, Joshua Small took a step back and called out urgently.

'Will! Come here, quick!'

His brother had been standing in the scene-room watching more experienced hands at work. Nervously, he hurried up.

'We'll have to carry him,' Joshua said. 'You take his legs.'

Will gulped. 'Can't he get up and walk off?'

The other let out a muffled curse. 'Don't argue! Follow me, and do what I say!'

And watched by Betsy and Jane, along with others who had gathered in the wings, the two Smalls walked out on to the stage and took positions at either end of Rigg's motionless body. At Joshua's signal they lifted him up, whereupon, in his eagerness to get out of sight of the audience, Will Small started off in the wrong direction. Rigg's feet slipped from his hand to land with a thud on the stage, prompting a roar of laughter from the pit. Voices rose and fingers were pointed as, red-faced, the fellow grabbed the feet again and waited for his brother. Fuming visibly, the older Small moved forward at a brisk pace, and without further mishap Banquo's body disappeared into the wings, followed by loud applause and more laughter.

In the scene-room, however, no one was laughing. William Daggett had appeared with a face like thunder, while actors and backstage folk alike tried to keep their faces straight. Will Small's employment at the Duke's Theatre looked as if it were likely to end the day it had begun.

But Betsy's eyes narrowed: for suddenly, instinctively, she knew that something was wrong. Rigg had been laid gently on the floor; but instead of getting up and chiding his bearers for their clumsiness as everyone expected, he remained still — apart from his limbs, which were trembling, while his eyes rolled in their sockets . . . and then at last, the penny dropped.

A hireling woman screamed, while men darted forward, everyone staring at Mr Joseph Rigg — who, it now transpired, was not acting at all.

He was really dying.

CHAPTER FOUR

A numbness seemed to settle upon the company, as they stood about the hushed scene-room. Actors and actresses began appearing in various states of undress, and there were gasps of disbelief as the news spread. Quite quickly, two things became clear. The first was that Joseph Rigg was apparently stricken in the same manner as Tom Cleeve had been only the day before. The second was that the performance might have to be cut short, even though the palace screens were already in place and Macbeth, Lady Macbeth and their attendant lords were about to make their entrance.

When Rigg was carried into the scene-room, Thomas Betterton had been among the first to notice the man's condition. William Daggett was another. But even as the stage manager hurried forward, Betsy Brand moved quickly to Betterton.

'I think Tom Catlin's in the playhouse,' she said.

Her mentor gazed distractedly at her, before his eyes fell upon Silas Gunn, who was staring down at Rigg alongside the dumbfounded Small brothers.

'Go and seek Doctor Catlin . . . he's likely in the gallery. Bring him here, quickly!'

Silas shook himself and moved off as John Downes the prompter appeared, wearing a sickly expression. Betterton addressed him at once.

'We cannot continue. The play must be halted!'

Downes swallowed, then nodded. 'Will you tell them, sir? I think it's best . . .'

After a moment, Betterton signalled his agreement. He glanced at Aveline Hale who was standing close by, apparently horror-stricken. 'Mistress Hale,' he began uneasily, 'are you unwell, too?'

Mistress Hale's eyes were fixed upon Joseph Rigg, who was mumbling incoherently. Then, without warning, her eyes closed and she fell into a faint. Luckily, Julius Hill, who was standing nearby, caught her swiftly.

'Take her away!' Betterton cried. Betsy's old mentor looked angry now; and in his anger he was always decisive. She watched as, drawing himself to his full height, he walked out on to the forestage.

The audience had grown restive at the delay in proceedings. When Betterton appeared, a crackle of applause broke out, before realization dawned that something was amiss. Then the man raised a hand, and silence fell. In a sorrowful tone he spoke of Mr Joseph Rigg's being taken gravely ill, and of the company's great distress. In view of the circumstances . . .

A murmur rose, people turning to one another. But though there were some voices of discontent, particularly from fashionable city men in the side boxes, there was no danger of serious protest. Betterton's presence had a sobering effect, so that Betsy, watching from the wings, breathed a sigh of relief. And now Doctor Tom Catlin came into the scene-room with Silas Gunn in tow, took in the situation quickly, and dropped to his knees beside Rigg.

Suddenly, it seemed that this was like some gruesome repeat performance — not of Rigg's death scene as Banquo, but of Cleeve's real death the day before. Again, the gradual stiffening of the body, again the desperate look in the man's eyes as his voice failed, then finally his breath . . . and Tom Catlin, his mouth set tight, could do nothing but take Rigg's hand, and watch his rapid descent. Finally he felt the great artery in Rigg's neck, before leaning back in silence.

Standing close by, Daggett the stage manager let out a cry of despair. From Betsy's side there came a sob; she knew it came from Jane Rowe. Then she blinked, as the tears started from her own eyes. And as one, the Duke of York's Company — men and women, actors and artisans — began to give vent to their emotions. The audience outside was forgotten, even when the noise of their leave-taking arose, so that when Thomas Betterton joined his fellows, he found himself as helpless as the rest. He could only stand with them, still wearing his Macbeth costume, and stare down at Rigg's lifeless body.

* * *

An hour later, the actor George Beale found himself under suspicion of murder.

The audience had melted away; no doubt news of what had happened would soon spread throughout London and its suburbs. In the playhouse itself, doormen stood by the entrance, under Betterton's orders to admit no one. The entire company, actors and backstage folk alike, sat on the pit benches in silence until their leader came to address them. Like the others he had shed costume and make-up. His face was taut, and his tone was severe, for reasons which would soon be apparent.

'I'll not dwell on the manner in which our dear friend Joseph Rigg expired,' he said. 'I am as broken by it as any of you. You saw what happened, as many of you saw what happened yesterday, to Tom Cleeve. And though my first thought was that some terrible sickness had afflicted both men, what I have now heard from Doctor Catlin has forced me to revise my opinion.'

There was a stir, and the company glanced uneasily at one another, but Betterton raised a hand. 'Mr Beale,' he said quietly. 'Would you be good enough to tell me what was the cause of your grievance against Mr Rigg?'

There was an intake of breath, as thirty pairs of eyes shifted towards George Beale, seated at the front. After a moment the young man rose stiffly and faced Betterton.

'You confound me, sir,' he said, somewhat sharply. 'For there was no grievance. I had nothing but admiration for Rigg and his abilities.'

'In which case,' Betterton retorted, 'Why did you stab him with such force in the murder scene that the knife pierced his flesh?'

There was a gasp. Beale paled, but stood his ground.

'How can that be, sir?' he asked. 'You know as well as I do that it's a stage dagger, blunted and with no edge to it. While I confess I may, in the heat of the moment, have been somewhat enthusiastic in my thrust, there's no possibility that the weapon did serious damage.'

'Yet the man was bleeding,' Betterton countered. 'And I for one would—'

'Mr Betterton, may I speak?' All heads turned, for it was Tom Catlin who had interrupted. The doctor rose from his seat at the end of the front row.

'I merely mentioned that the knife had drawn blood,' Catlin said mildly. 'But the wound was shallow, little more than a scratch. It could not have been fatal.'

Betterton was frowning. 'Could it not have brought on some seizure, or sudden flux to the head?' he asked. 'You saw the way the man fell, staggering forward in a manner he had not practised. It's my opinion Rigg ceased acting very soon after Beale stabbed him. Otherwise, he would never have failed to deliver his last line — it was utterly unlike him!'

'God in heaven, sir, this cannot be borne! Do you accuse me of murder!?'

Beale's face was flushed now, with fear as well as anger. Betterton made no reply, and a murmur arose. Some people glanced at the two hirelings who had played Second and Third Murderer, sitting together in shocked silence.

'I can only repeat,' Catlin said, 'that the stab-wound to Mr Rigg's chest was not serious. As you stated, the manner of his death was akin to that of Cleeve yesterday, the cause of which—'

'Very well, doctor!' Betterton nodded. 'I thank you for your assistance.' He faced the company again. 'I must give credence to the doctor's findings,' he went on. 'And' — this with a look at Beale — 'I accuse no one of murder.'

He lowered his gaze, the strain upon him now obvious to all. 'We have suffered a terrible shock,' he said, 'and no doubt you wish to go to your homes. Yet I ask you all, in view of what has happened, to be ready to answer questions: the forces of law already view Cleeve's death as suspicious—' he broke off. Anxious looks were flying about, but George Beale, who was still on his feet, addressed Betterton again.

'Sir, I am in torment yet, and I will be heard!' he cried. 'You have already come close to accusing me of despatching Rigg with a blunted dagger. Do you now intend to ask whether I had some grudge against Cleeve too?'

'Of course not.' Betterton maintained a level tone. 'Yet since you press me, I note you have not answered my question: even if we accept the doctor's view that your dagger thrust could not have inflicted serious injury upon Mr Rigg, I ask again: what was the nature of your grievance against him? For from what I have learned today, I feel certain there was one!'

Beale's face reddened further. 'I resent this deeply, sir!' he answered, 'as I resent the suggestion that, even if there had been any discord between myself and Rigg, I would have allowed it to encroach upon our professional endeavours—'

'Yet you did so!'

A high female voice rang out. In surprise everyone looked round at the unexpected sight: Louise Hawker, the shy little tiring-maid, on her feet in the middle of the group, pointing at George Beale. Aveline Hale, who had recovered from her fainting fit and was sitting beside the girl, gaped at her in astonishment.

Beale stiffened, and some looked perplexed: there was more to this than they had imagined. Betterton gestured to Louise to come forward, but the girl shook her head.

'They were like two cockerels that fight over a hen!' she cried. 'I heard them in the street — they did spit and cry insults at each other, so that I thought they would draw their swords! Beale called Rigg a rook and a bulker, and swore he would have his blood!'

Now voices rose in dismay, as well as in anger. Betsy looked round and saw that while some were casting suspicious looks at George Beale, others appeared unmoved, as if Louise's revelation was not news to them. Among those who kept silent, she noticed, were Joshua Small, William Daggett and James Prout . . . and Samuel Tripp, who sat in a corner. Apparently unfazed by anything that had been said, the playmaker wore his habitual cynical smile.

'Is this true, sir?' A hard look had spread across Betterton's handsome features. 'Answer me!'

Beale's mouth had gone dry. He moistened his lips, then seeing Betterton was about to repeat his demand, spoke up.

'Very well!' he cried. 'It's true we were at loggerheads, but it was of no consequence. A quarrel between two friends over a loan of money — nothing more. I swear it!'

When no one spoke, the man sought to defend himself further. 'I've never harmed a soul in my life!' he shouted. 'You may ask anyone who is acquainted with me. I confess I was angry with Rigg. What man wouldn't be, when he plays at cards with a fellow who can't make good his debts? I made him a loan in good faith, and he failed to repay it! And moreover—'

'Moreover,' a voice chimed in, 'you coveted Rigg's role, and felt you had more right to it than he!'

It was James Prout who had spoken. All turned to the dancing-master, who still wore his rhinegrave dancing-breeches.

'Forgive me, sir,' he said to Betterton, 'yet I cannot remain silent. Rigg was a fine tragedian, and it was a measure of the man that he laughed off the jibes of a mere supporting actor, who is not worthy to play his page-boy!'

Betsy glanced from Prout to Beale, who had gone white. Louise Hawker sat down hurriedly. This was threatening to escalate into a verbal battle. Fortunately, Betterton was equal to the task of defusing it.

'I thank you, Mr Prout,' he said briskly, 'yet I fear we make little headway. However, one thing at least is clear to me.' He looked deliberately at Beale, who flinched.

'I will not question you further, sir,' he said. 'If the forces of the law wish to take up the matter of your quarrel with Rigg, that is their right. We in the company will mourn the passing of our fellow, before gathering the strength to continue — as we have done before in the face of adversity, and will again!' Seeing that his words met with approval, he went on: 'Yet I will not have personal conflicts spilling on to the stage of the Duke's Theatre. You will not play here, ever again. You are dismissed, sir — and further, you are barred from entering this building. I wish you good day!'

A tense moment followed. Beale gave Betterton a long look, of impotent anger mingled with shame; then at last he puffed out his chest, turned on his heel and strode to the side entrance. The walk was a long one; and by the time he had reached the door, a doorman had flung it wide. From outside, the cries of the watermen could be heard from the river, before Beale disappeared from sight.

There was a general sigh of relief. Some of the actors rose, and by the look of them, were bound for the nearest tavern. Betsy, too, felt that she had heard enough for one afternoon, and Jane Rowe's expression suggested that she was of similar mind. Yet as voices rose, Betterton raised his hand again.

'I will not keep you here any longer,' he called. 'You of course understand that the run of *Macbeth* is over. We will not play tomorrow, nor the day after, which is in any case the Lord's day. Yet it is my wish that next week we may gather with renewed vigour, and prepare a favourite piece from our repertoire—'

But at that moment there came a sonorous voice from the doorway, and the sudden entrance of an imposing personage put paid to that notion in an instant.

'I regret that will not be possible, Mr Betterton. The theatre must close until further notice, by order of the Lord Chamberlain.'

The silence that followed was one of dismay. All eyes fell upon a stocky, handsome man in his middle forties, richly dressed in a maroon suit, flat-crowned hat and gold stockings. Lord Caradoc, the Master of the King's Revels, was a familiar face at the playhouses, even if his presence was not always welcome. Yet the man's good humour and wit were such that few could find it in their hearts to dislike him. Unhurriedly, His Lordship walked forward.

'My lord.' Betterton made his bow, and other men rose to follow suit while women curtsied. But Caradoc ignored the formalities, and it was clear from his grave expression that he had heard the news.

'I am sorry for it,' he said, 'as I am for your tragic loss.' He hesitated. 'For do I hear correctly, that Mr Rigg was not merely taken ill, but has since died?'

In reply to that Betterton's brief nod was all the man needed.

'Then, even though the Lord Chamberlain has yet to be appraised of the matter,' Caradoc continued, 'I take it upon myself to anticipate his will. In view of the fact that two deaths have occurred here in as many days, there can be no other course of action.'

Nobody spoke. The theatre's closure was more than a passing inconvenience for the Duke's Company: it meant the loss of their income. Many of them, from the older actors to Louise the tiring-maid, were the breadwinners for their families. Betsy caught Tom Catlin's eye, then she glanced at Lord Caradoc, and found his eyes upon her.

She sighed; she was not the only unmarried actress to have been propositioned at one time or another by the noble lord. Yet in contrast to someone like Samuel Tripp, he had always made his advances with such gallantry that Betsy had usually felt flattered. He had also taken her rebuffs with good grace, saying he was a sporting man who enjoyed the chase, and could laugh in the face of defeat.

But now there was nothing more to be said. Betterton and Caradoc moved aside in private conversation. After a moment John Downes joined them, along with Daggett. The rest of the company made for the doors in a subdued body. Betsy took Jane's arm. As they neared the doorway Louise the tiring-maid hurried past them, eyes downcast. Yet, Betsy reflected, few in the company would have cause to doubt the girl's words, knowing George Beale as they did — and Joseph Rigg too. Nevertheless, though few would miss Beale, she knew all would miss Rigg as much as she would.

Soon the two were outside, with the breeze in their faces. Each was busy with her own thoughts, but one was uppermost, as it would be on the mind of every member of the company: an uncertain time lay ahead, without work or wage. So when the familiar, ranting voice of Praise-God Palmer rang out in the lane Betsy and Jane exchanged exasperated looks, before following the rest of the company to the Hercules Pillars.

It was mid-afternoon, yet the inn was crowded. One of the largest ordinaries outside the walls and close to the theatre, it was the usual haunt of actors. As the two pushed their way inside, they adopted their most brazen manner: nothing less would suffice, for women unescorted. Almost at once there came a male voice from behind, but it was Tom Catlin, somewhat out of breath, who had evidently been trying to catch them up.

'Let's find a quiet corner,' he said. 'I must speak with you.'

A few minutes later the three of them had squeezed behind a table by the window. Catlin called for mulled sack, then began without preamble.

'I examined Tom Cleeve's body,' he said, 'and found something I didn't like. But before I tell you what it is, can either of you remember who was close to the man, before he fell down?'

Jane looked taken aback. 'We weren't near enough to see, with everyone milling about,' she answered. 'As I recall, he was talking with the other scene-men.'

'Apart from one,' Betsy put in. 'Joshua Small was making his way towards us — he's got designs on Mistress Rowe here.'

Catlin was wearing what Betsy called his 'puzzling-out' face. 'I looked his body over, from head to foot,' he said after a moment. 'And apart from a few old scars, I found nothing amiss — until I chanced to take a look at his arm. There was a tiny hole above the elbow — little more than a pinprick, but it was recent. Looked like he'd been pierced with a bodkin, or something similar.'

Then, seeing the looks on the two women's faces, he shook his head. 'No, it couldn't have killed him, any more than that blunted dagger killed Rigg. What was odd was the appearance of the puncture. I had to put a lens to it, before I saw it plainly: a trace of some brown substance, about its edges.'

'But . . . you said the wound was so tiny, it couldn't have caused his death,' Jane objected.

'Whatever he was pricked with couldn't have . . . at least, not in the upper arm,' Catlin said. 'But if it was coated with something poisonous, that's another matter.'

Betsy drew a sharp breath. 'You thought Long Ned was poisoned,' she said. 'And I found out today that they knew each other well. In fact, they went back a long way.'

'What's Long Ned to do with it?' Jane asked.

In a few words, Catlin told her how it was he who had been called to attend the man at the bathhouse, but two days previously, and how the manner of his death was almost identical to Cleeve's. 'At the time, I thought there was no mark upon his body, either,' he added. 'But then I didn't search it for anything as small as a pinprick.'

A tapster appeared with three steaming mugs of sack and set them down. 'Betterton told me this morning that rumours were already abroad,' Betsy said, 'of some foul play being practised upon the Duke's Company. Long Ned used to work for him, back at the old theatre, while Cleeve—'

'Ned, then Tom Cleeve . . . and now Rigg,' Catlin broke in, nodding. 'I'm not a gamester, yet I'd lay odds that if I were to examine Rigg's body, too, I'd find a pinprick exactly like the one on Cleeve's arm. Their symptoms were too alike — and in any case, I don't believe in coincidence.'

Jane Rowe looked aghast. 'Are you saying they were all poisoned?' she demanded.

But Betsy turned to her, and answered for Catlin. 'He's saying they were murdered. And I believe him!'

CHAPTER FIVE

Thomas Betterton's house stood to the north of Covent Garden, where many handsome new residences had been built in London's rapid westward expansion. Here he lived in comfort with his actress wife Mary, the celebrated Mistress Saunderson. But though Betsy had visited their home several times, on the morning after Joseph Rigg's death she approached the heavy door with some trepidation.

She had taken breakfast with Tom Catlin, a rare occurrence, as it was the doctor's habit to rise early. But though Betsy had passed a restless night, and there was no performance at the Duke's, the two of them had matters to talk over. They agreed that Betsy would tell Betterton what they had both learned, and let him decide what course to take. So after Peg had dressed her hair in side-locks and helped her into her tight-boned bodice, Betsy put on her second-best chemise and a cloak of midnight blue, and walked by Wych Street and Drury Lane to Long Acre.

The door was opened by Betterton's ageing manservant, Matthew. As he showed Betsy into the parlour, the old man bent to whisper in her ear. 'You're not the only visitor, Mistress Brand. Alderman Blake's here . . . in high dudgeon, too.'

Betsy knew the alderman of the ward of Farringdon Without, where the Duke's Theatre stood, only too well. He was an old-style Puritan who, though lacking the zeal of men like Praise-God Palmer, nevertheless viewed the libertarian ways of actors with distaste. If Blake had heard of the deaths of Tom Cleeve and Joseph Rigg, it was likely he had seized the opportunity to make one of his frequent demands for the closure of the theatre. In which case, Betsy thought wryly, he was too late.

Now she heard voices raised and, putting on a broad smile, walked into the sunlit room. As she entered, Betterton rose to greet her. 'My dear Mistress Brand,' he was smiling, but there was a warning look in his eye as he indicated the florid-faced man in black, who occupied a chair by the window. 'You know Alderman Blake.'

Betsy faced the Alderman, and made her curtsey. 'Of course, how do you, sir?'

Blake made no reply, nor did he rise. To a man like him, an actress was no different from a whore, except that she was likely to earn more money. He glanced at Betsy, then continued to address his host.

'I will press my case once more, Mr Betterton, and once only, for I have more important matters to attend to. You tell me the closure of the Duke's Theatre is but a temporary measure: I say that for the good of our community, it should be permanent!'

Betterton crossed the room to fetch another chair for Betsy, who accepted it graciously. Unhurriedly he returned to his own chair, before meeting the other man's gaze.

'In that respect I fear you will be disappointed, sir,' he answered. 'As you know, the Duke of York is our patron. He often favours us with his presence — as indeed, does the King himself, whose affection for the drama is well known. Hence I feel certain they would wish us to continue—'

But Blake snorted. 'I wondered how long it would be before you brought their names up!' he said in a contemptuous tone. 'Well, two may play at tennis! I am well acquainted with the Duke of Buckingham, who has the ear of the King, and, I may say, sees a deal more of him than do you, sir. More to the point, he's a good friend of the Lord Chamberlain — and hence I mean to seek an audience with him, this very day. In view of the dreadful events that have occurred, I believe he will see matters as I do, and agree that it is prudent — nay, imperative — that the Dorset Gardens Theatre remains closed. And furthermore, that it be boarded up like a plague-house. Only then—'

'Plague-house?' Unable to stop herself, Betsy interrupted. 'There's no sickness at the Duke's Theatre, sir.'

Blake turned a fiery eye upon her. 'Two deaths in two days, in the same manner,' he retorted. 'What cause would you propound?'

But instead of answering, Betsy let Betterton know by a glance that she had come with tidings for his ears alone. Whereupon her mentor stiffened and spoke up.

'I have no doubt that a cause will be discovered in time,' he said to Blake, 'and that any fears of infection will be allayed. Besides, you were not present when either of those tragic deaths occurred, sir. Hence you cannot comment upon them with any authority.'

'Authority!' Blake bristled. 'I have all the authority I need, sir — and I'll take no instruction from the son of a cook!'

There was a short silence before, to Blake's increasing fury, Betterton favoured him with a faint smile. 'Not just any cook, sir,' he answered mildly. 'My father was a *royal* cook.'

Betsy stifled a laugh. It was well known that Thomas Betterton was of humble birth; but like others loyal to the first King Charles, he had benefited from the Restoration and the reopening of the theatres, a decade ago. That in itself, Betsy knew, was more than men like Blake could stomach.

The man got to his feet, glaring. 'You insult me, sir, as you do my office!' he cried. 'And I shall take steps to see that you regret it!' But he was blustering, and he knew it. With perfect dignity, Betterton stood up himself and met the man's eye.

'I look forward to seeing how you accomplish that, Alderman,' he said. 'Now, since you claim to have more pressing matters — as do Mistress Brand and I — we'll not impose upon you any longer. Will you permit me to summon my servant?' And without waiting for a reply he called for Matthew, who appeared with such speed it was obvious he had been listening outside.

The alderman was fuming. He swung his gaze towards Betsy, who smiled politely and inclined her head. Beside the open door, Matthew waited in silence; and at last, eyes blazing, Blake turned and swept out of the room, and out of the house.

Betsy waited until her host turned and let out a long breath. 'Well, my dear,' he said, 'will you take a morning draught with me?'

* * *

A half hour later, the two of them were still sitting in Betterton's parlour. It had not taken Betsy long to tell her mentor everything she had learned from her visit to Hannah Cleeve in Clerkenwell, nor to speak of Tom Catlin's discovery. By the time she had finished, her old mentor was frowning.

'I will speak with Lord Caradoc again,' he said at last. 'He has always dealt fairly with us, and it's right he should know the worst.' He grimaced. 'I fear he has less influence with the Lord Chamberlain than our friend the alderman. He's but a deputy for the Master of the Revels, old Sir Henry Herbert, who, as you know, farms out his office.'

He sighed. 'Do you know what some of the actors are saying?' he asked. 'That *Macbeth* is an unlucky play, and we should not perform it again. Moreover, according to Blake, having witches on the stage calling up spirits and hatching spells amounts to blasphemy, and meddles with the devil!'

Betsy smiled. 'Perhaps you should heed Praise-God Palmer,' she replied. 'Forsake the theatre, fall upon your knees and beg forgiveness.'

But Betterton was serious. 'And yet, there's no denying that evil of some kind has befallen us,' he said, with a shake of his head. 'Ned Gowden, Tom Cleeve and now Joseph Rigg! Why, the man had his faults, but I know of no one who disliked him — or at least not enough to murder him! If, that is, I give full credence to Doctor Catlin's theory . . .' he broke off. 'It's too strange and too terrible — I wish I could reject it.'

'Tom Catlin's the cleverest man I know,' Betsy said. 'He's not given to flights of fancy.'

'So,' Betterton broke in, 'must we assume the rumours were right from the outset, and someone hates the Duke's Company enough to kill two of us?' He rose and took a few paces about the room, finally turning with a look of despair.

'I may as well confess to you, Betsy,' he said, 'that I have no idea how to proceed. The constable — Gould, I mean — is no fool, but neither is he a friend. The alderman wants to close us down. To whom then may we turn? For someone must find out how and why these deaths have been inflicted upon us.' He looked up. 'Suppose there is one with a grudge? Whatever the cause of it, might this only be the beginning? If he's able to strike down his victims with such ease, how many more might perish?'

Betsy said nothing. But there was an appetite within her that she barely understood. It had been growing ever since the death of Thomas Cleeve. 'I . . . I would like to follow the scent, and try to discover what lies behind these deaths,' she said quietly. 'That is, if you'll permit it. With the help of Doctor Catlin perhaps I can, as he would put it, puzzle the matter out.'

Betterton stared at her. 'You?'

'Well,' Betsy gave a little shrug, 'while the Duke's is closed I haven't a great deal else to occupy me, have I?'

* * *

Tom Catlin returned that evening to find Betsy waiting for him. He was tired, and barely muttered a greeting before dropping his bag in the hall and removing his hat and Brandenburg coat. Then he went into the parlour to pour himself a glass of sack. Betsy followed, to find as she hoped that he had poured two glasses. Without a word she picked hers up and sat down on one of the fireside chairs, while her landlord struck a flame and lit a couple of candles. Outside the light was fading, and Fire's Reach Court, gloomy at the best of times with its overhanging jetties, was already in near-darkness. Betsy took a sip from her glass and waited.

'I'd have come home hours ago,' Catlin said at last, 'but I took a hackney to Aldgate Street, where Rigg's body lies.'

'I thought he had lodgings in Hatton Garden,' Betsy said.

'He did. But there I learned that his body had been taken across London, to his father's house. He's a magistrate, did you know that?'

'No, I didn't,' Betsy answered in surprise.

'He's a magistrate,' Catlin repeated, 'but his name isn't Rigg. He's Sir Anthony Griffiths, who until yesterday had disowned his son, the celebrated actor. Joseph Griffiths, it seems, had taken a different surname, on his father's instructions — or risk being cut out of Sir Anthony's will.'

'Moreover,' the doctor went on, as Betsy took in the news, 'Sir Anthony has asked me to make it plain to those connected with the Dorset Gardens Theatre that they will be unwelcome at his son's funeral. In fact, should they presume to attend, they'll be turned away on pain of arrest. In view of which' — Catlin paused, then gave a little smile — 'I confess myself surprised to be granted permission to examine the body of the deceased. At first I was refused, until that is, the deceased's father learned that I was the one who attended his son in his dying moments. Whereupon he gave me to understand that as a member of the Royal College of Physicians, he expected me to pronounce a verdict of death by some common but non-contagious cause. That is, he wished it to be known that Joseph died an unfortunate but *acceptable* death. Hence he may be buried with all honour, and laid to rest in the family vault in Essex, where their country house lies.'

Betsy met Catlin's eye. 'So, what was your verdict?'

'Apoplexy. Brought on by the strain of a particularly energetic performance.'

'And was that deemed acceptable?'

'It was.'

Carrying his glass to the chair opposite Betsy, Catlin sat down. 'It seemed the least I could do for Mr Justice Griffiths,' he said, 'for whatever you may think of him he is a grieving father, who wishes his son's memory to be untainted.'

But Betsy could hardly contain her curiosity. 'So, you examined Rigg's body?'

'I did.' Catlin raised an eyebrow. 'You seem mighty eager to hear about it.'

Taking a breath, she now told the doctor what had passed between her and Thomas Betterton that morning. By the time she had finished, the man was frowning.

'Might it not have been prudent, or at least polite, to ask my approval before enlisting me as your co-intelligencer?' he enquired drily.

'But I know how much you enjoy a riddle,' Betsy answered, favouring him with one of her disarming smiles. 'Don't pretend your own curiosity isn't aroused . . . and has been ever since Long Ned expired so mysteriously at the bagnio.'

Catlin considered. 'Well then, I'd better tell you what I found . . . even though it will merely add to the riddle,' he said. 'For there wasn't just one of those odd little pinpricks on Joseph Rigg's body: there were at least three of them, very close together.'

'Three?' It was Betsy's turn to frown.

'In his right side, just below the ribs. Again, I'd say the perforations alone couldn't have caused death. But again, there was discolouration about each . . . dark brown, like the one on Tom Cleeve's arm.'

'So again, you think whatever pierced him could have been coated with some poisonous substance?'

'It seems plausible.'

'But how could that have happened, on the stage in full view of hundreds of people?' Betsy asked. 'George Beale may have stabbed Rigg with too much force — he admitted as much. But from what you say, the puncture wounds—'

'Were a long way from the scratch made by the dagger,' Catlin finished.

For a while, neither of them spoke. 'Those other fellows playing the murderers,' Catlin said at last. 'The tall one and the short one: might they—'

'They weren't allowed to stab him,' Betsy replied. 'That was Beale's task, with the blunted dagger. They're hirelings, just there to speak the words and make Banquo's death look real.'

'It was certainly that,' Catlin observed, meeting Betsy's eye again. 'So, Mistress Rummager — perhaps I will call you that henceforth — how will you begin your investigations?'

Betsy thought for a moment. 'Perhaps I should take the deaths in the order they occurred — starting with Long Ned's — and try to question those who were present at each one. That way I may build up a picture of what happened.'

'You don't intend to seek admittance to the *hammam*?' Catlin raised his eyebrows. 'Only one type of woman goes in there.'

But Betsy fixed him with her most brazen look. 'Then I shall need all Peg's skills as a dresser,' she said, and got briskly to her feet.

* * *

An hour after dark, with a stiff breeze blowing from the river, a shambling figure moved along the Strand and turned into Brydges Street. The woman wore an old pink gown trimmed with tattered Colberteen lace, divided and tied back to show a bright red underskirt. Her breasts bulged at the neckline, thrust upwards by bone stays. If the shiny golden hair was her own, it looked somewhat unnatural, perhaps owing its colour to the old nostrum of white wine and rhubarb juice. Her face was whitened, the lips coloured with Spanish red. Even without the vizard-mask which dangled from the woman's wrist, her profession was obvious to all. It was a new role for Betsy Brand, and one she had not rehearsed; this time, she had only her wits to rely upon. For a moment she hesitated, then, adopting a bold manner, strolled up the dark thoroughfare to the corner of Russell Street.

She turned the corner, and the familiar night-time sounds of Covent Garden assailed her. Traders called from their stalls, gallants in garish coats and long periwigs strutted about talking loudly, while from the Rose Tavern came laughter and voices raised in song. Here and there *bona fide* members of the street-walking profession plied her trade, accosting first one man and then another. Quickly, Betsy turned left and walked along Little Russell Street towards the piazza, and at once the broad, lantern-lit square opened out before her, thronged with people.

On the left-hand corner by the Little Piazza was her destination: a large house which had known many uses and many owners, before Robert Jenkins turned it into his famous bath-house, the *hammam*: a men's haunt like the Coffee-houses, but one where certain women were admitted as required. In fact, a man with shillings to spend could get anything in the bagnio: not merely a steam bath, but food and drink, a bed for the night, and someone of either sex to share it with. At the entrance a broad-shouldered doorman stood, and now Betsy drew a deep breath: she was on.

'Well, my duck,' as the fellow turned to her, she addressed him in an accent that hailed from somewhere east of Limehouse. 'Are you letting me in, or what?'

The man frowned. 'Who're you?'

'Mary Peach. I've got business with a gent within.'

'Peach? Never heard of you,' the other snapped. He was a heavy-browed man with a pocked face. 'I don't care to admit one I don't know . . . you could be a fireship.'

'I don't know you, neither,' Betsy told him, 'but I'll live with it.' She scowled. 'And I ain't a fireship, fustilugs — I'm clean as silver!'

The man hesitated, and a hint of a smile appeared. 'So what's it worth to let you take your goods to market?' he asked, his eyes straying downwards to her cleavage.

'What would you want?' Betsy countered.

'What d'you think?'

She appeared to consider the matter. 'When are you free?'

'Any time you like,' the man answered, his smile broadening. 'I can soon get someone to take my place.'

'All right,' Betsy said. 'I'll be out in an hour — wait for me.' Still grinning, the fellow stepped aside; and with a brazen step, she entered the bagnio.

At first she could see little, for the place was dimly lit. Then she felt a blast of warm, humid air and, glimpsing a doorway ahead, stepped into a room which she guessed to be the *tepidarium*. There were low voices, and figures wrapped in linen sheets were visible, moving to and fro. In a far corner somebody was playing a lute. She moved slowly, allowing her eyes to adjust to the gloom — whereupon, close by, a voice she knew stopped her in her tracks.

'Looking for someone?'

Betsy swung round to see none other than James Prout, the dancing-master of the Duke's Theatre, lounging on a wooden bench. He was bare-chested, the lower half of his body concealed by a white robe. Beside him sat another man, younger, and a deal more handsome. The two men's arms were linked and, as Betsy looked quickly from one to the other, both of them laughed.

'No need to look crestfallen, Miss,' the young one said. 'There's others within will be glad to see you.'

For a moment Betsy thought of revealing herself to Prout, then swiftly rejected the idea. She had arrived incognito and would remain so. And a little thrill of satisfaction ran through her that even the dancing-master did not recognize her.

'I ain't been here before,' she said. 'I'm looking for a friend . . . used to work at the old Duke's Theatre in Portugal Row. Know him, do you? Brown fellow, name of Long Ned.'

There was a pause before Prout blew out his cheeks and looked away. Only now did Betsy realize that he was rather drunk. But the younger man was alert.

'Heavens, girl, haven't you heard? The poor man's dead, three days since. Expired in there.' He pointed to an inner doorway. From within came a hissing, as of water being poured on to hot coals.

'Dead?' Betsy's mouth fell open. 'He can't be!'

The other nodded. 'It was very sudden. He was stricken with a seizure of some sort.' He indicated Prout. 'My friend here was close by when it happened, weren't you, old fellow?'

Prout peered up at Betsy with bleary eyes. 'I didn't see it,' he said. 'Hill did,' he frowned. 'What are you staring at? You'd best ask within.' He waved a hand irritably towards the steam room.

But in her new role as Mary Peach, Betsy was emboldened. Here was an opportunity, and she would not waste it. She faced Prout's young friend again.

'Where've they took his poor body, sir?' she whined. 'For I'd dearly like to look upon him again, and say my farewell.'

The man shrugged, but just then Prout lurched to his feet. 'Time for my sweat,' he muttered. 'Are you coming?'

The other got up, and put an arm about Prout's shoulder. But thinking fast, Betsy stayed both men.

'Wait, masters,' she said. 'For I'll confess to you I was worried about Ned. That's why I've come, see. He was uneasy when I saw him last . . . looking behind, like someone was after him. D'you know aught of it?'

Prout was frowning at her, and it was a surprise to Betsy to see how different the man's manner was here. His habitual good humour and talkativeness seemed absent. But the other man spoke up.

'If that's true, he hid it well,' he answered, 'for I saw no sign of a nervousness on his part.' He thought for a moment. 'One thing I know was that Ned was working every hour of the day for his passage money. He was burning to leave England . . . for the tropics I'd wager, whence he came.' He put on a wry smile. 'It's a sad tale is it not, for he would have succeeded in time. It's easy to turn a shilling in here, even a sovereign come to that. But I've no need to tell *you*, have I?'

Then he turned, for Prout was tugging at his arm. Without another glance at Betsy both men moved off, to be swallowed up by clouds of steam.

Betsy sighed. It looked now as if her notion of wandering about the bagnio asking questions was foolish, if not dangerous; and all she had learned was that Long Ned was trying to save enough money to leave England.

She turned about and left the bagnio. But only when she stepped out into the cool night air did she remember the doorman. She looked round sharply, as the fellow moved forward to block her way. 'That was quick,' he said in a suspicious voice. 'I thought you said you'd be out in an hour.'

But Betsy drew a breath — then reached up and tugged off her golden wig. With the other hand she fumbled in her pockets. As the doorman's jaw dropped, she said in an imperious voice: 'Enough play-acting, for I'm bored with it. I'm Lady Theodora Knightley, fellow, and I require a chair to take me home. Find one, and there's a shilling for you!'

The man stared, then his expression changed in an instant. 'Course, your ladyship . . . right away,' and he made a clumsy bow and hurried off towards the piazza. He did not see Betsy walk smartly off to Little Russell Street and round the corner. Only when she had turned into Brydges Street again did she relax. And at last her spirits flagged, for it seemed that her first foray as *Mistress Rummager* had proved fruitless.

CHAPTER SIX

The following morning, Betsy awoke from a troubled sleep with the realization that Peg had failed to rouse her. Stumbling downstairs, she found Catlin's servant on her knees scrubbing the kitchen floor. As Betsy entered, Peg looked up grumpily.

'The Doc told me I shouldn't disturb you,' she said. 'Reckoned you'd be worn out after traipsing round Covent Garden. Profitable, was it?'

'Not especially.' Betsy stifled a yawn, she sat down at the well-scrubbed table and poured herself a cup of milk. She had a vague notion of seeking out Julius Hill to ask him further about the death of Ned Gowden, since he had been one of those close to the man when he died. Or perhaps she would visit Jane Rowe.

'You look like I feared you would, after the theatre was closed,' Peg said, sitting up. 'Nothing to do but mope about. You need to watch that, or you'll end up with the mulligrubs.'

'I've plenty to occupy myself,' Betsy told her. 'Then I wouldn't be working anyway as it's Sunday, in case you've forgotten.'

'You've no cause to rail at me,' Peg replied. 'Especially since I've got news that'll cheer you. A boy came an hour since with a message: you're invited to supper.'

Betsy raised her eyebrows. 'Invited, by whom?'

'Lord Caradoc, at his mansion. Bread, or something—'

'Bredon House,' Betsy gazed at her in surprise. 'Are you sure that's right?'

'Course I'm sure,' Peg retorted. 'The boy said he was sent by Mr Betterton, to tell you there's a supper in honour of someone. You're to go to Betterton's house at six, and ride with him in a coach.' She put on her most scathing look. 'Aren't we the grand lady? Dining with Lords. Who's next, the King?'

But Betsy ignored her. She was already wondering what to wear.

* * *

The reason for her being invited to Lord Caradoc's grand house, however, was less flattering than she had first imagined. She discovered that soon after arriving at Betterton's in her farandine chemise, with a full lace bertha and her silver-grey velvet cloak. This time it was Mistress Mary who received her, and showed her into the parlour.

'Thomas is dressing, and will be down presently,' she said. 'So I thought to appraise you of the situation.'

Betsy had always respected Mary Betterton, the former Mistress Saunderson, one of the first female actors in London. Tutored by Betterton himself, she had pleased him so well he ended up marrying her. An attractive woman with fine auburn hair, she had retained her dignity, and served as an example to the younger actresses like Betsy who followed her on to the stage. It was some time before Betsy realized there was a steely hardness beneath Mistress Mary's charm that was directed at furthering her husband's career above all else. Nowadays she rarely acted, but was an accomplished hostess. She fixed Betsy with a smile, while she delivered her news.

'You are to partner Mr Tripp.'

'Tripp!' Betsy's face fell. 'Must I?'

'Listen, Betsy,' Mrs Betterton's smile did not waver, 'this supper has been arranged in haste for all our benefits. It will require considerable diplomacy, for it has but one purpose: to placate Alderman Blake, who will be the honoured guest. Yesterday, as you know, Blake made it clear he would petition the Lord Chamberlain to have the Duke's shut down. Lord Caradoc, who merely deputizes for the Master of the Revels, may find himself over-ruled, and so Blake may get his way. A disaster for us all, I'm sure you'll agree.'

All at once, Betsy had an inkling of what was coming.

'So,' Mary continued, 'His Lordship proposes to use his charm — a considerable weapon as you know — to win the alderman over. We are invited to add weight to his arguments, as well as smoothing over the rift that exists between the Duke's Company and the alderman. Mr Tripp—' she hesitated, and Betsy spoke up.

'Mr Tripp, famous for his wit, is there to flatter the alderman into letting us reopen, so that we may put on his new play.' When Mary made no reply, she added: 'And so . . . am I to be placed beside the alderman while he grows tipsy, and grant him an unobstructed view down my front? Or did you have something further in mind?'

Mary's smile faded. 'Is your opinion of Thomas so low,' she asked sharply, 'that you imagine he would act as pander, and serve you up on a plate?' When Betsy did not answer, the woman went on: 'It was Mr Tripp's idea that you accompany him. He's an unmarried man, of course — you will not be left alone with him. Nor with the alderman, for that matter, who is a widower. But besides, both His Lordship and Thomas think it prudent that you join the party. You are educated, and can help our case. If you wish, we will take you home afterwards, thus ensuring that whatever hopes Tripp may have in regard to your person, he'll be disappointed. Does that satisfy you?'

But Betsy did not voice her thoughts: that it was not Tripp she was wary of, so much as Lord Caradoc. Then, surely even His Lordship would not flirt with her in front of his wife?

'I take it Lady Arabella will be present?' she asked.

'Of course.' Mistress Betterton cocked her head at the sound of footsteps descending the stairs. 'So, for the good of the Duke's Theatre,' she went on briskly, 'can we count on you?'

After a moment Betsy nodded, wondering why she had been foolish enough to think there might be another reason for her being invited. Avoiding the woman's eye, she turned to greet Betterton as he strode in, dressed in a fine camelotte suit.

But had she known what the evening would bring, she reflected later, she would have been sorry to miss it.

* * *

The mansion of Charles Langdon, Lord Caradoc, was in Piccadilly between Clarendon House and Berkeley House. Here also resided His Lordship's wife, the formidable Lady Arabella, as well as his children (one son was at Oxford) and numerous servants. Less well known was the proximity of his mistress, who had her own modest set of rooms across St James's Park by the Spring Garden. As the coach Betterton had hired for the evening rattled through the imposing gates of Bredon House, Betsy gazed at the great building, its entire frontage lit by torches. She glimpsed a knot garden, trees shaped into cones, and water gushing from a statue of some mythical beast. The coachman heaved at the reins, the vehicle halted on a drive of washed gravel, and a liveried footman hurried out to open the door. Descending from the coach, Betsy made an effort to appear unimpressed, though the manifestation of such wealth subdued her. It occurred to her that His Lordship might intend it to weaken her resolve, so that the next time he contrived to catch her alone, she should bend to his will. In silence she followed Thomas and Mary Betterton through the front entrance, into a hall ablaze with light.

The meal was more than a mere supper; it was to be an entertainment. Caradoc had left little to chance, either in the richness of his dishes or his selection of wines. As the guests took their seats in the candlelit dining-room with its gilt-framed pictures and finely carved furniture, a trio of spinet, bass viol and fiddle began to play. Betsy had to hide a smile when they struck up one of the pieces from *Macbeth*.

But she had little opportunity to admire her glittering surroundings, for no sooner had she entered the room than Samuel Tripp, in a burgundy suit and a new black periwig, appeared at her elbow. Thereafter he rarely left her side, and Betsy was correct in her prediction when she found herself at one end of the table with Tripp on her left, and Alderman Blake, in the guest of honour's seat at the table's head, at a right angle to her. So she had no choice but to maintain polite conversation first with Tripp, who was the picture of attentiveness, and then with Blake who, as the evening wore on, began to turn his sharp little eyes in her direction.

The alderman's very presence surprised Betsy. As a man of Puritan disposition, and very conscious of his office, she expected him to despise the richness of these surroundings and to regard his hosts as frivolous people. This description might have fitted the Lady Arabella, who had evidently been at her closet for hours. She wore a voluminous, low-cut, flowered gown, parted to reveal a bright yellow underskirt. Her red hair was newly dressed, the false side-locks standing out like branches on either side of her whited cheeks, on which were stuck tiny heart-shaped patches of black silk. Betsy, in her pale-blue farandine, felt almost dowdy.

As the meal progressed, however, she began to modify her opinion of Alderman Blake. At first he ignored her and conversed with Lady Arabella, whose musical voice, even Betsy would have admitted, could soften the hardest of hearts. But as the wine flowed and glasses were refilled by Caradoc's attentive servants, the alderman showed himself to be a man of wider knowledge than Betsy expected. And eventually, somewhat red in the face, he began to converse with her.

'Mistress Brand, I confess myself taken aback to learn who your father is.' When Betsy looked up from her plate of stewed carp, he added: 'Is he not the same Mr William Brand who was assistant to the King's Surveyor-General?'

'*Was* is correct, sir,' she answered. 'My father lost his place some years ago. He's now a bookseller in the New Exchange.'

She lowered her eyes; she did not want to speak of her family, especially her father, an embittered man who had lost everything in the Great Fire. But she soon discovered that the alderman's thoughts ran on a different track.

'Yet he was a man of substance,' Blake persisted. 'Hence my surprise, to learn that he permits his daughter to go upon the stage.'

'My father's views on my profession are indeed old-fashioned, sir,' Betsy replied. 'Yet even he can see that as a result of it I'm able to keep myself in comfort, and not rely on him for my bed and board.'

'Capital. Keep it up, and mention *bed* as often as you can.' Betsy gulped, for Tripp had whispered in her left ear, while apparently listening with rapt attention to Lady Arabella's court gossip. Further along the table, Betterton and his wife were paying equal attention to Lord Caradoc's tales of the King's exploits at Newmarket.

The alderman took a pull from his glass and set it down rather clumsily. 'Bed and board should be the least of a gentleman's concerns,' he answered with an attempt at severity, though his eyes strayed towards Betsy's ample bosom. 'When his daughter's honour is at stake, that is. Surely you intend to marry at some future date? More, you expect to marry well.'

'I seldom give the matter much thought, sir,' Betsy answered, retaining a polite smile. 'My work is so absorbing I have little time for anything else.'

The alderman cleared his throat, but was then diverted by the Lady Arabella, who turned from Samuel Tripp to point out a dish that Blake had apparently missed.

'Do take some lobster, Alderman,' she urged. 'It's most rare at the moment.'

Blake blew out his red cheeks, and his eyes scanned the well-laden table. It was indeed a feast: savouries, fish and meat dishes vied for attention along with tarts, salads and sauces. Finally the man nodded and turned to his hostess.

'I'll bow to your advice, ma'am,' he said, 'once I've despatched this turbot.' He lifted his glass again and stuck his nose in it. 'And I must allow, your Navarre is splendid.'

Lady Arabella acknowledged the compliment gracefully. Betsy returned her attention to her plate, trying to ignore Tripp as he breathed in her ear once again.

'See how the old fool slavers,' he whispered. 'Yet I'll lay a sovereign the cause is his proximity to your body, and not the lobster.' The playmaker made a show of taking up his glass and studying it. Then he bent forward and whispered again. 'Ride home with me tonight. You'll sleep between silk sheets, breakfast on oysters.'

And then it was all Betsy could do not to yelp. Tripp's hand had gripped her thigh under the table. Taking a breath, she picked up her own glass — then deliberately spilled it over the man's burgundy coat.

'Oh dear — pray forgive my clumsiness!' She turned to Lady Arabella with an apologetic smile. 'I fear I am at sixes and sevens tonight.'

Lady Arabella lowered her spoon of rabbit fricassee. 'Think naught of it, my dear.' She beckoned to a footman, who hurried up. 'Refill Mistress Brand's glass,' she ordered, 'and fetch a cloth for Mister Tripp.'

Tripp cursed under his breath. But Lady Arabella caught Betsy's eye, and signalled with a glance that she understood perfectly well what had happened. She was no fool, Betsy thought — and wondered fleetingly how much she knew about a certain mistress, across the park.

Tripp had by now withdrawn his hand, allowing Betsy to pay attention to her carp. Small wonder, she mused, that Lord Caradoc invited actors to his table: for she, and to some extent Thomas and Mary Betterton, had been acting since they stepped out of the coach.

There was a stir as a footman approached the table carrying a great silver dish with a large pie upon it. Another servant cleared a space, and the platter was set down before Alderman Blake, who blinked at it.

'My Lady!' He looked at Lady Arabella, and decided to make an attempt at humour. 'My stomach is almost filled. I pray you do not expect me to despatch this, too?'

Lady Arabella peered at the monstrous pastry in some surprise. 'I confess I know not what it contains, sir,' she answered, then smiled faintly. 'And yet I have an inkling it's some treat my husband has ordered, in your honour.' She glanced at Lord Caradoc, who appeared not to have noticed the dish's arrival. Lady Arabella then turned her gaze upon Samuel Tripp and Betsy, favouring them both with a wink, and at once, Betsy guessed what was afoot.

It was a *blind-bake*: a false pie, part of which had been partitioned off with a wall of pastry and filled with dried peas or other ballast. After it was cooked, the crust would have been opened and the filling removed. Then something — and no one except the organizers of the jape would have known what — was put into the empty space, and the crust replaced. Thus when the pie was set upon the table, the moment it was opened the diners would receive a surprise — one which they were unlikely to forget.

A straight face was called for, and Betsy kept hers. Lord Caradoc was known at times for his boisterous manners, and no doubt had privately ordered his cook to prepare this treat for his guest. Whether the action was wise, however, she doubted; for Blake, unlike his host, was not a man noted for his sense of fun. Samuel Tripp, too, seemed ill-at-ease at what was going to happen, no doubt wondering as Betsy did what was waiting to leap, fly or even slither out of the pie. Mice, small birds, frogs, even a snake: the live ingredients depended on the host's humour, not to mention that of his guests. However, noting Lady Arabella's growing excitement, Betsy guessed that there was nothing to fear. And more, she knew that she and the other ladies would be expected to scream hysterically, and provoke roars of laughter from the men. Acting, again.

Betterton and his wife, now aware of the silence that had fallen at the other end of the board, turned to see what had caused it. Lord Caradoc, brows knitting in surprise, looked down the table at Alderman Blake, who, despite being fuddled by drink, had now begun to sense that all was not as it seemed. As if by arrangement, the little orchestra had stopped playing, while servants stood about, seemingly awaiting instruction. Finally, seeing that no one else seemed about to give it, Lady Arabella gestured to the nearest footman.

'Well don't just stand there, man, cut the pie open!'

The servant bowed, took a knife from the sideboard and came forward. As he did so, Lord Caradoc called to his wife in a voice of some concern. 'You have become most quiet down there, madam. Is anything amiss?'

Lady Arabella, no doubt realizing that she was to feign ignorance of the prank, smiled at him. 'We're all quite taken with this pie, my lord,' she answered. 'I confess I did not expect it.'

But Caradoc did not return her smile. 'Is that all?' he asked. 'Let our guests take what they will, though it's somewhat late for such a large dish, is it not?'

Then it was, that with a sudden quickening of her pulse, Betsy knew something was wrong — for Lord Caradoc did not appear to know any more about the blind-baked pie than his wife did. In fact, he was irritated that something so trivial had dampened the conversation. And Betsy knew well enough that His Lordship was no actor. In which case, who had arranged this little diversion?

Blake had been watching the footman, oblivious of the likely consequences. Now he looked embarrassed to find all eyes upon him, or upon the pie. The joke, familiar enough to those who had perhaps attended more riotous feasts than the alderman had, was now understood by all. And so the tension rose, as rather nervously the footman thrust his knife into the pie crust — and reacted in surprise. For the blade, having met with nothing but empty space, disappeared to the hilt.

There was an intake of breath. Not knowing what else to do the man removed the knife, then using it as a lever, prised off part of the pie's lid. The pastry broke at once — and involuntarily Betsy drew back, even as Samuel Tripp and Lady Arabella did the same. But in fascination, though clearly he had still not understood the cause of it, Alderman Blake stared at the pie . . . then gave a start, as if he had been struck. And the shriek that followed from Lady Arabella was as piercing as it was unfeigned — as was Thomas Bettertons's cry of alarm, and Samuel Tripp's oath, while Lord Caradoc stood up so abruptly that his chair overturned with a thud.

Betsy stared, and saw what everyone else saw: a shiny, sinister-looking lizard, oily black save for lurid orange blotches from head to tail, crawling out of the pie and on to the table cloth. The footman jerked back, raising his knife as if to ward the creature off, while the other diners now followed Lord Caradoc in springing to their feet.

'God in heaven.' Caradoc turned upon his servants in fury. 'Who has done this?!'

Nobody answered. And a vision flew into Betsy's mind of the banquet scene in *Macbeth*, when Banquo's ghost appears at the table unseen by all save the host, who cries out in similar fashion: *which of you has done this?*

As one, the watchers drew back from the table, eyes fixed upon the lizard-like creature. Apparently confused by its emergence into the light, it crawled slowly across the tablecloth between plates and cutlery, its splayed toes grasping clumsily at the linen. Its thick tail moved lithely from side to side, then uncannily the creature changed direction, and moved towards Alderman Blake.

But Blake did not move. He was frozen to his seat, and robbed of the power of speech. And as the others' gazes shifted from the monstrous lizard to the alderman, the fork fell from his hand. Slowly, painfully slowly, he rose from his chair.

Whereupon, as if at some unspoken command, the spell was broken. Both Tripp and Betterton seized knives from the table, but Caradoc's footman was quicker. Coming to his senses at last, the man raised his knife and brought it down violently upon the back of the animal, piercing it and pinning it to the table. There was another shriek from Lady Arabella, and a groan from the men, but the danger was passed. The creature writhed in agony, while a noxious-looking fluid welled from its body, staining the tablecloth. Then the wriggling ceased and, with a final twitch of its tail, the lizard was still. Everyone, servants and guests alike, gazed dumbly at the exotic-looking animal; whatever it was, it could not harm them now.

But Betsy's eyes were on Alderman Blake. For a moment the man remained rigid, half-risen from his chair, his hands gripping the arms. His face had turned from its usual florid hue, to a sickly yellow. Then he started shaking, and everyone turned in alarm, for it seemed that he was suffering some kind of seizure. Finally, when it looked as if he would collapse, Caradoc shouted an order, and servants started towards Blake. But the horror-stricken man raised a trembling hand, and pointed at the table.

'The Salamander,' he said hoarsely. 'He lives, and he sends me a sign!' And as the others watched, he fell back into his chair, staring vacantly into the air.

CHAPTER SEVEN

A short while later, at Betsy's suggestion, Lord Caradoc's coach was despatched to Doctor Tom Catlin's house with a message that his services were urgently required. Meanwhile, Alderman Blake had been laid on a couch in a downstairs parlour at Bredon House, where he remained motionless, his face drained of all colour. Betsy and the Bettertons stayed by him, but it was clear they could do little. Lady Arabella had retired to her chamber, overcome by the excitement. Her husband, furious at the disaster the evening had become, spent some time shouting at his hapless servants before disappearing to another part of the house. After a while he reappeared, striding into the room with a look of exasperation.

'This business grows stranger by the hour,' Caradoc cried. 'For my cook denies that he made the pie! Says he knew nothing of it until it was delivered from a bake-shop, soon after we sat down to dine. He didn't even trouble to ask the fellow who brought it, which bakery it came from! He assumed the dish was something special I'd arranged, and ordered it to be carried to the table. What think you of that?'

Nobody answered, until Betterton cleared his throat. 'If you trust the man, my lord, then what else can you do but accept his account as true?'

'Of course I trust him,' Caradoc snapped. 'He's been with me for years.' He peered at Blake. 'Has he still not spoken?'

'He appears to be in a shocked state, my lord,' Mary Betterton answered. 'Then who would not be, who witnessed what we all did?' She turned to her husband. 'What in heaven's name was that fearful-looking animal?'

Betterton threw her a helpless look. 'My lord, I fear there's little we can contribute here,' he said. 'With your leave, I would like to take my wife home.'

Caradoc nodded. 'We will speak again, of this.' He frowned. 'From my end of the table I couldn't hear what he said, when he pointed to the creature. Did you hear?'

Both Betterton and his wife shook their heads. Samuel Tripp, who had been sitting to one side of the room wearing his customary cynical expression, merely shrugged. But Betsy spoke up. 'The Salamander, my lord. That's what he called it.'

'Salamander?' Caradoc's frown deepened. 'But that's a mythical beast, isn't it? I'm no scientist, but what crawled out of that pie was a lizard of some kind. Anyone who's walked in the country knows that!'

'I fear you are mistaken, my lord,' came a voice from the doorway. Betsy looked round, to see Tom Catlin in his Brandenburg coat. As the others turned, the doctor came forward and made his bow.

'I've seen them on the continent, in warmer climes than ours,' he added politely. 'They are not lizards, but a type of newt, I believe, and quite harmless.'

'The devil, you say!' Caradoc stared at him, then gestured towards the prone figure of Alderman Blake. 'But if this man knew what it was, why was he so afflicted? I know a look of terror when I see one.'

'I can't say, sir,' Catlin answered. 'With your leave, may I examine him?'

'If you please.' Caradoc stood aside, while the doctor took a chair and placed it close to the patient. As he sat he glanced at Betsy, who at once understood.

'Might I remain, my lord?' she asked. 'I may be able to assist the doctor in some way.'

Caradoc nodded absently, then turned to the Bettertons, who were ready to take their leave. Tripp too, seeing he was surplus to requirements, rose and made his bow. The playmaker accepted Betterton's offer of a ride home. As he followed the others out he threw Betsy a pointed look, which she ignored.

The farewells over, Betsy and Catlin were alone with the patient. Having listened to the man's breathing and heartbeat, the doctor turned to her with a raised eyebrow. 'Will you tell me what happened?'

For the first time since entering Bredon House, Betsy relaxed. Without hurrying, she gave Catlin a full account of the evening's events, up to the alderman's collapse.

The doctor listened in silence. Then, after prodding Blake in various places, peering into his eyes and his mouth, he sat back. 'I've seen similar cases. When he'll emerge from this paralysis — or even whether he will — I've no idea—' he broke off as Lord Caradoc re-entered, and both he and Betsy rose to face him. Quickly, the doctor gave his verdict: Alderman Blake was in a static condition, supposedly induced by severe shock. It was impossible to tell whether he could hear or see what went on around him. Hence there was little the doctor could do but recommend the man be taken to his own house, under the care of his servants and his own physician. In time, perhaps, he would recover.

Lord Caradoc looked down at Blake, and shook his head. 'My thanks to you, Catlin,' he muttered. 'My coachman will drive you, and Mistress Brand too, of course.' He glanced at Betsy, then added: 'I'll make arrangements to have the alderman taken home, and his physician notified.'

But as the other two realized, His Lordship had more to say. 'This business confounds me,' he went on. 'For reasons that elude me, it would seem that someone arranged for that pie to be made, placed this . . . this salamander inside it, then had it conveyed to my house, to a private feast,' he spread his hands. 'But why? You say the creature's a species of newt?'

Catlin looked thoughtful. 'What have they done with the animal?' he enquired. 'Might I be permitted to look at it?'

'Well, if it hasn't been destroyed, I see no reason why you shouldn't,' His Lordship replied. 'Do you think it important?'

Now Betsy spoke up. 'My lord, I did not repeat everything I heard the alderman say when he pointed to the animal,' she said. 'But now it strikes me as curious. His words were: *The Salamander — he lives, and he sends me a sign.*'

His Lordship stared at her. '*He* lives?' he echoed. 'What can that mean?'

Now Catlin was intrigued. 'I cannot guess, my lord, but it grows deeper by the minute. I confess I won't be able to put the matter from my mind until I learn the cause of it.'

At that, Caradoc's manner grew brisk. 'Then follow me,' he said. 'For I'll not rest until I've got to the bottom of it, either!'

* * *

As luck would have it, the dead salamander had not yet been disposed of. A short while later, the three of them stood round a table in Lord Caradoc's library, staring down at the sorry-looking creature. A servant had carried it from the dining-room in a box. After a moment, His Lordship wrinkled his nose in disgust. 'Well, is there anything you can tell us?'

Catlin's brow had furrowed the moment the animal was brought in; now he looked almost excited. Despite the evening's events, Betsy had to suppress a smile. Especially when the doctor startled Caradoc by picking the salamander up by its tail and peering at it.

'My curiosity increases, my lord,' he answered, as he lowered the lifeless creature back into its box. 'For unless I'm mistaken, this is a fire salamander. One sees them in France and Italy, though they are generally marked with yellow rather than orange.'

Turning to face Caradoc, he went on: 'The ancients believed it one of the elementals, defined by the sage

Paracelsus. As gnomes were said to inhabit the earth, nymphs the waters, and sylphs the air, so the salamander's domain was fire.' He shrugged. 'Pure superstition, of course. The belief that the fire salamander was born of fire comes from its habit of hibernating in crannies such as wood piles. When logs were carried indoors and put on the hearth, the creatures would scuttle out. But they are harmless amphibians, as I said.'

'And very colourful,' Betsy put in thoughtfully. 'Small wonder those marks would suggest a poisonous nature.'

'Yet we are no nearer to discovering why it was sent to frighten us,' Caradoc muttered.

One thing, however, was clear to Betsy. 'None of us knew what it was, save Alderman Blake,' she went on. 'Perhaps it was sent only to frighten *him* — and he alone saw some significance in it: *He lives, and sends me a sign.*'

'I believe Mistress Brand is correct,' Catlin said with a nod. 'It was a message — and a most cunningly contrived one.'

'But it's bizarre,' Caradoc said irritably. '*He* lives? It makes no sense!'

Catlin thought for a moment. 'I will visit the alderman in a day or so,' he said. 'If he speaks, then perhaps we might learn more of the business.'

'Well, if he does, be sure to acquaint me of it,' Caradoc said grimly. 'For whoever invades my house with such tricks will live to regret it!'

Soon after, Betsy and Tom Catlin took their leave of Bredon House. Lord Caradoc accompanied them outside to the coach. A west wind was blowing, with a promise of rain. As they clambered inside, His Lordship said: 'Whatever you can discover, doctor, and you too, Mistress Brand, I am most keen to hear it . . . and I will reward you for your trouble. This wicked prank has made my flesh crawl!'

He signalled to his footman to slam the door, and in a moment the coach was rolling out of the gates into Piccadilly.

Now Catlin turned to Betsy, as if he had been waiting until they were alone. 'I didn't tell His Lordship all that I knew,' he said, 'for it seemed not the time to do so.'

When Betsy showed her surprise, he went on: 'You said Blake cried out: *He lives, and he sends me a sign.* Assuming that the fire salamander was the sign, then perhaps there is an explanation.'

He put a hand to his forehead, as if probing for the memory. 'During the Great Fire, I recall something — someone, I should say — known as "the Salamander". It could be because he — was it *he*? — seemed to thrive on the conflagration, as if somehow he relished it.' He shook his head. 'But it's vague; I might even have imagined it.'

'Could it have been a looter?' Betsy asked. 'One who took advantage of the catastrophe to prey on people, and to rob their houses?'

'Perhaps,' Catlin sighed. 'But then, those terrible days have become forged into one fearful memory, as no doubt they have for others. It was as if we all stood on the brink of Hades.'

Whereupon Betsy took his arm in a sisterly manner. 'Yet we survived it,' she said. 'And London is rising from the ashes, to become the great city that it was.'

The doctor gave a nod, and gazed out of the window.

* * *

A rainy Monday morning, with no performance to prepare for, was not to Betsy Brand's liking. But she rose early, her mind filled with the events of the previous evening. Tom Catlin saw her briefly before leaving the house, saying he would 'poke about' if he found time. So after breakfast she put on a cloak and hood and walked down to Fleet Street, intending to go into the city and call upon Jane Rowe. Talking to Jane always helped her put matters in a clearer perspective.

As she crossed the bridge, her gaze wandered up the narrow, choked expanse of the Fleet River, to fall upon the forbidding bulk of the prison. The Fleet was one of the most notorious gaols in London, and among its inhabitants was

Jane's sweetheart, a handsome but feckless rogue whose name Betsy sometimes forgot. Hall, that was it. Cobus Hall. She sighed, thinking of Jane's devotion to a man who was unlikely to bring her anything but grief. How was it, she wondered, that the best women seemed so often to pair with the weakest of men? Then her mind jumped to Hannah Cleeve, and she stopped in her tracks.

In her mind's eye she saw Hannah, telling of Tom Cleeve's frightened behaviour just before he died: of his 'babbling' about Long Ned, and of the Fire. But then, as Hannah said, what Londoner didn't dream of that? Nevertheless, instead of walking through Ludgate, Betsy turned left into Old Bailey, and made her way northwards along the wall. Soon she was threading her way through the crowds in Smithfield and past the Three Bars into Clerkenwell, until once again she stood in Turnmill Street, at the entrance to Cooper's Court.

The place looked even grimmer than when she had last been here. The alley was a quagmire, its drain choked with refuse. Even the trulls had kept indoors out of the rain. Picking her way beneath the jetties and avoiding dripping water, Betsy reached the familiar door and knocked. This time there was no noise of children, but after a moment the door opened a couple of inches, and Hannah's face appeared. Without a word she drew back and allowed Betsy to enter.

The baby was asleep in a corner, but the twins were conspicuous by their absence. To Betsy's enquiry, Hannah gave a shrug.

'I hire 'em out to a lame beggar,' she said. 'They can put on a good enough show . . . bump his takings up. We'll get a shilling or two out of it.'

Without preamble, Betsy told Hannah something of what had occurred during the past days: of Joseph Rigg's death, and her discovery that Long Ned had been intending to leave England. She did not speak of what Catlin had found, nor did she mention Alderman Blake, let alone what had befallen him at Caradoc's.

But Hannah was barely interested. She had never heard of Rigg, nor did the man's true name of Griffiths mean anything to her. As for Long Ned intending to leave the country, she gave a snort. 'Who wouldn't go, who'd come from somewhere warm and sunny like Ned did?' she asked. 'Wouldn't you?'

Betsy nodded, then in a casual tone said: 'I heard something, to do with the Fire. Or I should say, I heard of someone . . . the Salamander, that was it. Does it strike a memory in you?'

There was a moment, then to Betsy's surprise Hannah threw back her head and gave a shout of laughter.

'The Salamander! What've you heard about him?'

'Well . . . that he was about, during the Fire—'

'About!' Hannah gave another laugh. 'He was that, all right. He was everywhere!'

'I don't understand,' Betsy said.

'He's a fable,' Hannah told her. 'A sprite you conjure up to frighten children. Show me someone who says he's seen the Salamander, and I'll say he was pickled as a herring!'

The woman sniffed, and wiped her nose with the sleeve of her old chemise. 'I suppose it's unlikely you'd have heard of him,' she added. 'You mix with folk of all stations, Betsy Brand, and you never scoff. But your father was a gent, and you're a well-bred lady at heart, that once lived in a big house. Isn't it so?' When Betsy did not answer, she went on: 'In the lanes and ginnels where tenant folk like my family dwelt, it's another tale. Those who had precious little to save, who left their old houses with naught but the clothes on their backs, watched 'em burn without much sorrow, often as not.' She sighed, then went on: 'After a couple of days, when the fire spread to the west wall, that was when those tales started up: the Salamander, hopping in and out of burning buildings free as you like, because the flames couldn't touch him. Every purse, every bit of silver that went missing . . . blame the Salamander, for he must've took it! Why, there's even women who claim they were violated by him, while the house next door burned.' She broke off, fixing Betsy with a wry smile. 'You believe in the Salamander, Mistress, you'll believe anything!'

'Perhaps I shouldn't have listened to rumour,' Betsy said ruefully.

Hannah was silent for a while. 'There was so much panic then, so much fear,' her face clouded. ' 'Twas the devil's work . . . and there were those who found a ready scapegoat when something valuable disappeared. They could always blame the Salamander. Some swore blind they saw him, but when it comes to describing him, they'd turn a bit forgetful. Odd, that, wouldn't you say?'

'Looters, you mean?' Betsy met Hannah's eye. 'Is that what you meant when you said Tom and Ned were thick as thieves?'

'Here, don't you go calling Tom a looter,' Hannah muttered. 'He never told me what he did during the Fire, and I never asked.' She gave another sniff. 'Is that all you came for?'

'You asked me to pass on anything I learned,' Betsy replied. 'But since it seems it's nothing to do with what happened to Tom, I'll take my leave.' Whereupon Hannah spoke in a softer tone.

'You know me, Betsy,' she muttered. 'I've a mouth on me that'd stop a horse and dray. Look for me in a week or two, for I'll likely be working the Black Spread-Eagle. We'll take a mug, and laugh about old times.'

Betsy frowned; the Black Spread-Eagle was an evil tavern, notorious for the coarseness of its whores. 'What of your children?' she began, but Hannah shrugged.

'They'll have a roof and a bite to eat. That's enough, isn't it?'

* * *

A half hour later, Betsy was in Jane Rowe's house in Butcher's Hall Lane, with a welcome cup of ale in her hand. The house was new, one of those rebuilt in the years following the Fire.

Jane's brothers were at their work, helping their widower father at his stall in Newgate Market. Hence the two actresses could talk at leisure, and in a short time Betsy had acquainted her friend with all that had occurred since they last parted, at the Hercules Pillars. But on hearing of the curious fate of Alderman Blake, Jane grew thoughtful.

'Well now, I don't know how this salamander business fits, but I do know Blake's made enemies in his time. Then, he makes such a show of being a pious, God-fearing man you'd guess the old blatherer was a fake, wouldn't you?'

'A fake?' Betsy raised her eyebrows.

Jane shrugged. 'He made most of his money importing wines . . . but not all of it. He had the rights to Newgate felons, for transport to the colonies,' she fumbled for the word. 'Franchise, that's what they call it.'

'You mean, he was paid for shipping them out?' Betsy asked.

'Paid by the head,' Jane told her. 'More, he had a sideline in selling the shackles for old iron.' She gave a grim smile. 'You ask my Cobus what those in prison think of Blake, let alone what they'd do to the bastard if they had the chance!'

Betsy took a drink. 'But if it was a matter of revenge,' she said thoughtfully, 'say a freed felon, or a relative of someone he'd sent away, why not just wait for him after dark with a cudgel? If the live salamander was a message, as Tom Catlin thinks, it seems a mighty strange message to me.'

'And a deal of trouble to go to,' Jane agreed. 'And now you've reminded me, I might have heard those tales too, about the Salamander. But they didn't trouble me. Our family were lucky, Betsy. My father and brothers worked fast and we got out before the flames reached us, carried everything we could to Moorfields. Lived under a tent for more than a year.' She frowned at the memory. 'Then, nothing that happened in those days surprises me. We'll never know all that went on, will we?'

It was true. Every Londoner had memories of that fearful conflagration, and Betsy's were less terrible than most.

After a moment she said: 'Let's suppose that the Salamander was real, can we?' When Jane looked sceptical, she went on: 'If there was someone — a looter, say — who saw easy pickings as people fled the flames, would it not suit such a man to be thought a sprite . . . a mere fable? He could even have spread the tales himself.'

Jane made a face. 'You've never been one to let your fancies fly away with you, Betsy,' she remarked. 'Could it be that watching Tom Cleeve's death, then Rigg's, has shook you up more than you know?'

'I don't think so,' Betsy answered. 'But I yearn to know what connects them. Remember the pinpricks Tom Catlin found?'

'What does a pinprick matter?' Jane asked. 'Whether there's a brown stain about it or not, does that speak of murder? I've thought on it since, and I'll take a deal more convincing than that!'

It did not surprise Betsy that her down-to-earth friend remained sceptical. Was it likely that the three men — Long Ned, Cleeve and Rigg — had all been murdered, in the space of as many days? She looked up, to see Jane smiling.

'Now don't fall into the mulligrubs,' she said. 'Whatever you do, you know I'll help if I can.'

'I know it,' Betsy said, returning the smile — whereupon Jane looked thoughtful. 'There's some in prison could tell you more,' she said. 'About looting, I mean.' She frowned. 'I don't mean my Cobus! He's no angel, but he never did worse than pocket a bit of silver,' she hesitated. 'There's one I could name knows more than most. Then you wouldn't want to go looking for him.'

But Betsy's pulse quickened. 'Who is that?'

Jane looked uncomfortable. 'Pay someone else to go seek him,' she said, 'for he's a wicked fellow, and I wouldn't sleep knowing I set you after him.'

'Please . . . tell me who the man is,' Betsy persisted. 'Then let me worry about how to find him.'

Finally Jane sighed, and met her gaze. 'Dart,' she said finally. 'His name's Dart, and he'll likely be in the Bermudas, where the law can't get at him.'

Then, as if regretting what she had said, she put out her hand and gripped Betsy's arm. 'But if you go seeking that one, Betsy, promise me you'll take someone to watch your back,' she said urgently. 'Or Lord knows what might happen!'

CHAPTER EIGHT

When Betsy told Tom Catlin that she intended to disguise herself and go into the Bermudas, he was mortified.

'Have you taken leave of your senses?' he demanded. 'The Straits is a lawless enclave! At best you'll be robbed, at worst . . . well, I won't name it. But I imagine you can guess.'

Betsy waited for him to regain his customary calm. She had spent much of the afternoon walking in St James's Park, thinking. Now night had fallen, supper was over at Fire's Reach Court and the candles lit. She remained seated while the doctor paced about. Finally he picked up his mug and took a pull.

'It's a foolhardy notion, Betsy, and I urge you to abandon it. As a friend of your father's, I must have an eye for your safety. Going on a hunt in that warren for some fambler or biter you've never set eyes upon — it's madness. Even if you find him, he'll likely take your money and tell you nought but lies!'

'Fambler or biter?' Betsy smiled. 'I didn't know you were so *au fait* with criminal speech.'

'It's because I know something of the netherworld of rogues that I'm qualified to warn you off!' the other retorted. He sighed, then sat down facing Betsy.

'Think what you do,' he said. 'Your little expedition to the bagnio proved fruitless. This time, even if your disguise fools those you meet, which it may not, you're taking a far greater risk. The Bermudas may claim old rights of sanctuary, but there's nothing holy about the place — quite the reverse. Only the desperate go there.'

'Which is precisely why I may find some clue to the puzzle that has kept me awake half the night,' Betsy told him. 'Don't pretend you're not curious yourself.'

'Curious, perhaps,' Catlin allowed. 'But I haven't lost my reason.' His brow knitted. 'There's something very dark behind this whole business. The deaths, I mean.'

'And now Alderman Blake being scared out of his wits,' Betsy broke in. 'Do you think there could be some connection?'

'I don't see how.' Catlin hesitated, then added: 'I went to see Blake today, as I promised Caradoc. There's no change. The man's like a living statue . . . it's almost as if he's given up, and simply wills himself to die.'

'And if he should die, that would make four deaths,' Betsy answered. 'All of them linked in some way with the Duke's Theatre!'

'A tenuous link,' Catlin objected. 'Long Ned was employed briefly at the old theatre, it's true. But Blake's only connection was a desire to see the Duke's shut down.'

'Perhaps not,' Betsy said, and at last told the doctor what Jane Rowe had told her, about the alderman's grisly trade of shipping felons from the gaols to the colonies.

Catlin was stunned by the revelation. 'The old hypocrite!' he exclaimed. 'To my mind, that makes him little better than the wretches he packed off.' He met Betsy's eye. 'But I still don't follow your reasoning. What makes you think those tales of the Salamander have bearing on the deaths of Ned, Cleeve and Rigg?'

'The Fire,' Betsy replied. 'I don't know how, but all threads seem to lead back to that. Hannah Cleeve wouldn't speak of it, but it's my belief Tom was involved in looting at that time. And he and Long Ned were thick as thieves, Hannah said . . . literally. In which case—'

'In which case,' Catlin interrupted, 'your theory falls flat! For Joseph Rigg — or Joseph Griffiths, the magistrate's son — had no connection with Ned or Cleeve, back then. The notion that he'd consort with looters is preposterous.'

'Yet you found the same pinpricks on his body that you found on Tom Cleeve's.'

After a moment Catlin lifted his mug and drained it. Then he got up again and took a few paces. 'Well, Mistress Rummager, you have me there.' He stopped pacing. 'One thing occurs to me: with Blake out of the way, it seems likely the Duke's will reopen soon, does it not? Which will be of great relief to quite a number of people.'

Betsy started. 'You think one of our company was behind that cruel joke at Caradoc's?'

'How many would know where the alderman was dining that evening?' Catlin countered. 'Let alone be able to arrange the blind-baked pie in time, and have it sent to Caradoc's.' He shook his head. 'An elaborate plan, carried out with such cunning — a sharp intellect's behind it, that much is clear to me.'

He paused, whereupon Betsy spoke up. 'I know you have my safety at heart, yet I still mean to go to the Bermudas and look for this man Dart,' she said gently.

The doctor sighed . . . and gave up. 'Then you must not go alone. I'd better accompany you — and I will be armed.'

But Betsy shook her head. 'You're too well known about the Strand and the suburbs,' she objected. 'And even if we fashioned a disguise for you, you're no actor.' She thought for a moment. 'If I must have a companion, it should be another woman who can pass herself off as one of Hannah Cleeve's calling.'

At that moment the door opened, and Peg lurched in with cap awry and sleeves rolled, glaring at them both. 'If master and mistress have finished,' she said acidly, 'I'd like to clear the supper table.'

Betsy looked at Catlin, who let out a sigh of exasperation.

* * *

Reprising her role as Mary Peach was easy enough for Betsy; persuading Peg Brazier to accompany her was another matter. Only with Tom Catlin's promise of a day off, and Betsy's of a new petticoat, would Peg consent to the enterprise. Even then, as the two women made their way through Covent Garden that night, she made plain her contempt for the whole business.

'What d'you think to do?' she asked. 'Knock on every rotten door in the Bermudas and ask for Mr Dart? They'll think you're cracked as an old pot!'

Betsy's mind was busy, however. She was mulling over not only her conversation with Catlin, but those she had had earlier with Hannah and Jane. Despite her fears, which she could not admit to Peg, she felt elated. She was on the scent; and though she did not know where it might lead, it excited her.

Peg's presence was a mixed blessing. Though she looked the part of a street-walker well enough, in a torn taffeta chemise and an old red wig, her heart was not in the role. And what Betsy feared was that the first man who accosted her might receive a kick to the shins followed by a mouthful of abuse. Her advice was that Peg should wear the vizard-mask they had fashioned, and let Betsy do the talking. Her one concession had been that Peg could take an old dagger of Catlin's, which was strapped to her thigh under her skirts. Thus armed, the two sallied forth among the night-time crowds, and were able to make their way unhindered to Maiden Lane, parallel to the Strand. Turning left into Half Moon Street, which was less crowded, they arrived at the large inn on the corner which bore the same name. The Half

Moon was a disreputable tavern, despite being directly opposite the fashionable New Exchange. The difference between the south side of the Strand, lined with grand houses that gave on to the river, and the north side, was never more marked than it was here.

Now both women tensed as they walked the last yards to the dark opening of Round Court, the south entry to the lawless little community of the Bermudas. Debtors had once fled to the distant Islands of Bermuda; and though this less balmy district was on the fringes of London, it had earned the nickname because it too offered a haven, a respite for those wishing to escape the reach of the law. With a glance at each other, Betsy and Peg entered the rookery. And though there was no obstacle, Betsy felt as though she passed through some invisible barrier. More alarmingly, the feeling grew that unseen eyes were upon her, and that henceforth her every movement would be watched.

Gingerly, they walked under creaking, overhanging jetties, past boarded windows. But soon there was light ahead: a lurid red glow. The two of them emerged in Round Court, a rough quadrangle with several exits, and doorways opening on to what looked like noisome hovels. Now came a hum of low voices, and at last there were people: a group of men standing about an iron brazier, warming their hands at the fire within it. As the two women emerged from the alley the men turned, and some laughed at sight of a pair of blowsy-looking trulls, who appeared to be lost.

'Whom do ye seek, Miss?' The questioner was a rat-faced little man in fustian. When Betsy hesitated, he grinned. 'Come into the light — or d'you wish to hide your charms from us?'

Behind, Betsy heard Peg mutter under her breath. Quickly she summoned a Mary Peach smile, and stepped forward. 'Looking won't cost you, master,' she said. 'But don't think there's any laced mutton for free!'

Another man, less good-humoured than the first, glowered at her from across the fire. 'If you want the Red Sash it's back the way you've come, in Long Court.'

'I know that,' Betsy said. 'I'm looking for a fellow. I've brought news for him.'

'Who's that then?' the first man asked. His glance strayed past Betsy to Peg, who hung back.

'Dart,' Betsy answered, and was quickly alert, for all of the men stiffened.

'Dart, eh?' the rat-faced fellow seemed to ponder the matter deeply. 'Sure it wasn't "fart"?'

'It's Dart,' Betsy said. 'Are you deaf, or sumfing?'

The man gave a laugh. But now Betsy heard Peg draw close behind her. 'We haven't got all night, you little weasel,' she said caustically. 'Either point us to him, or go tug yourself off.'

There was a brief silence before the men reacted, most with amusement. Finally the weasel spoke.

'Give me your news and I'll pass it on,' he said. But his smile was fading, to be replaced by a hard look. Betsy glanced round, and stifled a groan. For Peg had disregarded her instruction: not only was she not wearing her mask, she was twirling it impudently about her wrist.

'I'd tell you to boil your ears,' she retorted, fixing the small man with a stare to match his own. 'If I hadn't guessed you'd lost 'em already. Nailed to the Charing Cross pillory, were they?'

Now there was danger in the air. The men gazed at them, until, cursing inwardly, Betsy rounded on Peg.

'Shut it, buffle-head!' she cried. 'You've got a mouth on you like Bow Bell.' She turned to the others. 'She don't mean nothing by it,' she said. 'She's not been right in the head since she got sent to Bridewell.'

'Is it so?' the little man answered, looking both women up and down. And though Betsy read the menace in his gaze, she stood her ground. Beside her, Peg was breathing hard.

'I think he's Dart,' she said abruptly.

Betsy blinked, then saw that Peg had seemingly guessed right, for the man allowed a grin to spread over his features again. 'Well, you're a sharp one,' he said. 'How come I've not seen you before?'

Peg sniffed. 'I've my own place, away from here — and you couldn't afford me!'

Some of the men had relaxed, but one or two still wore ugly expressions. And now the glowering one, who had assumed they were seeking the Red Sash, took a step towards them.

'You see about your news,' he said over his shoulder. 'I'll do business with the other.' And both Betsy and Peg stiffened as he approached them, fumbling in a pocket.

'I can afford you,' he said, holding up a gold coin. 'In fact, I can buy half a dozen like you. So let's take a turn down the alley there.'

Betsy glanced at Peg, but with a jerk of her head Peg silenced her. Meeting Betsy's eye, she gave her to understand that they should go with both men. What she had in mind after that, Betsy did not know. But she trusted Peg; and despite her fears, she still felt a thrill of discovery. She had found Dart, and it had been easy. What more might she discover?

'Well then.' She flicked her skirts, allowing Dart a brief glimpse of her leg. 'If you gents know somewhere a bit private we'll all go together, shall we?'

A look of uncertainty crossed the small man's features. But the other one's eagerness merely increased. Drawing close to Peg, he put a hand to her waist, and ran it upwards to her breast. 'Follow me,' he said, with a look that would have quelled a woman of lesser spirit. 'But know that I'll make you earn every penny, you mouthy young bulker.'

Peg drew a breath, took the man's hand from her bosom and held it. 'Lead on, then,' she said in a flat voice. 'And let's see if you're all you claim to be.'

And watched by the other men, some of whom now wore envious looks, Betsy and Peg allowed themselves to be led away from the firelight, into a narrow opening. The walls and the low roof closed about them at once, so that both had to bend their heads, and in a moment gloom swallowed the four of them up. Betsy was already considering her escape when Dart, who had been holding her arm, stopped. There was the squeak of a latch, and the four of them squeezed through a doorway into a noisome room that smelled of old sacking. As the door closed behind them, the taller man fumbled for a tinderbox and struck a flame. Both women blinked . . . then Betsy caught the gleam in Peg's eye, and steeled herself for what would happen.

The man had found a tallow dip, and was lighting it. As the walls came dimly into view, Betsy saw they were in a cluttered storeroom, with a ladder in one corner leading to an upper floor. But even as she glanced round, she was pushed over, to land on her back on something soft. She gasped — then realized her 'customer' was standing over her.

'Not yet,' she said, keeping a level tone. 'We haven't talked money,' but the small man was already loosening his belt. Hurriedly, she sat up — then to her alarm there was a loud crack, followed by a grunt. And she was both surprised and highly relieved to see the taller man sinking to the floor — and Peg standing over him with something in her hand. And as the other one turned in surprise Peg dropped the weapon, lifted her skirt and whipped the dagger out.

'I'm nobody's bulker,' she said in an icy tone. 'Now sit down, Mr Dart, and hear my friend out, for it's you we seek!'

But to both women's dismay, the man laughed suddenly. His eyes went to the dagger Peg brandished, then he looked up.

'I'm not Dart,' he said cheerfully, and pointed to the prone figure by the wall. 'He is!'

* * *

There was nothing else for Betsy to do, once the rat-faced man had convinced her of her mistake, but to dig out her purse.

Within minutes she had paid him what she could spare, and extracted a promise from him to leave her and Peg alone with the other man. She swore that she had been paid to take information to Dart, and that the two of them would then be gone, never to return. Finally the fellow shrugged, clinked the coins in his hand and went out, pulling the door shut. Only then did Betsy turn to vent her anger upon a subdued Peg.

'So you thought you'd try a little deduction of your own, did you?' she demanded. 'Not only did you get the wrong man, you managed to knock the one we want senseless!'

Peg looked down at the tall man, who lay where he had fallen, knocked unconscious by the broken stool she had picked up. 'You were as taken in as I was,' she retorted. 'How do I know what's what, in a nest of rogues like this? Anyway, it's no use bleating. What're we going to do with him?'

'Let me think, will you?' Betsy sat down heavily on a sack of something. But there came a groan, and both women looked round in alarm. Betsy scrambled to her feet, even as Peg picked up the stuttering lamp and held its feeble flame aloft.

'He's coming round,' she said, and reached for the broken stool. But Betsy stayed her.

'Wait. I'll bind him while you hold the dagger. Tell him you'll poke his eye out.'

'Suppose he doesn't believe me?' Peg demanded. But without further delay Betsy lifted her chemise, grasped her underskirt and tore at it. In a moment she had produced a strip several feet long, and falling to her knees she held it above the figure of Dart, who was trying weakly to raise himself.

'The dagger!' she cried. 'Quick.'

Peg knelt beside her victim and held the dagger out. Both of them waited while the real Dart struggled to raise himself, groaning as he did so. Finally he opened his eyes, trying to focus. But at once Betsy threw her strip of linen about his shoulders, pulled it tight and tied it. At the same moment Peg stuck the dagger in front of Dart's face.

'One move and I'll slit your nose,' she breathed.

The man's mouth fell open. Clumsily, he sat up, then fell back against the wall with a grunt. He tried to move his arms, and found them restricted. Finally he seemed to come to his senses and gave a sigh, gazing from one woman to another.

'You,' he winced, his mouth twisted in anger. 'What do you want of me?'

But Betsy, on her knees, faced him with suppressed excitement. 'I want you to tell me about the Salamander,' she said.

There was a silence, then: 'Why should I?'

She drew out a coin and held it up. 'There's this if you do. If you won't, my friend here will stab you a couple of times, since you've upset her so. Then we'll be gone and you'll still be lying here, looking a prize fool.'

Dart glared. 'Untie my arms,' he demanded.

Peg shook her head, then caught Betsy's glance. With a wry look she held the dagger out while Betsy tugged at the knot, and finally freed the strip of linen.

Dart sat up, rubbed his head and winced again. Then seeing both women watching him, he seemed to come to a decision. 'Most thought he was dead,' he muttered, 'but I knew better,' he grimaced. 'So he's back, is he?'

After a moment, Betsy gave a nod.

The man's eyes strayed to Peg, then back to Betsy. 'Who the devil are you?' he demanded.

'Never mind,' Betsy said. 'Tell me what you know of the Salamander.'

After a moment, Dart looked away. 'The Salamander's a Dutchman,' he said. 'Name of Aanaarden. He served at sea in the Dutch wars . . . had a skill with fire-ships, so I heard.'

Betsy caught her breath. So that was how he was able to move about so readily during the Fire. She gazed at Dart, whose eyes narrowed.

'Well now,' he murmured. 'It looks to me as if you know a thing or two about him already.'

'He was looting, wasn't he?' Betsy asked.

The man met her eye. 'I never asked him.'

'Yet there are things you know,' Betsy persisted. 'Tell me, or I'll—'

'You'll what?' Dart broke in. To the dismay of both women, he had begun to relax. 'You won't use that,' he said, with a nod towards the dagger. 'And in any case, from the look of it, it wouldn't cut rancid butter!'

'She mightn't use it, but I would,' Peg said quietly.

The man shifted his gaze towards her. Then after a moment, he gave a leer. 'You should've took my offer, Spindle-shanks,' he said. 'You don't know what you missed.'

Peg flared up. 'You miserable dunnaker,' she snapped. 'I'd rather shove my hand in boiling tar.' And before Betsy could stop her, she had moved the dagger so that its tip rested on Dart's cheekbone. In spite of himself, the man flinched.

'It may not cut,' Peg said in a voice of ice. 'But I wouldn't want it stuck in my eye!'

Dart had stiffened. Both women smelled his sour breath, as slowly he brought up his hand to rub his stubbly chin. Then he threw a look of hatred at them, tempered only by his instinct for self-preservation. Betsy remembered Jane Rowe's words, even as she saw the truth of them: *He's a wicked fellow*.

'The Salamander worked the houses,' he said harshly. 'While folk fled out the doors, he was climbing in the back windows . . . even as the fire took hold, he was busy. Began to think he was immortal, to my mind, and that was his undoing. He got careless: slipped into one place, and there were a couple of looters already there, breaking open a chest. One was a black-skinned fellow.'

With an effort Betsy hid her excitement, hoping that Peg would do the same. But oddly, Dart seemed to have forgotten them both. There was a far-off look in his eyes, as if speaking of the Fire had jolted memories even he preferred not to dwell upon.

'They set on him,' he muttered. 'One — not the black fellow, the other — would have killed him, save they heard the beadle in the street, shouting was there anyone left inside, for the flames were close. So those two biters left him there and legged it. They thought the fire would finish him; but the beadle and his men came in, saw the chest broke and took him for a looter. Took him to Newgate.' He grimaced. 'That's where I knew him.'

Dart paused, and an odd look came over his features. 'I was the one he told his tale to,' he said softly. 'I, and no other! He thought he was talking to a dead man, for I was facing the rope . . . only no one expected that within days the fire would reach Newgate too! And God bless it, I say, for burning that stinking pile down!'

The change in the man was startling. There was a wild look in his eye now, a mixture of pride and defiance, so that when Peg finally took the knife away, he barely noticed.

'I escaped the Three-legged Mare,' Dart said, nodding to himself. 'But I was the one the Dutchman told his tale to. So when he was shipped off to the Indies, only I knew who he really was,' he laughed harshly. 'Thought they'd seen the last of the Salamander, did they? Perished in the Fire? Well, I knew he'd be a sight harder to kill than that.'

He lowered his voice to a whisper. 'And if he's back, I wouldn't want to be in their shoes, the two who left him for dead. Or anyone else he'd a mind to take his vengeance on, for that matter!' He looked up suddenly, fixing Betsy with a glare.

'Whatever your interest be, woman, my advice is forget it — and quick! For if you cross the Salamander's path, you won't be laced mutton much longer: you'll be rotten meat!'

CHAPTER NINE

The next day, Alderman Blake was found dead.

Betsy did not learn of it until late in the morning, when Tom Catlin came home to find her in the kitchen with Peg, taking a tardy breakfast. The two of them were tired after the previous night, but at the sight of Catlin's expression Betsy was soon alert. With barely a glance at the two women, he sat down and told his news.

The alderman had passed a peaceful night. In fact, his servants believed they had detected signs of progress throughout yesterday, though to Blake's physician that seemed mere wishful thinking. By morning Blake was stone cold, which suggested he had died some hours earlier, a consequence of the shock he had received at Caradoc's. But Tom Catlin had a more sinister explanation.

'His physician resented my presence,' he said, 'which was no surprise. I told him it was a courtesy visit, since I was the one who attended the alderman when he was taken ill, but that only annoyed him further. So there was no point in asking leave to examine the body, for I knew I would be refused.'

He paused. 'Yet you did so,' Betsy said, intrigued. 'So tell me of it, for I've much to tell you.'

'I respected the physician's wishes,' Catlin went on, 'and took my leave. Save that I didn't leave . . . not right away. I merely spent time downstairs with Blake's servants, offering my sympathies. Then when the physician went out, I returned to the alderman's bedroom. A few minutes was enough to find what I sought.' He sighed. 'I imagine you can guess what that was.'

'The same pinpricks?'

'Just one,' Catlin corrected. 'And so tiny it was little wonder the physician didn't notice it. It was on the neck, by the great artery that carries blood to the head. And the wound was fresh, inflicted during the night.'

'So the Salamander got to him eventually,' Betsy said. 'And now, I think the blind-bake trick was but a warning. He wished the man to suffer, to ponder his fate awhile, before he was dealt the death blow.'

Catlin eyed her. 'I think it's time you told me what you've discovered,' he said. 'Let's go to the parlour.' He glanced at Peg, who picked up a bowl and busied herself mixing something in it.

'And leave nothing out,' Catlin added. 'For I've yet to see whether certain people have earned a day's holiday or not.'

Peg met the doctor's eye, and pulled a face.

* * *

It took Betsy some time to give Tom Catlin an account of her night's adventures. By the time she had finished, the man was frowning at her.

'It was a foolhardy enterprise,' he said. 'You're both lucky not to have been violated . . . or even murdered.'

'Oh, cods,' Betsy retorted. 'None of those we met doubted we were what we appeared to be. And after Dart told us what he would, we left the Bermudas without being accosted.'

'I still say you were lucky,' Catlin insisted. 'And I hope you don't intend to make a habit of playing such a role.'

But Betsy brushed it aside. 'You're a man of logic, so will you view the matter as I put it before you?' she asked. 'For it seems clear to me that the Salamander — or the Dutchman, Aanaarden — has returned from the Indies where he was transported as a felon, to wreak vengeance on all those who had a hand in putting him there.' When Catlin said nothing, she went on: 'It's too close for coincidence! I'm certain the two looters — a black man and a white man — were Ned Gowden and Tom Cleeve. Tom beat Aanaarden and left, expecting him to die in the Fire. Then after he was caught and imprisoned, Blake was responsible for having him shipped across the ocean in chains, surely a terrible fate. If somehow the man managed not only to survive — and it sounds to me as if he could survive most things — but to escape as well, then surely it's possible that he could make his way back to England, in disguise, perhaps. Assuming he speaks English well enough, he could have hidden his true nationality.'

'Yes, yes. It all sounds plausible.' There was impatience in Catlin's voice. 'You wish to appeal to my logic — then ponder these sticking-points.' He turned to her, and began to lay out his own set of facts.

'Let's say this Dutchman has returned, embittered by his experiences. This, of course, assumes that your unsavoury informant Dart spoke the truth . . . but let's say he did. So Aanaarden returns, keen to pay back those he considers responsible for his misfortunes. Firstly, London is almost unrecognizable since the Fire reduced most of it to ashes. Few people reside where they did, back in the year this man was transported. Hence our avenger must first find out the whereabouts of those who wronged him, assuming he knew who they were, that is. Ned Gowden, for several reasons, is not difficult to trace: he works in the bagnio, not far from where he did before, in the old Duke's Theatre. Tom Cleeve has since found employment at the new Duke's Theatre, so perhaps he's not so difficult to trace either.'

'Indeed,' Betsy interrupted. 'And it accounts for Tom's terrified state. When he heard about Ned's death, he guessed he'd be next!'

'Very well,' Catlin held up a hand. 'But what of Blake? He was unknown to most people at that time. He has only become prominent since being made an alderman, and because of his opposition to the theatre . . .'

He broke off, seeing Betsy's growing impatience.

'Yet you admit that a man as cunning as the Salamander — Aanaarden — surely is, could have tracked down his intended victims,' she countered. 'So—'

'The method!' Catlin said. 'Think of the method he has used to kill. Then ask yourself how he could have gained access to all those men, and pricked them with a poisoned bodkin, or whatever it is, without anyone noticing. Secondly — the timing. Why kill all of them in such a short span of time, and thus draw attention to the deaths? If they were spaced months or even weeks apart, it's likely no one would have made a connection. Thirdly—'

'Enough!' Betsy put her hands to her ears. With a wry look, Catlin broke off.

'You assume he always thinks rationally,' she went on. 'Yet he may be so consumed with a lust for vengeance that he cares not.' She brightened suddenly. 'Or, he wants everyone to know he's back! If there were any doubt, after the first deaths, he sends a sign as plain as a playbill to Blake, before finishing him off.'

'Perhaps.' Catlin nodded slowly. 'Though I'd be interested to know where he obtained a fire salamander, which is not found on this side of the English Channel . . .' he hesitated. 'But that isn't important. One thing you have yet to account for: why did he kill Joseph Rigg?'

'I don't know,' Betsy admitted. 'Perhaps there was some feud, some link between them, about which we know nothing.'

'It doesn't sit well with the other deaths.' Catlin was shaking his head. 'Though clearly,' he added, 'the same means was employed . . . a most powerful toxin. Perhaps he obtained it in the tropics, where I hear there are noxious substances distilled from strange plants, even taken from the skins of certain creatures, such as toads.' he looked up. 'Not salamanders, however. Though they produce a secretion when roused, it isn't dangerous to humans.'

There was silence, Betsy and Catlin each busy with their own thoughts. 'I've tried to form a picture of this man,' Betsy said at last. 'And yet, I can't see his face. He was a housebreaker, skilled at slipping in and out of places undetected. Hence he is agile, and cunning. But no one seems to know what he looked like. Even Dart, who knew him better than most, didn't trouble to describe the man,' she frowned. 'I wonder now that I didn't ask him to. Somehow, it didn't seem important.'

'Perhaps because he's so ordinary that no one noticed him,' Catln suggested. 'For he has the ability to move freely without drawing attention to himself. And hence . . .' he hesitated. 'I was about to suggest, that since all the deaths are linked — however tenuously — to the Duke's Theatre, your man might even be one of the company. That would have given him ready access to two of his victims, at least. But I doubt it, for such a plain individual would be an unlikely find among the peacocks that populate your world.'

'You've never had a high opinion of us, Tom Catlin,' Betsy said wryly. 'But we're agreed that the victims have connections with the Duke's. So I hope there's no one else on the Salamander's list. Another murder would be the end of us. All of London would think us accursed, and we might never reopen.' With a sigh she got to her feet. 'Indeed, it's time I went to Dorset Gardens to see if anyone's about. I promised to tell Betterton of anything I discovered.'

Catlin eyed her. 'Do you think he'll thank you for it?'

Betsy did not answer. Within the hour, deep in thought, she was making her way across muddy Fleet Street, and along Water Lane to the Duke's Theatre.

* * *

But the moment she walked through the door into the pit, news awaited her that drove even the Salamander from her thoughts.

'Tammy Tupp?' Betsy faced Thomas Betterton, aghast. 'You wish me to play the part of a fat whore, with false warts and a runny nose, and—'

'Perish the thought!' The voice was that of Samuel Tripp, who was standing beside Betterton, wearing his driest smile. 'You can play her thin, not fat.'

'But I thought you wished me to play the Lady Althea.'

'Then you're mistaken,' Tripp replied. 'Mistress Hale is perfect for Althea.'

'Is she indeed!' Betsy's temper was rising. She had not forgotten Tripp's hand grasping her thigh beneath Lord Caradoc's supper table.

'My dear Mistress Brand,' Betterton was conciliatory. 'Think of our position. After the travails of the past week, our best course is to stage a robust comedy, and so divert the minds of our audience — and ourselves — away from *Macbeth*. And to stage it quickly! Mr Tripp's new piece, *The Virtuous Bawd*, more than fulfils my hopes. Hence I've already called a rehearsal for this afternoon. The role of Tammy would suit you admirably — you'll have them roaring with mirth! And besides . . .' he glanced at Aveline Hale, who was entering by the street door. Betsy looked round, and saw Jane Rowe coming in behind her.

'Besides, what?' she asked.

Betterton cleared his throat, and smiled. 'You may think differently, when I tell you that Mr Tripp's comedy has been written especially with the Duke's actresses in mind. In short: it will be played by an entirely female cast!'

Betsy blinked. 'No men at all?'

'None! There are breeches roles, which will be taken by Mistress Rowe and some of the hirelings.'

Still smiling, Tripp now spoke up. 'So you see, Mistress Brand, I have your best interests at heart, as always. You will not be required to cross-dress. And after your taxing but splendid performance as First Witch, the role of Tammy — one of the Doves of Venus — should be a true pleasure. As Mr Betterton says, you'll have them falling off their seats . . . with laughter, I hope.'

Betsy ignored the jibe, as she digested the news. From behind the stage came the sound of sawing: already the carpenters were at work. She was about to greet Jane, when she remembered.

'Have you heard that Alderman Blake has died?' she asked Betterton.

'I have not.' His brow knitted. 'A consequence of that dreadful jest, at Caradoc's?' Then catching the look in Betsy's eye, he started. 'Does His Lordship know of it?'

'I expect he does by now,' Betsy answered. 'Doctor Catlin viewed the man's body this morning. He'll send word.'

But Tripp stirred, and his smile merely broadened. 'Most unfortunate,' he said. 'But not for the Duke's Theatre. Surely there will be little opposition now to your reopening?'

Betterton stiffened, not liking the man's tone. 'Very likely,' he replied. 'Now, with your leave . . .' And turning his back on the playmaker, he moved away to greet Aveline Hale. Betsy followed, throwing Tripp one of her most withering looks. But the man merely gave a mocking bow, and walked off.

* * *

So it was arranged: rehearsals would begin at once for *The Virtuous Bawd*, with a cast made up entirely of women. Though such performances had taken place before at court, this was a new venture for the Duke's Company. There was already an air of excitement about the theatre, which intensified later when Betterton gathered all the actresses on the forestage. Even Louise the tiring-maid was being given a small role in the play, which filled the nervous girl with fear. But all the women approved, when it transpired that Mary Betterton herself would take a part, sharing principal billing with Aveline Hale. Some eyebrows were raised at this news, though Mistress Hale appeared delighted. The reason for that soon became clear; and even Betsy was impressed by the announcement.

'A royal performance! How splendid!' Aveline favoured Betterton with a radiant smile.

'Indeed!' Betterton raised his hands to quell the chatter that had broken out. 'Hence we must be on our mettle. The King and the Duke will both attend, along with many of their friends.' He too was smiling now. 'I have great confidence in you, ladies. There's hard work ahead, but the rewards will be substantial.' His gaze wandered to his wife, who was standing to one side. 'And we have a wealth of acting experience between us, to make *The Virtuous Bawd* our finest endeavour!'

But Jane, standing close to Betsy, spoke in a low voice. 'I wonder how much money they'll save by employing only women?' she mused. 'It could be the cheapest show ever!'

Soon afterwards, however, they were obliged to put speculation about *The Virtuous Bawd* aside. For Lord Caradoc arrived at the theatre, and sent word immediately that Betsy should join him and Thomas Betterton in private conversation.

* * *

They sat in one of the empty side boxes, while below them James Prout the dancing-master took the hirelings through some steps upon the stage. Betterton and Lord Caradoc listened in silence while Betsy told them all she had learned of the Salamander, and what she and Catlin had theorized. By the time she came to the end of her account, both men were subdued.

'If it's a matter of vengeance,' Betterton said at last, 'this man, whoever he is, must be consumed with hatred!'

'Indeed.' Caradoc was troubled. Glancing from Betterton to Betsy, he said: 'And I ask of you both that we keep the matter secret. The company would be greatly distressed if they learned of this. And I ask you, Mistress Brand, to make the same request of Doctor Catlin.'

'Doctor Catlin's servant already knows of the matter, my lord,' Betsy said, 'though I trust her completely.' She did not add that Jane Rowe also knew of it. In fact, rather a lot of people knew. She bit her lip, thinking that in her eagerness to investigate the matter she might have been somewhat careless.

But Caradoc wasn't listening. With a frown at Betterton, he said: 'The notion that one of your company may be a murderer, sir, fills me with horror.'

Betterton looked dismayed. 'Surely it cannot be. Even George Beale, whom I dismissed for his behaviour . . . I'm certain he would not be capable of such wickedness! It's bad enough to learn that Cleeve's a criminal, let alone Ned Gowden, who was hard working and courteous, even if he could be a sly one at times. As for Rigg . . .' he fixed Betsy with a bewildered look.

'His death remains a mystery,' Betsy admitted. 'Yet with your leave, and yours, my lord,' she added tentatively, 'I would like to try and follow the scent as far as I may.'

'But it grows more sinister by the day,' Caradoc objected. 'And I would not have you put yourself in further danger.'

'Nor I!' Betterton gave Betsy a severe look. 'Had I known you'd act so recklessly, I would not have asked you to investigate at all.'

'It was my own notion,' Betsy told him. 'And I see now that a woman may sometimes uncover matters more easily than a man, just as she gains access to certain places.'

'If she impersonates a woman of the streets, perhaps,' Caradoc said drily. 'You should not take such risks again!'

But Betsy could not help giving Betterton a dry smile. 'And yet, my performance should serve as good preparation for my role as Tammy Tupp, should it not?'

For once, even the great actor was lost for a reply.

* * *

By the time the afternoon's rehearsals were over, Betsy had decided on a course of action. Her talk with Tom Catlin had set her thinking there were certain trails she might pursue to find some clue to the identity of the Salamander. Though after the conversation with Caradoc and Betterton she thought it best to make her enquiries without telling anyone . . . at least, not yet. So after taking farewell of Jane, she slipped out of the Theatre, made her way down to the Whitefriars stairs and hailed a boat. Within minutes she was being rowed downriver on an outgoing tide, with the bridge looming ahead.

She was not certain of her destination save that it would likely be below the bridge, close to the wharves where the larger seagoing vessels landed their wares. But after casual enquiry of her waterman, she discovered that there was a dealer of the type she sought near St Botolph's. A short time later she was clambering ashore and making her way up Billingsgate stairs. Then, with the tang of fish and tar in her nostrils, she walked the crowded quays, seeking the whereabouts of a Mr Thomas Vane, purveyor of exotic beasts.

The shop was a revelation. Creatures from foreign lands, brought back by sailors, were not uncommon in London. Like most people, Betsy had seen monkeys and parrots, just as she had been taken as a child to gape at the royal menagerie in the Tower, especially its famous lion. But nothing prepared her for the smell and the cacophony of noises that greeted her as she entered Vane's cramped premises. In cages stacked from floor to ceiling were creatures of many kinds, from the commonplace to the bizarre: squirrels, a polecat that spat and marmosets that shrieked. From a corner, a large ape gazed mournfully at her. Brightly coloured birds in willow cages swung above her head, some singing melodiously, others screeching. Towards the rear was the most unsettling sight of all: a great shiny snake in a box, with strange markings along its back. Though the creature never moved, it was all Betsy could do not to flinch as she passed it. But here at last was Mr Vane, a smiling man in a chestnut-brown coat and horsehair periwig, rising from a stool to greet her.

'What do you seek, mistress? A furry creature to share your bed on these cold nights, perhaps?' Betsy blinked, whereupon the man laughed. 'I mean no slight,' he said. 'How can I be of service?'

'A fire salamander,' she said shortly. 'Have you ever had one?'

'A salamander?' the fellow echoed. 'Heaven forbid! Who would wish to own such a creature?'

'I understand they hide in stacks of wood. Have you heard of any being found in cargo, for example?'

Vane considered. 'If so, I imagine whoever found one would kill it. Are they not poisonous?' When Betsy feigned ignorance, he added: 'Well, I fear I cannot help. If you're set upon obtaining such, perhaps you could ask at the timber wharves,' he brightened. 'But if it's a woolly monkey you seek, or a guinea pig — that's a charming little animal from South America — then permit me to show you . . .' he broke off, for Betsy was shaking her head.

'Another time, perhaps,' she managed a smile. 'In the meantime, can you point me to the timber wharves?'

Vane sighed, and accompanied her out to the street.

But the timber merchants were a disappointment.

There were many, and they were busy men. So when Betsy made her enquiries, she met with rather less courtesy than she had received from Thomas Vane. Did she not realize, several demanded, that since the Fire, London was in the throes of a building boom the like of which had not been seen for centuries? If it was wood she wanted, then they might do business. But as for lizards scuttling out of stacks of timber . . . had she nought better to occupy herself, than to ask such questions?

Discouraged, Betsy took her leave of a dealer by the Customs House Quay, deciding to make him the last one. But as she was about to walk to the stairs and hire a westward boat, unexpectedly the man called her back.

From his accent she had guessed he was German. A heavy-set man with thick blond hair, he waited until she had retraced her steps towards him. Then she saw a second man approaching: younger and slimmer, but so like the other in his features that he had to be the merchant's son. Leaving this one to do the talking, the older man walked off.

'You asked about salamanders, mistress?' the young man asked. His manner was civil, and when Betsy smiled and nodded, his face softened. 'My father is from the Black Forest country,' he said. 'There are salamanders there. They hibernate in the wood piles against the houses. When logs are brought in for the fire they run out and scare the children. They're most colourful — yellow spots from head to tail.'

'Indeed.' Betsy warmed to her new informant at once. 'Have you ever seen any here, in England?'

The young man shook his head. 'Never.'

Disappointment threatened again, but Betsy tried a final question. 'Do you know of some that have orange marks?'

The other considered. 'I've heard of such. But they come from the south, from countries like Spain and Portugal.'

At that, Betsy caught her breath. 'I thank you,' she said after a moment. 'You've helped me more than you know.'

The young man smiled broadly. 'I'm honoured,' he said. 'Perhaps you would care to stay for a mug of—' then he broke off. For Betsy had turned quickly and was walking off, to vanish between stacks of timber.

She had not meant to be sharp, but the young man's words had struck a chord: perhaps the journey downriver had not been wasted after all. For in Covent Garden there was a man who sold strange things from foreign lands: jewellery, trinkets and carvings, bought by the wealthy to beautify their houses. He was called Lopez, and he was a Portuguese Jew.

CHAPTER TEN

The morning brought grey skies and a chill breeze from the river. But by ten o'clock Betsy had left Fire's Reach Court and was walking briskly towards Covent Garden. Emerging from Russell Street into the piazza, she turned right along a row of shops, above which hung a series of brightly painted signs: a white hand denoting a glover, a stag for a breeches-maker, a civet cat for a perfumer. But the one she sought bore no sign: only a little gold bell over the doorway, that tinkled in the wind. In a moment she had passed through the entrance into a windowless interior, lit by a couple of small lanterns.

Shimon Lopez had been a part of Covent Garden for almost a decade. Earlier — almost twenty years back — Oliver Cromwell had invited the sage Menasseh ben Israel to lay the foundations of a new Jewish community here. After King Charles's restoration, others — refugees from the Dutch provinces, who had aided him in his exile — were made welcome in their turn. Some were now wealthy men, merchants and importers. But Lopez had never sought advancement beyond the modest premises he had obtained, and from where he still sold the curious assortment of goods for which he was noted. As Betsy paused to let her eyes grow accustomed to the dimness, the man came forward in his long coat and inclined his head.

'How may I aid you, mistress?'

'I'm looking for a rare animal, sir,' Betsy replied, meeting his unblinking eyes. 'And I was told you were the man who could find such. Or you might know where to direct me.'

Lopez raised his heavy eyebrows. 'It's called . . . ?'

'A salamander.'

The other digested the information. 'And this *salamander* — what manner of animal is it?'

'Like a lizard . . . dark, and spotted with orange,' Betsy told him. 'Though it isn't a lizard, but a newt.'

Lopez watched her. Then, when it became clear that he was waiting, Betsy added: 'Its proper name is the fire salamander. It's found in warm countries like Spain . . . and Portugal, which I think was your homeland, Mr Lopez.'

The man made a polite movement of his head. 'And might I ask what you wish to do with this spotted newt?' he enquired.

'I would put it in a pie, to frighten my dinner guests,' Betsy told him.

At that, Lopez started. 'Most peculiar.' He put a hand to his beard and rubbed it, his smile gone as quickly as it had appeared. Finally he said: 'Permit me to make a guess, mistress: my guess is that you do not wish a salamander for yourself, but information about another who did. Am I correct?'

'If that were so,' Betsy asked after a moment, 'would you be able to help me?'

Lopez hesitated. 'If you were a customer of mine, perhaps,' he began.

'Of course,' Betsy smiled. 'I see a charming little ivory fan there. How much might that cost?'

Lopez returned her smile, and ushered her towards a table to begin negotiations.

When Betsy emerged from the shop a quarter of an hour later, she was so preoccupied that she walked in the wrong direction, across the piazza almost to the entrance of St Paul's church. Realizing her error, she turned and retraced her steps towards Russell Street. She was still pondering the intriguing information she had gleaned from Shimon Lopez.

Some weeks ago, a man had come to him and asked him privately to obtain several fire salamanders, for which he would pay whatever price Lopez wanted, and in whatever currency. Lopez had tried: such an order took time, he explained, and was most difficult to fill. In the end, through various contacts, he had managed to purchase three such creatures, but disastrously, in transit from the Bay of Biscay, two had perished. So he was able to supply his customer with only one living salamander. Such was his mortification that he refunded the generous down payment the customer had provided, taking only a small sum for expenses. Hence, in view of the outcome of the affair, he no longer felt bound to such secrecy as the customer had insisted upon, and found himself able to give Betsy a fairly full account. Yes, it was a black and orange fire salamander, about ten inches in length . . . and the man had indeed claimed that he intended it for a joke, to frighten an old friend at a party. The customer . . . ?

Lopez had shrugged, scratched his chin, and reflected a little. The customer was a man of middling height, simply dressed, with no particular distinguishing features. But his name, yes, his name he remembered, for he knew it was not the man's real name. In fact, he felt vindicated that he was not truly betraying his customer, for it was but a title the man had used. *Histrio*, he called himself, perhaps not realizing that Shimon Lopez knew Latin. And when Betsy pressed him, the dealer had favoured her with a knowing smile. Why, he said, *histrio* means 'actor'.

* * *

Betsy arrived at the theatre a short time later, still mulling over what she had learned. Even when rehearsals began, and she was obliged to fling herself into the outrageous role of

Tammy Tupp, she was unable to forget the matter. For the stark fact that refused to go away was that the Salamander appeared to be one of the Duke's Company after all.

It had to be! Who else had such close access to Tom Cleeve and to Joseph Rigg just before they died? An actor would also have known Alderman Blake, at least by reputation, and easily discovered his address. And as for Long Ned, the bagnio was open to all. Hence this man who was so undistinguished that few seemed to notice him, let alone remember what he looked like, had been able to observe his victims, and choose the time of their deaths at his leisure. But then, Betsy knew all the actors of the Duke's Company, and the King's too, for that matter. In which case, she asked herself for the twentieth time, who in heaven's name could the Salamander be?

So preoccupied was she that it soon became evident her mind was not on her work. And after an unproductive hour, James Prout the dancing-master and Downes the fat prompter, who were sitting at the front of the pit, called a halt and suggested everyone take some refreshment. As Betsy was about to leave the stage, Prout called to her.

'Mistress Brand, a moment if you please.'

She walked to the edge of the forestage and looked down. 'Mr Prout?'

Prout wore a glassy smile. 'We are mindful of your efforts to breathe life into Tammy,' he said. 'Nevertheless we feel, Mr Downes and I, that the part demands a little more than you are giving. She's a woman of the streets after all, hence—'

'You wish me to lower my chemise further, so that my bosom falls out?' Betsy enquired.

'Indeed not!' Prout pretended to be shocked. 'Perhaps the key lies in Tammy's speech, and the manner of its delivery.'

Betsy felt her hackles rising. 'Her speech,' she retorted, 'is a poor rendering of the language of the jilts I've known. In fact, being well enough acquainted with the playmaker,

I'd say that if he spent more time observing their language and less on their charms, he might have crafted a better work than this jiggalorum!'

'Would you, indeed, Mistress Brand? Then perhaps you should instruct me!'

Betsy looked towards the side door, where Samuel Tripp was standing. How long he had been there she did not know. But as the man came forward, nodding to Prout and to John Downes, she curtseyed elaborately.

'I regret sir, that I've not the time for such endeavours,' she replied. To Prout, she added: 'Yet I'll do my best. If you'll allow me a little more time to study the part.'

'Of course,' Prout nodded, diverted by Tripp's arrival. And Betsy was quickly forgotten as both the dancing-master and the prompter stood up to greet the playmaker.

She walked backstage into the scene-room. The marked absence of male actors made the area seem half-empty, as well as producing a somewhat lackadaisical atmosphere. The Small brothers, Joshua and Will, were smoking their pipes. Joshua exchanged gossip with Silas Gunn, while Will was flirting openly with Louise Hawker the tiring-maid. As Betsy appeared, the girl looked up quickly.

'Is it time for me to practise my scene?' she asked.

Betsy shook her head. Then Gunn caught her eye, and for some reason a thought flew up. 'Silas,' she smiled at him. 'May I trouble you for a moment?'

Silas's pleasure was so apparent, Joshua Small sniggered. At once the old man hurried over to Betsy. 'Whatever service I can perform mistress, consider it done!' he declared.

Drawing him aside, towards the steps to the Women's Shift, Betsy spoke low. 'There's something I remember hearing,' she said in a casual tone. 'Am I right in thinking you were once at close quarters with the Dutch?'

Silas looked surprised. 'I fought in the first Dutch war,' he said. 'Fifty-two . . . a terrible year.' He shrugged. 'Close quarters? You could call it that. My ship was boarded and I was took prisoner. Ransomed soon after, though.' He gave her a doubtful look. 'You don't want to hear about that, do ye?'

'I've no wish to stir bad memories,' Betsy replied. 'I merely wondered if you knew any of the Dutch language.'

'A word or two, maybe,' Silas said vaguely. ''Tis a mighty strange tongue, to an Englishman's ear.' Then he stiffened as Betsy bent her head closer.

'Aanaarden,' she said quietly. 'Does that word mean anything to you? It doesn't mean *actor*, by any chance?'

Silas thought deeply for a moment. 'Nay, Mistress Brand. I might have heard the word, but I don't recall what it signifies.' He stood, somewhat crestfallen, as Betsy thanked him and started to climb the steps. Then all at once he brightened. 'Here . . . wait a minute!' he cried. And when Betsy turned he added: 'I know what it means — yes, Aanaarden. It's Dutch for *hill*.'

* * *

Thomas Betterton was expected at the Duke's Theatre at midday, to see how rehearsals for *The Virtuous Bawd* were progressing. Betsy, whose presence was not required on stage, was waiting for him by the street door. In a short time, the two of them had gone up to one of the side boxes, where she told him all she had discovered.

Her mentor was stunned, but soon shock began to give way to disbelief. 'Julius Hill?' he muttered. 'No . . . I cannot countenance it. The fellow's harmless! Why, I've never even heard him raise his voice. Indeed, I've had to instruct him to speak up when he's on the stage, so that he might be heard!'

'Not much of an actor, though, is he?' Betsy ventured.

'Perhaps not,' Betterton allowed. 'He was previously unknown to me, it's true . . . claimed to have some experience touring in the country. I offered him a modest role at a modest wage, which he seemed glad enough to accept,' he frowned. 'Are you asserting that he took a job with our company merely in order to do murder!?'

Since Silas Gunn had told her the word *aanaarden* meant 'hill', Betsy's mind had been in a whirl. For now, it seemed to her that several things fell into place. She drew a long breath and looked Betterton in the eye. 'The more I think on it,' she said, 'the more it seems to fit. Hill was in the bagnio, when Long Ned died. Prout told us that he was closer to Ned when he fell, though when Hill gave an account of the matter in the scene-room, he seemed unwilling to say any more than he had to. The place is gloomy — I've seen that for myself. Hill could easily have brushed past Ned and stabbed him with a poisoned spike, or whatever it was, without anyone noticing.'

'This is speculation, Betsy!' Betterton wore a look of distaste. 'Think of the risk, in such a public place.'

'Furthermore,' Betsy went on firmly, 'Hill was in the scene-room when Tom Cleeve fell! There was a crush — again, he could have pricked Tom in passing and no one would have seen.'

'Then what of Rigg?' Betterton countered. 'Hill was nowhere near him when he collapsed. It was that young pup Beale, and the two hirelings.'

'Agreed.' Betsy nodded. 'Let's leave Rigg aside for now — think of Blake. It would not have been difficult for a skilled housebreaker like the Salamander to climb through a window in the night, and spike the old man in his neck.'

'Betsy, I pray you!' Betterton was aghast. 'These are wild leaps of imagination. You have no proof, nor are there witnesses . . .' he broke off, then laid a fatherly hand on her arm.

'Think on what you say,' he went on in a gentler voice. 'The man's the unlikeliest candidate for murder that I ever saw.'

'Precisely!' Betsy's eyes were alight. 'That's his skill, this unassuming manner, the ability to remain in the background without anyone noticing him. In fact, it seems to me now that he's the best actor we have!'

Betterton fell silent. 'There is one thing,' he said finally. 'If he's indeed the one who purchased the salamander to taunt or frighten Blake, calling himself *Histrio*, then I see vanity behind it. As if he has a weakness for nicknames — like "the Salamander". If Aanaarden were his real name, then surely calling himself "Hill" amounts to a considerable risk? How long did he think it would be before someone discovered the connection?'

At that, Betsy started. 'Perhaps that's what excites him: he gambled on it . . . and he has won. For now that the actors have dispersed, we may be too late!'

Betterton looked unhappy; but finally he came to a decision. 'You have a sharp mind, but then, you always did. And though I still find it hard to believe your theory, I will at least test it.' He thought for a moment. 'I'll send word to Caradoc, but first I'll go to Hill's lodgings myself with a constable. Then we may question him, and see what account he gives of himself. Will that content you?'

At which, Betsy could not resist a smile of satisfaction.

* * *

Fortunately, she did not have long to wait. For in the mid-afternoon Betterton sent a scribbled message to Fire's Reach Court via a link-boy: Julius Hill had paid off his landlord two days ago, vacated his lodgings in Aldersgate Street, and left no word as to where he was going. The message added that Mistress Brand should come to Betterton's house that evening, to talk further of the matter.

Catlin was home, and stood in the hallway while Betsy read the message. When she passed it to him he scanned it quickly, then turned to the messenger who was waiting.

'D'you wish me to take a reply, sir?' the boy asked.

Catlin nodded, and felt in his pocket for a coin. 'Tell him Mistress Brand will be there,' he said. 'And Doctor Catlin will accompany her.'

The boy hurried off, while Betsy met Catlin's gaze in some surprise. But before she could speak, he said: 'Don't imagine that I'm convinced by your theories . . . or at least, not entirely.'

Whereupon Betsy nodded felt a surge of excitement. The trail may have gone cold for a while, but somehow she knew it was the right one.

* * *

That evening in Betterton's parlour in Long Acre, she and Catlin listened to her mentor's account of his visit to Julius Hill's modest rooms in Aldersgate Street, close by the Cooks' Hall. According to his landlord, the actor had been a model tenant: absent much of the time, and when he was home, so quiet the family barely heard him. Nor did he entertain visitors. In fact, if truth be told, the landlord could not be certain when Hill was home and when he was not. After some hesitation he had conducted Betterton and the constable to Hill's rooms, which had been cleared of every trace of their occupant. All that remained were ashes in the fireplace, as of some papers that had been burned.

'It's odd, I have to admit such,' Betterton mused. 'The man said nothing to me about changing his lodging. He had every reason to expect further employment, if not with me, then at the King's Theatre. Why leave so abruptly, unless . . .' he eyed Betsy, who sat opposite him.

'Unless he didn't want to be found,' she finished.

'What else do you know about this man?' Tom Catlin asked.

Betterton shrugged. 'Not a great deal, I now realize.'

'You say he was in the bagnio when Ned Gowden died,' the doctor went on. 'Was he in the habit of frequenting the place?'

'If you mean did he seek the company of molly-men, rather than of women,' Betterton replied, 'I'll confess my ignorance. You might ask James Prout.' He turned to Betsy in some embarrassment. 'Can you shed any light on the man's tastes?'

'Are you asking if he has ever put his hands on me, or any of the other actresses?' she asked. When Betterton merely raised an eyebrow, she made a wry face. 'Not to my knowledge, but that proves nothing. I always thought him a timid man, for an actor. Now I see it may have been a clever mask.'

Catlin was nodding. 'I saw him on your stage, in the role of the Doctor in *Macbeth*,' he said to Betterton. 'It struck me as an indifferent performance. Yet if we give credence to Mistress Brand's suggestion that he was acting a part in the first instance — the part of Julius Hill — then he must be a very clever fellow indeed. For he was acting the doctor, as Hill would have acted him.'

'And if he's Dutch, as I was told,' Betsy put in, 'he conceals it well enough to pass for an Englishman.'

'Moreover,' the doctor continued while Betterton frowned, 'when I was called to the bagnio after Ned Gowden fell ill, I have no recollection of seeing Hill there. It was as Mistress Brand said, as if he could vanish into the background.'

'And now he has vanished from his lodgings,' Betsy put in, eying Betterton. 'Do you still doubt this is the man we seek?'

Finally, her mentor spoke up. 'Well, one thing is clear at least,' he sighed. 'He must be found, if only to answer for himself.' He rose, and drained his glass. 'I'll confer with Caradoc, who I'm sure will put matters in motion. Likely he will order a search.'

'With your leave, I'd like to make one enquiry of my own,' Betsy said. When both men looked to her, she added: 'I believe you were right that Mr Prout could tell us more about Julius Hill. The two of them spent some time together, during *Macbeth*.' she put on a winning smile. 'And if you're concerned for my welfare, doubtless Doctor Catlin will accompany me.'

Catlin met her eye, and sighed.

A half hour later, Betsy and the doctor descended from a hackney coach outside James Prout's rooms in Whitecross Street by Cripplegate. The house was an old timbered structure with an overhanging jetty, this being a district that had been spared the ravages of the Great Fire. Lights were visible in the upper storey, but when Catlin knocked loudly there was no answer. He knocked again, and finally with a squeal of rusty hinges the door was opened by a tiny girl in a bonnet and a nightgown too long for her.

'If you seek the fiddler, he's not home,' she said.

'The dancing-master,' Betsy said kindly. 'Is he home?'

The girl sniffed. 'Him? He must be, for I heard him doing his steps a while back . . . top floor.'

She stood aside, permitting Betsy and the doctor to enter the dimly lit passage. Soon they had climbed a narrow stair to the second floor, finding themselves in a broad chamber that overlooked the street. It was comfortably furnished and lit by several candles, but there was no sign of the occupant.

'Mr Prout!' Betsy called, looking about.

No answer. Catlin too was taking in the surroundings. Part of the room, presumably the bedchamber, was screened off by an oak panel. With a glance at Betsy, the doctor crossed to the screen and peered round it. Then he stiffened, and Betsy felt a chill run down her spine like cold silk. Slowly she walked to his side . . . but already she had smelled the sharp, iron tang of blood, and steeled herself for what she might see.

What she saw was James Prout, lying across his bed with a fixed look of surprise on his face. As for the blood, his body, and the bed, were awash with it.

CHAPTER ELEVEN

It was late that night before Betsy and Tom Catlin returned home. Peg had gone to bed, but enough glowing embers remained in the parlour fireplace for the doctor to stir it into life. He poured a mug of sack for each of them, before lighting his pipe. The room was soon filled with pungent blue smoke.

They had sent word to Betterton, then waited at Prout's lodging for him to arrive with a constable from nearby St Giles. The owner of the house, and father of the diminutive girl, also returned soon afterwards to learn what had occurred under his roof. The man was horror-struck: his tenants were all respectable folk, he insisted. There had never been trouble in his house before. As for murder . . .

Catlin had examined the body, and concluded that the dancing-master had been stabbed through the heart with a narrow blade. It was a brutal attack, but far from frenzied: the killer knew where to strike. Moreover, the body was still warm, which testified to the crime being recent. Indeed, the young girl's account of hearing the dancing-master 'doing his steps' shortly before, now took on a sinister hue.

'So, this time he had no need of secrecy,' Betsy said quietly. 'No poisoned pin . . .'

Catlin had been gazing into the fire. 'For that reason, can you be certain that Prout died by the same hand?' he asked.

'I can't,' she admitted, 'but in my heart I know it's the Salamander. Look how easily he made his escape, for one thing. The landlord didn't even know someone else had been in the house.'

'But why has he waited so long?' the doctor asked. 'If he's Julius Hill, he could have got close to the dancing-master at any time.'

'I can think of one explanation,' Betsy answered. 'If he and Prout were lovers, that's where he might have stayed the past two nights, since he left his lodging. In fact, perhaps he coveted Prout's company, going to the bagnio with him and so on, in order to make use of him. Use his home as a bolthole, if he needed it.'

'But why kill him?' Catlin objected. 'If he's done with his avenging, why not just disappear?'

'Perhaps Prout was too much of a risk. He was a quick-thinking man — he might have discovered Hill's real identity.' Betsy gave a sigh. 'One thing I know: I'll miss him, as will all the company. And his loss could be a death blow for us.'

Both of them fell silent. Betsy thought briefly of Betterton, who had been shattered by the news of Prout's murder. Even Lord Caradoc, who arrived on horseback soon afterwards, was shaken. After hearing a brief account of the matter he had ridden off to rouse the authorities, and urge them to scour the suburbs for Julius Hill. And if constables and watchmen should fail, he vowed to raise an armed body at his own expense. Since the business of the live salamander on his supper table, it seemed His Lordship took every turn of events as a personal affront.

After a while, Betsy rose to go to her bed. As she gave the doctor good night, he nodded absently, staring into the fire. Likely he would still be there in the morning, she thought, asleep in his chair.

Betsy slept fitfully, her dreams filled with foreboding. Once she sat up, thinking she heard someone at the window. But it was only the wind rattling the frame, and eventually she drifted into a deeper sleep that lasted until dawn. Then with a start she woke, hearing the door open. There stood Peg, wearing a grim expression.

'You'd best come down,' she said. 'There's a visitor.'

'At this hour?' Betsy muttered, shaking herself awake. But she clambered out of bed, threw on an old camelotte gown and stumbled barefoot outside to the stairhead.

Peg was standing in the hallway. Beside her, almost a head shorter, was a man in rough outdoor clothing, peering about in the dim light. His manner was tense, and when Tom Catlin emerged from the parlour in his shirt sleeves bearing a candle, the fellow shrank backwards towards the door. Then he heard Betsy's footsteps and glanced up quickly, whereupon her eyes widened. For gazing up at her was the weasel-faced man from the Bermudas, whom she and Peg had once mistaken for the informant Dart.

Slowly Betsy descended the stairs. Catlin was frowning at the fellow, who looked the very picture of a fugitive. As Betsy drew near he looked round, as if to make sure the door was still open at his back. Nobody spoke. Then at last the man summoned his courage, moistened his lips and said hoarsely: 'I helped you, didn't I? Now you must help me!'

If Betsy showed surprise, Peg did not. 'Help you, you wicked little stoat?' she growled. 'You've got some brass, coming here.'

'Listen!' the man was desperate. 'I've nowhere to go . . . all I'm asking is common charity.' He looked deliberately at Catlin. 'I heard you were a good man, who don't ask too many questions.'

The doctor glanced questioningly at Betsy, then realization dawned. He turned back to the ragged fellow. 'Are you Dart?' he asked sharply.

Peg gave an impatient snort. 'No he isn't — I made that mistake—' catching Betsy's eye, she broke off. Neither of them wished to dwell upon events in that fetid little storeroom in the Bermudas, three days back. But both started when the weasel-faced man dropped to a half-crouch, jabbing a finger.

'Dart's dead!' he cried. 'And if I don't get out of London I'll be joining him! Now . . . will you help me, or not?!'

* * *

A short while later the three of them stood in the kitchen while 'Weasel-face', as Peg called him, sat at the table eating ravenously. When asked, he had given the name Daniels, which was clearly one of convenience. Having drunk the curds Peg had grudgingly given him, he wiped the bowl with a hunk of bread, stuffed it in his mouth and sat back, eying each of them. Finally, he began to talk.

'I knew something wasn't right about you two,' he said, his eyes flicking from Betsy to Peg. 'I've met some rare trulls in my time, but none that would pay a man like you did. So when you left the Bermudas that night, I followed you.'

'You followed us?' Betsy echoed. 'To here?'

'Had a notion it might be useful,' the fellow replied, then glanced uneasily at Tom Catlin who, arms folded, was leaning against a side table watching him.

'After I found out whose house it was, I went back.' Daniels lowered his gaze. 'Then the next night, this cove comes to the Bermudas looking for Dart. And the minute Dart sees him, he near soils his breeches. I never seen him scared before, and that's a gospel truth!' He scratched his unkempt beard. 'Him and the other go off together. Then come morning, I find Dart in the back of Round Court, stuck like a hog! And no one saw or heard a thing!'

The man's fear was genuine. And now Tom Catlin spoke up. 'Can you describe this man who came looking for Dart?'

The other threw him a dour look. 'He looked a bit like you,' he answered. When Catlin looked blank, he shook his head. 'It was night, and he wore a hat pulled low. Rather, you should ask who he is. That'd be enough for most.'

'The Salamander,' Betsy said, to which Daniels's scared look was assent enough. She exchanged glances with Catlin. It was almost as if the very mention of the nickname was enough to conjure up the man's presence, here at Fire's Reach Court.

'You claim you'll be joining Dart if you don't get out of London,' she said to Daniels. 'You mean he's looking for you?'

The fellow swallowed the last of the bread, then faced Catlin. 'Hide me for a day and a night, Doctor,' he said in a voice that was almost a whine. 'That's all — by then he'll be gone. He can't afford to stay longer. He knows there's a net closing about him.'

Catlin frowned. 'He knows?'

The other nodded. 'If only half the tales I've heard be true, there's nothing that devil don't know. Always one step ahead, save in the Fire, that time.' He looked at Betsy. 'I talked with Dart, after I'd followed you home.' A sour look came over his pinched features. 'And it seems to me now, it's because of you he's dead!'

But at that, Peg, who had been watching the man with growing anger, took a step forward. 'You little crack-halter!' She pointed a shaking finger at him. 'What the two of you would have done to us if I hadn't knocked that other cove out, I don't—'

'Peg.' Catlin's voice was sharp. Peg fell silent, as the doctor turned to Daniels with a hard expression. 'Your friend Dart's death makes at least five that we know of, by the Salamander's hand,' he said coldly. 'So don't try to shift blame where it doesn't belong.'

The weasel-faced man wiped his mouth with the sleeve of his dirty coat. But feeling the doctor's eye upon him, he forced himself to meet his gaze.

'Now,' Catlin's manner grew brisk, 'You come here asking my help, so I do have questions. First, you say your own life is in danger — are you certain?'

Daniels nodded vigorously. 'I'd swear Dart told the Salamander about me,' he answered, 'but that isn't it.' His nervousness was such, he could barely keep still. 'You say there's five dead already,' he went on. 'Well, I'd wager a sovereign there's more, if you knew where to look for 'em,' he swallowed. 'Don't you see? He's got the taste for it now! Since he was transported over the sea, then got himself back, all those years, he's been feeding his anger like a fire. He won't stop, until someone stops him, and there's precious few could do that! A day is all he'd need, to hunt me down . . .'

The man broke off, and now Peg glanced at Betsy. All of them recognized the truth when they heard it.

'Very well.' Catlin nodded. 'You say that hiding here for a day and a night would be enough. Do you mean that the Salamander . . .' he frowned. 'I'll use his name — Aanaarden. Do you mean Aanaarden intends to leave London by then?'

Daniels' head bobbed. 'Not just London. He'll be gone from England, and we'll all sleep sounder!'

Catlin paused. 'Then I will help you . . . on one condition: that you lead us to him.'

Daniels' mouth fell open. 'Good Christ, I can't do that! You may as well sign my death warrant!'

The doctor surveyed him without expression. 'There's a coach leaves Bishopsgate tomorrow morning at six of the clock,' he said, 'bound for the North country. I'll pay your passage. But more importantly, I can give you a letter to a friend of mine in York, who might find work for you if you wish it. If you don't wish it, he'll shelter you for a day or two, until you decide where to go. And he too will ask no questions.'

But the little man was shaking his head mournfully. 'Don't ask this of me,' he begged. 'It's more than I dare.'

Catlin kept his patience. 'All I ask is that you point me to Aanaarden. Others will stand ready to arrest him, the moment he's identified. There's no risk to you—'

'No risk!' Daniels gave a short laugh. 'You don't know.' Seeing the eyes of all three of them upon him, he banged a fist down on the table. 'It's not just him!' he cried. 'If I spill the tale of the Rye road, I'm finished. I'll have such a price on my head, half the Bermudas will come looking for me!'

'The Rye road — is that all?' Catlin relaxed. 'You think someone who's been about the western suburbs as long as I have hasn't heard of it?'

Daniels did not answer, whereupon Catlin met Betsy's gaze. 'There's a man who arranges passages — for a fee, of course — for those who wish to get out of the country quickly, without being observed. You might term it an underground way, from rookeries like the Bermudas to the Kent coast, where a boat leaves for France after dark. It leaves from Rye, because Dover is generally watched.' He eyed Daniels. 'Do I hit the mark?' When the other said nothing, he added: 'I don't know the name of this trader in human cargo, nor do I know from where he despatches his charges. I merely ask you to conduct myself and others to the place tonight, where we will conceal ourselves. The moment Aanaarden appears, your side of the bargain is filled. I'll even have someone escort you back in safety. You can pass the night here, then in the morning take the coach for the North.'

The three of them waited, watching Daniels as he struggled with his predicament. It was odd, Betsy thought, that so much might rest on one who, despite her grim experience with him in a dark chamber in the Bermudas, now appeared such a pitiful creature. At last, he looked up.

'I'll take you,' he muttered, 'though you won't know him. He'll likely go in disguise.' He threw a baleful look at Betsy. 'If I'd seen through yours from the start, I wouldn't be in this mess!'

Betsy ignored him and turned to Catlin. The doctor seemed satisfied, but she felt a little surge of excitement.

Perhaps the Salamander's reign would soon be over after all.

* * *

By nightfall, matters had moved forward. At Bredon House, Lord Caradoc was waiting for word of the Salamander's capture. Having been fully appraised of events, His Lordship had vowed to stay up all night if necessary. At the same time, in more modest premises in Long Acre, an unhappy Thomas Betterton awaited the same news. The master of the Duke's Theatre had called off all rehearsals because of the death of James Prout, in the hope that this tempestuous period would draw to its close. Then, somehow, the company could regroup and try to return to normality.

Betsy's hopes, however, were more immediate. When she entered Catlin's parlour that night she was prepared for a battle, and had armed herself with a range of arguments. But in the end, she won the day more easily than expected. After allowing the doctor a period of nay-saying and head-shaking, she played her final card.

'I understand the danger,' she said. 'But upbraid me as you will, you can't prevent me coming along. You're my landlord, not my guardian . . . and in any case, after you'd gone I'd assume the guise of Mary Peach and follow you. Unless, that is, you were planning to lock me in my bedroom?'

'I swear, one day you will give me a seizure,' Catlin muttered.

'Oh, flap-sauce!' Betsy could not help smiling. 'You're savouring the prospect of catching this villain as much as I am. Why should you have all the pleasure of it? After all,' she added with a wry look, 'in a way it's Mistress Rummager who's brought matters to this point, is it not?'

Catlin's only reply was one of his looks of exasperation.

But it was settled: guided by Daniels, a party consisting of Catlin, Betsy and three well-armed constables sent by Caradoc would leave the house soon after midnight. Then they would conceal themselves at the place their guide still refused to name, until the Salamander made an appearance. After that, the little man declared, they were on their own. And further, he needed no escort but would make his way back to Fire's Reach Court by a roundabout route, and spend the rest of the night there. He also demanded that Catlin give him his coach fare in advance, so that he might change his plans if necessary. Then, having sealed his bargain with a mug of sack, he had fallen asleep in the kitchen.

The minute the old parlour clock showed midnight, the party left Fire's Reach and made their way by quiet back lanes towards the Strand.

The streets were windswept and empty; only a watchman's call, and distant sounds from Covent Garden, spoke of others being abroad at this time. Without incident, the little group followed a very nervous Daniels past the closed-up New Exchange, then down a causeway towards the river. But before reaching the water's edge, their guide turned into a noisome alley between darkened houses and hurried along it, crossing Buckingham Street and Villiers Street. Then he veered left, and led them down a dark pathway to a set of rickety-looking stairs. Below them the river showed, black and sluggish in the starlight.

There was a tense moment while the party looked about for hiding places. Catlin, muffled in his heavy coat and flat-crowned hat, gazed upriver briefly, then turned to Daniels with a sceptical expression.

'You mean to tell me this is where the Rye road begins?' he demanded. 'We're but a stone's throw from Whitehall, almost under the royal nose!'

'I noticed that too,' Daniels answered in a voice heavy with sarcasm. 'Now, with your leave, I'll get myself out of sight.' And at once he darted to the shelter of an overhanging jetty, to disappear beneath its shadow. No lights showed in any of the buildings that loomed over the stairs; indeed, from their appearance, they had all been disused for a long while.

The constable was a thin beanpole of a man named John Quinn. His assistants were younger men, both nervous. When Catlin pointed out a promising doorway, the constable nodded and sent the other two hurrying out of sight.

'Are you sure we can trust that little rat-faced fellow, Doctor?' Quinn asked in a doubtful tone. 'I don't care to take my eyes off him, not for a minute.'

'Mistress Brand here knows the man we seek as well as anyone,' Catlin answered. 'She can identify him. That's what matters, is it not?' When Quinn still looked uneasy, the doctor gave a grim smile. 'There'll be much credit to you, if you can take the Salamander.'

The notion seemed to encourage the man. 'You'd best stay close to our friend,' he said, and pointed to the building on the right-hand corner, which leaned dangerously out over the water. 'I'll find a den in there, where I can spy a boat if one comes,' he said. 'I'd prefer it if you didn't take any risks yourself, Doctor — or you, mistress,' this with a meaningful glance at Betsy. And without further word, the man walked off.

Betsy and Catlin had not spoken since leaving Fire's Reach. The doctor glanced at her, but saw no fear in her eyes: only a gleam of excitement.

'Well then,' he gestured in the direction Daniels had disappeared. 'Shall we find a vantage point?'

Drawing her cloak about her, Betsy accompanied him to the overhang. Beneath it was an open doorway, the door long since broken down. Stooping, the two of them ducked inside, finding themselves in what seemed to be a derelict warehouse, its floor littered with refuse. As they entered there came a sound from close by, and Daniels' voice floated out of the gloom.

'I'd find somewhere snug if I were you,' he said in a leering tone. 'We could be in for a long wait.'

* * *

It was the most uncomfortable two hours Betsy had ever spent — though little worse, she reflected later, than playing First Witch in *Macbeth*. Seated in a corner on some sacking she had found, she kept her eyes on the doorway through which the path down to the stairs could be seen. Catlin was closer to the street, having found a peephole through a badly boarded window. Daniels was somewhere opposite, crouching against the wall, though neither of them could see him.

After their arrival, nobody spoke again. But as the small hours passed, the unpleasant feeling came over Betsy that they could be on a fool's errand. She tried to push the notion aside, reasoning that Daniels would hardly go to all this trouble for nothing — unless he planned to sneak off. That caused her more serious doubt: having got his coach money from Catlin, the fellow could simply slip away. But then, she was sure the idea had occurred to Catlin. He wouldn't let the man get past him even in this dark, unless he had fallen asleep. After what seemed an age she was on the point of calling out and risking his wrath, when there came a sound from outside. At once Betsy sat up stiffly, relieved to hear a movement from Catlin's post by the boarded window. She listened — and her pulse quickened. For now there could be no mistake: someone was walking down the path. But the next moment she started: it wasn't one set of footsteps, but two!

Betsy struggled to her feet, rubbing the stiffness from her limbs, and moved to crouch beside Tom Catlin at the boarded window. Across the room she was aware of Daniels kneeling, peering through the doorway. In silence the three of them waited until the footfalls were almost opposite. Now they heard voices, and then a peal of laughter.

Beside her, Besty felt Catlin tense. She could only hope that Quinn and his men were alert at their positions across the pathway. Calling out was impossible, and belatedly she wondered why they had not agreed some signal between them. But in any case, it was too late.

In the half-light two figures came into view, walking arm-in-arm down to the stairs. One of them wore a loose-fitting gown . . . and one glance at the heavy make-up and the mask dangling from her girdle, was enough to tell her profession. Her companion, or rather her customer, was male — and Betsy's face fell in dismay: the man was not Julius Hill!

They waited, not daring to move, while the trull backed to the wall of the building opposite, drawing her cull along with her. The couple's voices were low, but it took little imagination to guess what was being said. The man, a scrawny fellow in a cheap periwig and bombazine coat, was fumbling in his pockets. From this short distance the clink of coins was easily heard. And at Betsy's side Catlin cursed audibly, and turned in Daniels's direction.

'So this is your Rye road, is it?' he whispered hoarsely. 'A quiet spot for harlots to do business?'

'I swear it's the place!' Daniels hissed back. 'But I never promised to deliver you the prize, did I?'

The couple now moved into the shadow of the building opposite, so that they were almost hidden. Disappointment threatened to overwhelm Betsy. She was tired and cold, and her limbs ached. She squinted into the dark, hearing the murmur of the man's voice as he fumbled with the trull's skirts. There was no other sound: presumably the constables had decided to stay put and wait until the unwelcome couple finished their business and left. But the next moment she turned her head sharply, towards the waterside. Catlin stiffened, he had heard it too. There could be no mistaking the splash of oars: a boat was approaching the stairs.

And in an instant, Betsy knew that they had been fooled — but not by Daniels. Even as she got awkwardly to her feet, her heart thudding, she saw the trull — who was no trull at all — hitch up her skirts, revealing thick stockings and heavy shoes, and start to sprint for the stairs leaving her 'customer', who at once ran off up the pathway.

There came a shout and the crash of a door flung open, and the constable's men ran from the house opposite, but Betsy knew they had failed.

Tom Catlin was running from the doorway, calling to her to stay back, but she ignored him. In seconds she, the doctor and the constables were stumbling on the uneven path, almost colliding with one another to get to the stairs, down which their quarry, his wig awry, was fast disappearing.

There came a thud, followed by a grunt of pain and another male voice raised in irritation, and the pursuers knew they were too late. For Aanaarden — alias the Salamander, alias Julius Hill — had leaped into the boat which bobbed below them, a few feet from the bottom of the steps. And Quinn, who came hurtling down the stairs behind them, cursing and shoving his hapless assistants aside, could only lurch to a halt on the lowest step and watch, pistol in hand, while the boatman dipped his oars.

With barely a ripple, the little vessel shot outwards on the Thames, and disappeared into the dark.

CHAPTER TWELVE

For a moment, nobody spoke. Then there came a deafening report as Quinn raised his pistol and fired. But since there was no lantern on the vessel's stern there was nothing to aim at. Cursing roundly, the constable turned on his fellows, who both looked as if they expected the worst.

'Don't stand there like a couple of maypoles!' he shouted. 'Get after the other one!'

Relieved to have something to do, the two younger men ran off. But Catlin and Betsy exchanged despairing looks: Aanaarden's accomplice, whoever he was, would have disappeared into some alleyway. And before they could speak there came another set of footfalls, scurrying from the derelict building which had been their hideout. The two of them turned sharply, just in time to see a slight figure running off into the gloom: Daniels had picked his moment to make himself scarce.

The doctor turned to Quinn. 'So that's the end of it all, is it?' he demanded. 'Anaarden guessed the stairs might be watched, so he plays us all for fools, jumps into a boat before our eyes and vanishes. Is there nothing you can do?'

The constable wore a sickly expression. 'They can't row fast in the dark,' he said. 'Besides, it's an incoming tide. I'll run to the next stairs and find a boat. There must be someone on the water.' He started to go, then looked back. 'Would you get word to His Lordship?' he asked lamely.

After a moment the doctor gave a nod, whereupon the other hurried off up the pathway. Betsy watched him disappear round the corner. 'Don't judge him too harshly,' she said to Catlin. 'We were all taken in by the disguise. If anyone should have seen it wasn't a woman in that garb, it's me.'

But the doctor didn't answer. And without further word, the two of them began retracing their steps in the direction of the Strand.

It was barely an hour before dawn when they returned to Fire's Reach Court, and there seemed little point in going to their beds. Betsy raked the kitchen fire into life and put on a saucepan of milk, while Catlin sat down at the table. Finally he looked up.

'I underestimated our quarry,' he said. 'I only set eyes on the man once, when he cut a poor figure as the doctor in *Macbeth*. It's easy to forget how cunning he must be. And yet there's one comfort: he knows how close he came to capture. He'll want to get himself out of England as soon as he can, likely never to return. So at least his murderous spree is over.'

But seeing the look of disappointment on Betsy's face he broke off. More than anything, she had wanted to be a part of the Salamander's capture. Yet he had eluded her as he had eluded everyone else, and taken another life too: that of James Prout. Wearily she sank down on a stool beside Catlin.

'I should get Samuel Tripp to write a play about it,' she said finally. 'A satirical comedy . . . call it *Escape of the Salamander, or the end of Mistress Rummager*. For I believe I've finished with chasing shadows.'

At that moment there came the thud of footsteps on the stairs, and Peg stumbled in in her nightgown.

'I thought some rogue had broken in!' she cried. 'Did no one think to tell me what was up?' Then seeing how tired both of them looked, she sighed. 'Weasel-face hasn't come back,' she said. 'Then, I never thought he would.'

She frowned at Catlin, but he merely turned away.

* * *

Feeling restless, Betsy left the house at mid-morning to walk to the Duke's Theatre. She expected few of the company to be there, but she wanted to talk with someone, especially Jane. The skies were heavy with thick cloud, and a breeze blew from the river. Absently she walked down Fetter Lane, turned into Fleet Street and trudged through the morning traffic, heedless of the shouts of the carters.

An hour ago she had stood in the hallway with Catlin when Quinn had arrived wearing a sheepish expression, to report that attempts to pursue the Salamander had failed. The boat could have crossed to the Southwark shore, he explained, or passed under the bridge to rendezvous with a larger vessel downstream. By now the fugitive would be well on his way on the Rye road. To Catlin's questions, he responded with increasing irritation. No, his men had not succeeded in catching the Salamander's companion either. It was hardly surprising, since none of them got a proper look at the man in the dark. As for the little rat-faced fellow, what did the doctor expect but that he would fly at the first opportunity? Finally the constable had taken his leave, claiming other duties, while a grim-faced Tom Catlin prepared to go to Bredon House and inform Lord Caradoc of the sorry chain of events.

With a heavy heart Betsy turned into Bride's Lane — to be confronted by a familiar, wild-eyed figure in black.

'Hark, ye brazen jade! Now another steeped in sin falls into the pit that is prepared for him, yet still ye come here to flaunt yourself! Will nothing make ye take thought for the morrow?!'

But Betsy merely gave a sigh. Whereupon Praise-God Palmer hesitated, tattered Bible in hand, and peered at her through narrowed eyes. 'Y'are troubled, woman; the weight of sin presses ye down. Heed me, and call on your maker for forgiveness!'

'Another steeped in sin.' The man's words suddenly registered in Betsy's mind. 'If you mean Mr Prout,' she retorted, 'he will be sorely missed, if not mourned throughout London!'

The ranter's brow furrowed. 'Mourned by painted theatre folk, perhaps,' he cried, 'but not by God-fearing men!' When Betsy said nothing, he added: 'Are ye still so blind that ye cannot see the design? This creature of fire is but God's instrument, that strikes down all those who forsake Him!'

Suddenly a wave of anger soared up from within Betsy, to burst like a cataract. 'How dare you!' she shouted, so forcefully that Palmer gaped and stepped back. 'How dare you appoint yourself judge and pronounce on matters of which you know nothing. God's instrument? None of those who've died did any harm to anyone.'

'Did they not?' Palmer had recovered quickly. 'Two thieves, a strutting peacock of a player, a prating alderman steeped in greed and lust, and now a sodomizing villain — wicked men all — who have paid the price! They shall not look upon the gates of paradise, nor shall they—'

'Oh, cods!' Betsy shouted, realizing that she had never stood up to Palmer's ravings before. 'What of Dart, a fugitive whose only link with the others was to tell what he knew?'

'I know naught of that,' Palmer snapped. 'Yet I say there is order and design in this web of evil, which y'are too foolish to see! And more, I say it is not yet ended, and shall not be, until the fire be quenched in the blood of Christ!'

'Not yet ended.' Betsy's heart skipped a beat. 'What do you mean?' When the man merely glared at her she repeated herself. 'What do you mean it's not yet ended, and how is it you know so much about those deaths?'

Palmer drew a breath and puffed out his chest. 'I walked through the Fire,' he said, as if delivering a sermon. 'And though there was evil abroad, I feared it not. I saw 'twas but

God's judgement, as it is writ in Kings: *And after the fire, a still small voice.* I saw the Almighty at His work, and I gave thanks that the city was razed to the ground so that it might be founded anew! And I . . . I would be that still voice!'

To Betsy's alarm a smile spread across the man's features, and his eyes filled with a strange light. 'I was spared,' he went on, nodding to himself. 'Though I looked in the demon's face, he would not slay me.' The ranter paused, seeming to remember Betsy, and fixed her with a stern expression. 'I saw him for what he was — God's instrument — and so I allowed him to do his work! And he in his turn smiled upon me and spoke to me, bidding me bear witness, so that now he takes his vengeance upon those who turn from the path!'

But Betsy was aghast; for only now did the man's words, which she had dismissed as the ravings of a lunatic, begin to make some sense. She drew closer, forcing Palmer to meet her eye. 'Do you tell me that you saw the Salamander — Aanaarden — during the Great Fire?' she demanded. 'That you spoke with him, and he spared you because you believed he was carrying out God's will?'

Palmer smiled at her. 'I saw him . . . like a sprite he ran through the flames unharmed, for the Almighty was his shield.' He peered at Betsy. 'And I see there is yet hope! For if the Lord's design is become clear to ye, ye may yet be saved! Come into yon church, woman, fall upon your knees, and—'

'You buffle-head!'

At Betsy's cry, Palmer fell back as if struck. In amazement he met her gaze, as she lambasted him.

'For days past, men have been scouring these suburbs to find a murderer,' she cried, 'one who's not satisfied with taking vengeance on those he believes wronged him, but is so glutted with killing that he cannot stop! And all along you've known who he is, and what he looks like? Did it never occur to you to tell someone?'

Palmer made no reply.

'Last night he escaped capture,' Betsy went on. 'And now he's free to kill again as the whim takes him, if not in

London, then elsewhere! How many more might die, before he is caught?'

At that, Palmer raised his Bible as if to ward Betsy off. 'Caught?' he echoed. 'Ye cannot stop God's instrument! Only when the hour is appointed shall he cease. There may yet be others who will fall!'

Then suddenly the man dropped to his knees in the dirt, clasped his hands with the Bible between them and closed his eyes. And ignoring Betsy, he began to pray in an undertone, the words tumbling so rapidly from his lips that they might have been in some foreign tongue. With a last look at the muttering figure in his battered hat, she walked away.

* * *

The theatre was deserted, though the side door was unlocked. Betsy entered to the echo of her own footsteps. With a sinking of spirits she walked through the empty pit, glancing up at the forestage. The candle-hoops had been lowered, and were unlit. At the rear, half-finished screens for the opening scene of *The Virtuous Bawd* were in place, but there was nothing on the darkened stage apart from sawdust.

But there was a sound from backstage. Betsy climbed the side steps and opened the door of the scene-room, to see a figure bent over a sawhorse. As she entered, the man started and turned. It was Joshua Small.

'Lord, Mistress Brand, you frit me near to death.' The scene-man peered at her. 'What d'you do here? There's no rehearsal.'

'I know,' Betsy replied. 'I merely wondered if any of the company had come by.'

Small shrugged. 'Will Daggett was here earlier. Never seen him at a loose end before. The Duke's is his life — mine too, come to that,' the fellow paused, then said in a different tone: 'You heard about Prout? An evil business!'

The man appeared very edgy. When Betsy did not speak, he went on: 'Tom Cleeve, then Rigg, now the dancing-master.

And 'twas Julius Hill murdered them. Not only that, but he's a Dutchman too! Who'd have thought such?'

Still Betsy made no reply. How much Small and other members of the company had learned by now, she could not know. Finally she said: 'He was nearly caught last night, but escaped by boat. He could be out of the country by now.'

Small was not cheered by the news: in fact, if anything his nervousness merely increased. 'Escaped, you say,' he frowned. 'Then he's still at large.'

'Not in London,' Betsy said. 'He knows he's a hunted man. And as far as we know he's paid off his scores.'

'So you say,' Small sniffed, and wiped his nose with the back of his hand. 'And what scores are they?'

'Grudges that go back years . . . to the Great Fire,' Betsy answered after a moment. But the man was barely listening.

'Aye, there's many a wound unhealed from that time,' he murmured. 'As there are those who still say the Fire was started on purpose. It may have begun in the shop of Farriner the baker, but how it is some fires started up in places the blaze hadn't yet reached? Can you answer that?'

There was both fear and anger in the man's eyes, the causes of which Betsy did not understand. But at once Small added: 'You've heard that black-clad fool who rants in the lanes — prating Palmer. He thinks 'twas God's vengeance on London. What if it was just the French, or the Dutch?'

'I know some think that,' Betsy answered. 'But it seems to me the reasons it started were simple enough. A dry summer, a high wind, an oven not put out properly.'

But Small was becoming animated now. 'Aye, but in the heat and the flames, with folk panicking and running every way, you'd not condemn a man for jumping to conclusions, would you?' he cried. ''Tis hard to reason straight, when you see everything you own, everything you know, falling to blazes!'

Betsy watched him. 'What is it you're trying to say, Joshua?' she asked. 'That you did something in the Fire you regret?'

There was a moment, then Small seemed to master himself. 'If I did, that's between me and my maker,' he answered, and suddenly his expression changed to one of hostility. 'I hear you've been busy toing and froing these past days, mistress,' he added. 'Betterton's willing horse . . . I should say mare. Taking supper at Caradoc's, too.' He gave a thin smile. 'Could it be you're looking to get yourself set up in a nice little house in Pall Mall, like others we could both name?'

Betsy put on a wry expression. 'I think it's time I left you to whatever it is you're doing, Joshua,' she said. 'What is it you're doing, by the way?'

Then without waiting for an answer, she walked out of the scene-room. Behind her she heard the man mutter an oath, which was soon followed by the sound of vigorous sawing.

* * *

That night after supper at Fire's Reach Court, Betsy talked with Tom Catlin. The news of Aanaarden's escape had been greeted with incredulity and anger by Lord Caradoc. Fortunately, having listened to the doctor's account of the matter, he did not blame him or Betsy, but the incompetence of John Quinn and his fellows. After offering Catlin half-hearted thanks, His Lordship had gone off to write letters. He would request that the Channel ports be watched for a man answering Aanaarden's description; though given the Salamander's talent for disguise, there seemed little hope of him being apprehended. In fact, Catlin surmised, it was more than likely the man would change his plans and flee the country by another direction.

Both of them were still tired after the previous night's adventures, and Betsy rose to go to her bed. Catlin stood up too, but at that moment there was a knocking outside. Followed by Betsy, the doctor walked out to the hallway just as Peg was opening the front door. On the step was a diminutive, tousle-haired boy. When Peg towered menacingly over him, the child shrank back. But at sight of Catlin he made a clumsy attempt at a bow. He was out of breath, and had clearly been running for some distance.

'You the physician, sir?' When Catlin signalled his assent, the boy went on: 'My father bids you come — quickly if you please. Mother's been in labour since this morning, and the baby don't come!'

Catlin nodded to Peg, who walked off. Then taking his coat from its hook he pulled it on, questioning the child as he did so.

'Is there a midwife attending?'

The boy shrugged. 'Likely so. Half the neighbours be crammed in the house — tis like the fair.'

'And is your mother in much pain?'

The boy nodded vigorously. 'She does scream the street down, sir. We fear for her life!'

Betsy had found Catlin's bag and was holding it out. With a glance at her he took it. 'I may be gone for some hours,' he said. 'Lock the door after me.'

She gave a nod and glanced down at the child, who was eying her without expression. Then as Catlin stepped through the doorway, he pointed up the street in the direction of Holborn and trotted off. The doctor strode after him.

Betsy closed the door, turned the key, then walked down the hallway to the kitchen where she caught Peg in the act of lighting a pipe. At Betsy's appearance she started, choked on the fumes and fell into a coughing fit. Finally the coughs subsided, whereupon Peg sucked hard on the pipe and blew out a cloud of smoke.

'What he don't know won't hurt him,' she croaked, and indicated Catlin's tobacco jar. 'Want a puff?'

'I'm for bed,' Betsy said with a shake of her head. 'The street door's locked. Will you bolt up the back, and see to the window latches?'

Peg nodded absently, frowning at the pipe. 'This Spanish tobacco's a mite strong,' she muttered, then glanced round. 'Tom'll be out a good while, won't he?' But Betsy was walking tiredly towards the stairs.

* * *

When she awoke, it was pitch dark. Groggily, she raised herself on one elbow, wondering what had startled her. She listened, but there was no sound; Peg must have gone to bed. As for Tom Catlin, it was likely he had not yet returned. Urgent calls upon his skills, sometimes at night, were not uncommon. Betsy yawned, sank back on to her pillow and closed her eyes — then sat up with a jolt.

It sounded like a cry. She cocked her head towards the door, and to her alarm, it came again. It came from downstairs, and there was no mistake: someone had cried out, in pain or in fear, she could not tell. But in an instant she had risen and was pulling on a gown. Groping about in the dark, she found her leather mules and stepped into them. Then she stumbled to the door and wrenched it open.

'Peg!'

There was no answer. Glancing along the landing, she saw no light from Catlin's chamber. Uneasily she made her way to the top of the stairs and looked down. There was a faint glow from the rear of the house. Standing on the top step, Betsy called Peg's name once more, and after a moment there came an answering shout, which made her pulse quicken.

'In the kitchen!'

It was almost a shriek. Betsy started downstairs, the wooden heels of her mules thudding on the boards. She imagined housebreakers, and briefly considered going into the parlour for a poker or a candlestick. Then chiding herself, she dismissed the idea. It was Peg's voice, so there must be some explanation. She reached the bottom step, saw that the parlour was in darkness, and turned towards the kitchen. The door was ajar, and the light came from there. Had Peg not gone to bed?

Now there came a muffled sound from beyond the kitchen door. Betsy hesitated, sniffing: there was an odour which at first she failed to recognize. Then she realized that it was lantern oil.

'Peg?'

This time there was no answer. Berating herself for her timidity, Betsy strode forward and pushed the door open. At first she saw nothing amiss. There was a candle on the table, its flickering light reflected off Catlin's best pewter dishes, racked above the sideboard. There too was the tobacco jar which Peg had plundered. She stepped into the room — then froze.

Peg sat motionless on a chair, still in her workaday clothes, staring wide-eyed at Betsy. Her hands were on her lap, tied together with an end of rope, and they were trembling. But that was not why Betsy stood rigid, struggling with the wave of cold fear that washed over her.

To Peg's right, and slightly behind her, stood the man Betsy had once known as Julius Hill; a supporting actor of indifferent talent, who had played the doctor in *Macbeth*. And he was smiling.

'Mistress Brand, you've taken your time. Do join us, won't you?'

His voice was soft. And having forced herself to meet his gaze — which did not waver — Betsy's eyes strayed downwards, to see the reason for Peg's immobility as well as her terror.

Hill — now that she saw him, she could think of him by no other name — had his left arm about Peg's shoulder, resting his hand upon her, almost affectionately. On the right hand, however, he wore a leather glove. It was a well-tailored glove, and it had been made to a most unusual design. For at the end of the middle finger was a little cap, somewhat like a thimble. Except that this was a thimble in reverse, so to speak, since it ended in a sharp point: a thick darning needle or a bodkin had been securely fixed therein, so that it stuck out alarmingly, a deadly extension to Hill's finger. It was a cunning device, and as she stared at it Betsy's breath caught in her throat, for in a trice, a mystery was solved.

Here was the means by which Tom Cleeve had been pricked as he stood in the scene-room, mug in hand, toasting the success of *Macbeth*. Here too was the means by which Alderman Blake had been pierced in the neck. No doubt this was how Ned Gowden had also received his wound, a quick stab by a customer who brushed by him, unnoticed in the semi-darkness of the bagnio. Somehow Joseph Rigg, too, had received his pinprick — several in fact, for good measure.

And now the fearful spike was levelled at Peg's neck, its tip barely an inch from her skin.

CHAPTER THIRTEEN

'The natives call it *curare*,' Hill said softly. 'In the jungles beyond the Spanish Main there's a vine. They extract a substance from it which they boil up, making a deadly ichor to dip their arrows in. Once the flesh of the victim is pierced, animal or human, it cannot live.'

Betsy stood still, her eyes flicking from Hill to Peg and back. She could think of no other course than to let the man talk.

'It took me a deal of trouble to obtain it,' he murmured, giving a bleak smile. 'A curious turnabout, is it not? For in sending me to the other side of the world, my enemies enabled me to find the means to take my retribution.'

Peg caught Betsy's eye, and there was desperation in her gaze. Somehow Betsy must distract the man, or at least get him to take the terrible pin away. Only now did she see the thick brown paste with which its tip was coated.

'Your enemies have paid a heavy price,' she said, managing to keep her voice steady. 'But Peg isn't one of them . . . she's done you no hurt. Will you not release her?'

Hill's smile faded, to be replaced by a hard look. And if Betsy needed further proof that he was not the unassuming, diffident man the Duke's Company had once taken him for, it was about to follow.

'You mistake me,' he said coldly. 'It's you who have done me hurt. Dogging my footsteps, poking about . . . even setting traps!' His face twitched, and Betsy resolved to tread carefully: this man was not merely dangerous, he was close to madness. As she watched, he withdrew his free hand from Peg's shoulder, keeping the other close to her neck.

'Stand up!' he ordered. 'And no sudden movements.'

Slowly, Peg stood up.

'Now — change places.'

For a moment both women hesitated. 'Change places, I said!' Hill cried. 'I've been put to enough difficulty already on your account, Mistress Brand, so sit down before I spike this maid's neck. Which would be a pity,' he added, 'for it's a pretty neck.'

Betsy walked round the end of the table and sat herself down in the chair Peg had vacated. At once, Hill gave Peg a shove which sent her staggering, and moved his gloved hand quickly to rest on Betsy's shoulder. She heard the soft scrape of leather, close to her ear. She even smelled the faint, aromatic odour of the poison.

'Put your hands forward, and press them together,' he ordered. When Betsy did so, he glanced at Peg and jerked his head towards the floor. 'There's another cord in there — take it out, and tie her wrists.'

Betsy had not noticed the open sailcloth bag which stood near the wall. Keeping her head still, she let her eyes follow Peg, who stooped with difficulty since her hands were still bound, and fumbled inside the bag. Drawing out the length of thin rope, Peg hesitated.

'Bind her!' Hill shouted, his voice filling the room. And now, both women sensed the well of pent-up rage within the man. Peg moved towards Betsy, and falling to her knees before her began to wind the rope clumsily about her wrists.

'Knot it securely,' Hill told her. With trembling fingers Peg managed to tie the rope. Then with a glance at Betsy she bent forward, gripped the end in her teeth and drew it tight.

'Beautifully done.' With a thin smile, Hill signalled to Peg to stand and move back. Then he bent, leaning so close to Betsy that she could feel his breath on her face.

'In a short time,' he said, 'this house will be aflame . . . and your bodies will burn with it. Your landlord, the good doctor, I have chosen to spare.'

At once Betsy understood: it was Hill who had sent the boy, and drawn Catlin away on a wild goose chase.

Keeping his hand on Betsy's shoulder, Hill looked round at Peg. 'You, too, I had a mind to spare,' he murmured. 'However, your little venture into the Bermuda Straits made you an accomplice, so you too must pay. I say this . . .' he turned to Betsy again, 'I say it because I wish you both to know why you will die. All those I've despatched had time — but a short time, I admit — to reflect upon their fate before they expired. Hence you too should be afforded that small luxury.'

Fighting panic, Betsy met Peg's eyes. If she was to act, it must be soon. But first the smell of lantern oil was explained, for with his free hand, Hill gestured Peg towards his bag.

'There's a bottle and some rags in there,' he said. 'Take them out.'

Peg stooped again and reached inside the bag. This time she took out a horseman's leather flask, fumbling with it in her tied hands, and placed it on the table. She returned to the bag and pulled out a bundle of dirty rags.

'Now,' Hill drew a deep breath, 'pour the oil out.'

Peg stared, as if she did not understand.

'Pour it!' he snapped. 'On the floor, about the door and the walls. If there's any left, drip it on the rags. Then take them and scatter them down the passage, as far as the door.'

Still Peg did not move, and suddenly Betsy felt Hill's hand tremble. Trying her best to sound calm, she spoke up.

'Julius Hill,' though she knew it was not his true name, she would use the one she knew him by, 'won't you give me some answers first? I want to know what hurt the Duke's Company have done to you. I know Tom Cleeve betrayed you . . . Long Ned too, but Rigg—'

'Be silent!' Hill's voice rang in her ear. 'I owe you nothing. I came back for vengeance, and I've taken it!'

'Joseph Rigg,' Betsy persisted. 'What quarrel had you with him?'

There was a moment, then Hill sighed. 'None,' he replied at last, then gave a short, barking laugh. 'You've seen how the fire salamander moves, I think,' he added. 'Ignorant folk have never understood its ways. Salamanders carry their young for eight months, almost as long as a human term. Yet they give birth not to one, but to many!'

Now, Betsy felt a chill along her spine. Peg was gazing at the man as if transfixed.

'You mean, there are others?' Calling on all her acting skills, Betsy kept anxiety from her voice. But Hill squeezed her shoulder with his bony fingers, making her flinch.

'Some may find that out, after I've gone,' he hissed. 'But you will die in ignorance!' He gestured impatiently to Peg. 'Now spread the oil, as I told you!'

Trying not to shake, Peg picked up the flask. Her eyes met Betsy's again, then they strayed to the candle, barely two feet away from her. And suddenly a look of understanding passed between both women. Holding Peg's gaze, Betsy signalled furiously with her eyes.

Hill was watching Peg suspiciously. 'One sudden movement,' he said, 'and I will pierce Mistress Brand's neck as I would yours. It makes no difference to me whether she dies by poison or by fire!'

Betsy began to talk rapidly. 'If you had no quarrel with Rigg, what then of Prout?' she asked him. 'Can't you see what ruin you've brought upon the Duke's Company—'

'Stop!' Hill cried, and Betsy felt the tremor along his arm. 'You dare to question me?' he demanded. 'You know nothing of what I've suffered. I'll take vengeance on anyone I choose! As for that simpering dandy of a dancing-master, he was no longer of use.' He turned abruptly to Peg. 'Enough delay — do as I ordered!'

Peg picked up the flask, drew out the stopper and tilted it. As the oil ran out on to the floor, she began to move round the table towards Hill and Betsy, spilling it as she went. Hill watched her as she moved past him — then suddenly she stumbled, and tipped a splash of oil over him. Some of it fell on his coat, more ran down his stockings and on to his shoes. The man gasped, and an oath flew from his mouth.

'You stupid girl!' Hill spat. 'By the Christ, I'll make you suffer for that!' He looked briefly down at his clothing, and that second was all Betsy needed. Tilting her head away from the deadly needle, she raised her right leg and brought the wooden heel of her slipper down as hard as she could on Hill's foot.

The man yelped, but even as he sensed the danger, Peg's tied hands shot out like a crab's claw and grabbed his wrist. And in a moment the two of them were locked in a battle for control of Hill's hand with its wicked device. But it was enough for Betsy: struggling to her feet, her arms thrust out before her, she lurched over to the table and seized the candle by its holder. At the same time, however, both Peg and Hill slipped on the spilled oil and crashed to the floor together, locked in a wild embrace that almost suggested the throes of passion.

It was a bizarre tussle. Hill seemed as surprised by Peg's strength as he was by her determination, though he made no allowance for her sex, cursing and hitting out at her with his free hand while she kept a vicelike grip on the one with the fearsome glove. But when Betsy came to Peg's aid, the man was outnumbered.

Putting the candle down, she ran to the struggling pair, dodging a chair which was sent flying across the floor by Hill's flailing leg. Desperately she kicked the man in his side. He grunted with pain, whereupon she kicked him again, causing her right mule to fly off and land somewhere across the room. Cursing under her breath, she commenced kicking him with her left foot, until to her annoyance the other mule came off.

'Oh, cods!' she breathed. The struggle was becoming ridiculous. Hill was a snarling figure, his breath coming in shorter bursts. To his consternation, he found himself on the defensive. And when Betsy dropped to the floor and grabbed his free hand between both of hers, bending it backwards until the pain made him cry out, he realized he was losing.

Peg scrambled to her knees, then levering herself up with her bound hands, fell deliberately on to Hill's chest. Her full weight drove the wind from him, and quite suddenly it was over. His eyes popping, the man let out a great gasp, fighting for breath, even as Betsy scrambled up and stumbled to the table. Peg too struggled to her feet — but Hill saw their intention. And if he had not already guessed that Peg's spilling oil on him was deliberate, he did so now.

Picking up the candle Betsy turned to him, as Peg let go of the man's wrist at last, and fell backwards against the kitchen wall, panting. But Hill's eyes never left the candle. As Betsy took a step, he got painfully to his feet, winded but fully alert.

'Stand still, or I throw it.'

Her voice was ice cold, and meeting her eye, Hill saw the steeliness in her gaze. Warily, half-crouching and still breathless, he watched as she raised the flame and held it out in front of her. The stench of lantern oil filled the room now, along with the waxy smell of the guttering candle.

'You won't,' he muttered, then winced with pain and pressed his ungloved hand to his side. It was clear Betsy's kicking had done him some hurt, before she found herself barefoot.

'If she doesn't, I will.' Peg's voice was hoarser, but equally resolute. Hill's eyes flicked towards her as she leaned against the wall, her hair sticking out in all directions. There the three stood, in silent tableau: the Salamander and his intended victims, bruised, breathless and smeared with oil. But then, Hill did something neither Betsy nor Peg expected.

Straightening up, his face relaxing into a grim smile, he eyed each of them in turn. 'Throw it,' he said softly. 'And let's see which of us walks through the flames.'

There was a brief silence. Then Hill raised his gloved hand and made a jabbing motion in the air.

'You can't kill the Salamander,' he said.

Betsy raised the candle higher. 'Your clothes will burn at once,' she said. 'You'll be a living torch.'

Still pointing, Hill closed three fingers and pressed them down with his thumb, so that only the middle finger with its wicked needle was extended before him. 'You lose,' he said, raising his voice slightly. 'Before you could throw, I would spike you!'

From near the wall, Peg gasped. 'Don't let him close,' she said, and took a step away. Fortunately for them both, they were between Hill and the doorway. The tension in the room was almost unbearable, but the Salamander seemed to feed upon it. It was as if a naked flame could do him no harm. Deliberately, he took a pace forward.

'I walked through the Fire,' he said; and the words of Praise-God Palmer rose at once in Betsy's memory.

'Since I was a child,' he went on, 'it has held no terrors for me. Many were the times I stood and watched a hayrick burn.' He was smiling broadly now. 'Stood with other villagers while men ran about, colliding with one another, spilling their buckets of water before they could dash them over the blaze, and no one guessed that the one who set the fire was standing among them!'

He gave a throaty laugh, then fixed Betsy with a scornful look. 'You think what you and your foppish fellows at the Duke's do is acting?' He shook his head. 'I was acting before I could walk!'

But Betsy held his gaze. 'That was in Holland, was it . . . Mr Aanaarden?'

'*Aan*aarden.' The other corrected her. 'The English have never learned how to pronounce my name.'

Betsy glanced at Peg, who had edged to the doorway. Holding the candle out, Betsy took a backwards pace too. But Hill stepped forward again, and his smile vanished. 'Enough talk,' he said, levelling his spiked finger at Betsy, then swinging it towards Peg. 'The Salamander is impervious to fire. But you'll both die a terrible death, like that villainous old skate Blake, like those two rogues who left me to the mercy of the law,' the words fell venomously from his mouth, and his teeth showed.

'You'll feel each part of your bodies stiffen, until you can't move,' he hissed. 'It starts with the toes, then the ears, then the eyes, the neck — you've seen it for yourself, Betsy Brand! When Cleeve choked his last breath you were there! And once again I stood among the watchers, laughing inside, for none knew it was by my hand, nor did they when the African perished among the molly-men of the *hammam*.'

He broke off, watching both of them with his small, pale-blue eyes. There was indeed madness in them, and Betsy struggled to think of some way to use it. The fellow was so steeped in vanity, it could be his weakness. She stiffened, as Hill took another step.

'For the last time,' he ordered, 'throw it, or set it down!'

But in a second, everything changed. For to the surprise of all three of them there came a noise from the far end of the passage, a rattling of the door, followed by a clatter. The key had been pushed from the lock, and fallen on to the hallway floor.

'Run!' Betsy dropped the candle and turned, even as Peg lurched round and bolted for the doorway. There was a moment which seemed to take an age — then a flame sprang up, filling the kitchen with a garish glow. But both Betsy and Peg were running down the passage without looking back. As they did so the front door opened, and to their immense relief Tom Catlin appeared, bag in hand and a frown on his face.

'How many times have I told you to take the key out when you lock this door?' he demanded. 'Lucky I had my own—' then he froze, taking in the bizarre sight: both women dishevelled and reeking of oil, with their hands tied together.

Then he saw the fire. Dropping his bag, he pushed Peg and Betsy aside and started along the passage. 'Go out!' he shouted. 'Get some help.'

But he was too late, for the open door had fanned the flames. The house was filling rapidly with smoke, and Catlin entered the kitchen only to fall back, raising his hand to protect himself. Coughing, he staggered backwards along the passage, eyes fixed on a most terrible sight.

There was a piercing scream, and a figure of flame appeared, staggering blindly through the kitchen doorway. In the heart of the flames could be seen a dark shape, limbs thrashing wildly about as it careered towards them. And Betsy and Peg, followed swiftly by Catlin, ran down the steps into the street. There were shouts as windows were flung open, but none of the three looked round. Their eyes remained on the dreadful sight of the Salamander, as he came screaming through the doorway in front of them, and tumbled down the steps.

All of them fell back, gazing helplessly at the human pyre. Once the figure tried to rise, then sank down again. And finally it collapsed into a blazing heap, in which it was impossible to distinguish burning clothing from flesh. The houses were lit by a lurid glare, but still Betsy, Peg and Catlin were unable to take their eyes from the sight until quite suddenly the screams ceased, and the shape stopped moving. Then it became merely a bonfire, its flames gradually subsiding. Slowly they lessened, until only a smouldering mass lay before Tom Catlin's front steps. Finally, all that remained was a charred and smoking heap that gave off a most unpleasant smell.

Peg was shaking; and as if noticing her for the first time, Catlin turned to her. Sobbing, she fell against him. After a moment he put an arm awkwardly about her.

But Betsy remained motionless, staring at the remains of the Salamander — who was not impervious to fire after all.

* * *

The house was saved, though the kitchen was a shambles. With the help of neighbours, Tom Catlin stamped out the blazing patches of oil and doused the floor with water. Then he opened the windows and retired outside to allow the smoke to clear. It seemed a cruel turn of fate, someone remarked, that this old street that had survived the Great Fire, had come close to being destroyed by fire at the hands of a madman. For once it became known that the Salamander had returned, the news spread like wildfire itself.

Betsy and Peg passed the rest of the night at a neighbour's house, where they were able to clean themselves and borrow some clothing. When dawn broke they went out to find Tom Catlin in the street, talking with the constable of St Dunstan's. Thankfully, the remains of the Salamander's charred corpse had been removed, and the three of them were able to enter the house and survey the damage.

The hallway was littered with burned rags and scraps of charred clothing, though the walls had only been scorched. The kitchen, however, was beyond use. But both Betsy and Catlin were surprised by the energy with which Peg set to work, throwing out the perishables and clearing the floor. Dinner was out of the question, she said, but supper was a possibility; meanwhile, would the doctor be seeking plasterers and painters to make good the walls and ceiling?

Leaving her to her work, Catlin went into the front parlour, signalling Betsy to follow. Now at last she was able to give him a full account of all that happened in the night. When she had finished, the doctor breathed a sigh.

'I should have known something was amiss,' he murmured. 'That boy was a sly little fellow, and he fooled me. Though by the time we were past Smithfield and almost at the Barbican, I had my suspicions. When we reached the house, there was indeed a woman in labour — but she was well attended, and in no difficulty. Having been dragged all that way, I thought I'd stay to help with the birth.' He frowned. 'It was after that I discovered the boy had disappeared. It wasn't his mother!'

Though Betsy nodded, she was past being surprised. Having reflected upon the Salamander's deeds, and looked him in the eye, she could believe anything. More, the man had almost succeeded in putting both her and Peg to a terrible death. The means by which he had gained entry to the house had also been explained: Peg had not secured the back parlour window. Though in view of what she had been through, Catlin had no mind to reproach her.

'Will you get word to His Lordship, and Betterton?' Betsy asked finally. 'They'll be mighty relieved.'

'I've already done so.' Catlin fixed her with a shrewd look. 'Are you sure you're well? You've had a shock.'

With an effort, Betsy smiled. 'It's thanks to Peg, and to you, I'm alive,' she answered. 'I haven't quite taken it in yet,' she sighed. 'And though the man burned to death in front of me, I still fear his works.' She met Catlin's gaze. 'There's danger for the Duke's Company yet, I'm certain of it.'

'You mean those hints he gave you about others carrying on his wickedness?' Catlin looked sceptical. 'It sounds like humbug to me . . . bravado and defiance. The man's mind was so deformed he seems to have believed himself immortal!'

But Betsy did not look convinced. 'He admitted he had no quarrel with Joseph Rigg,' she objected. 'So the question yet remains: who did?'

'Perhaps we'll never learn the answer to that,' Catlin said.

Then he too frowned. 'You haven't seen my tobacco jar anywhere, have you?'

CHAPTER FOURTEEN

The Virtuous Bawd was ready to open.

It was almost a week since the events in Fire's Reach Court, which had culminated in the death of the Dutch murderer Aanaarden, alias the one-time actor Julius Hill, but better known as the Salamander. The story of his wicked deeds and his terrible demise had spread through London and its suburbs, providing much fodder for *The London Gazette*. Yet it was not only people like Praise-God Palmer who saw the hand of divine justice in the man's death by fire. Memories of the city's fearful conflagration of September 1666 remained raw in the minds of many of its citizens.

In the past few days, Tom Catlin's house had been made habitable again, and life had returned almost to normality. Normality for the Duke's Company at Dorset Gardens Theatre, however, meant suppressed panic, and the kind of heady disorder that always preceded the opening of a new play. Four days earlier most of the company had attended the funeral of James Prout, the dancing-master. A supper at Thomas Betterton's house followed, in which their leader and his wife had been at pains to cheer everyone's spirits. Mr Prout, Betterton reminded them, would have been the first to urge his friends to put these dreadful events behind them, to throw themselves into their work, and fill the theatre again. The Duke's Company's reputation would soon be restored, and this unfortunate period of ill luck and scandal would be but a fading memory for the theatre-going public. Such was the man's optimism that the company took heart, and began to look forward to the success of Mr Tripp's new comedy. And once again, the word from Whitehall Palace was that the King himself would very likely be attending.

In the Women's Shift early on that Friday afternoon there was a mood of high excitement. Aveline Hale, splendidly costumed for her role of Lady Althea, was taking a glass of strong water to calm herself. Louise Hawker, in a red gown both garish and revealing, was even more nervous than usual in her part of a young dell, Foggy Moll. Jane Rowe, however, cross-dressed as Lord Feverish in breeches, velvet coat and long periwig, was in reflective mood.

'I can scarce believe it,' she said to Betsy, who sat beside her applying her make-up. 'Dart dead, too . . . but then if anyone had it coming, it was him. Mayhap there's justice, even in the Bermudas!'

Betsy nodded absently. Lately, she had found the chain of events of which she was a part so bizarre they seemed like a play in themselves, one that had run for longer than expected. Sometimes she woke in the night, imagining she heard a cry. And try as she might, she could not rid herself of the troublesome notion that the Salamander's spree of fear was not yet ended. Despite Tom Catlin's view, shared by Peg, that the man's hints about others following in his wake were but wicked boasts, she remained uneasy. Even readying herself for the role of Tammy Tupp could not drive the matter from her thoughts.

'At least we're working again, I suppose,' Betsy said, sticking the last of several false warts to her nose. 'And my landlord, for one, is mighty glad of it.'

Jane peered into the looking glass and adjusted her periwig. 'And if we show that a company of women can pack the Duke's out, it could be we'll have no further need of actors!'

There was a snort from the doorway, and the portly figure of Downes the prompter appeared. 'Give me actors any day,' he grunted, 'rather than this flock of harpies! Curtain's up in five minutes, and half of you still undressed.' He peered about, then fixed his small, piglike eyes on Louise.

'You'd best get yourself downstairs, girl. Scene One's the street, in case you needed reminding.'

Louise stood and picked up her vizard-mask. 'I'm not likely to forget,' she replied in a shrill voice, 'since it's my first time on the stage!'

Downes sniffed. 'Mistress Brand, you'll be showing her the ropes, I take it?'

'There's no need to fret, Mr Downes,' Betsy answered, picking up her own mask. 'We street trulls can shift for ourselves.'

And taking Louise's arm, she followed the prompter as he turned and clumped down the stairs. As they left, Aveline Hale's voice floated through the doorway. 'I'd not be the least surprised if the Duke of York attends too,' she breathed excitedly. 'Do you think this yellow will catch his eye?'

In the scene-room there was an air of quiet expectation. Joshua Small would raise the curtain, while Will Small and Silas Gunn stood by to shift the screens. William Daggett, his moustache twitching more fiercely than usual, was standing in the wings. Beside him, two hirelings who had non-speaking roles as street women were waiting. As Betsy and Louise appeared, Daggett nodded to them.

'Mr Betterton's in one of the boxes,' he said, 'and Tripp's with him.'

The sounds of an expectant audience outside were such that Betsy found sympathy even for the odious playwright, whose very livelihood depended on the piece's success. And at least he wasn't backstage fumbling with her skirts. She glanced aside, seeing Louise wetting her lips with her tongue. The poor girl was clearly terrified.

'I felt as you do when I first took a speaking role,' Betsy said, favouring her with a smile. 'You think you're about to empty your stomach, but the moment you speak your first line, you know all will be well.'

Louise looked at her, aghast. 'My first line,' she whispered hoarsely. 'I've forgotten what it is!'

Betsy told her. A minute later the orchestra struck up, the elder Small heaved on the curtain rope, and the trulls stepped out on the candlelit stage to shouts of male approval.

The Virtuous Bawd's first performance, however, was something less than a success.

The danger signals began before the end of the first act. There was a growing restlessness in some sections of the audience, and more than the usual number of hoots and barbed observations from 'Fops' Corner', the area populated by city gallants. The cast struggled on valiantly, pointing up the wittier passages and aiming for broad comedy whenever they could. By the time Betsy and Louise made their exits at the end of the act, the young tiring-maid was hoarse from raising her voice. She stood in the wings taking a breath, while Betsy offered words of encouragement.

'Here . . . take a mouthful of this.' Joshua Small was nearby, wearing a knowing look. Unstopping a small leather flask, he offered it to Louise.

'Thank you, but no.' She forced a smile. 'Your Nantes is too strong for me. I'll take a mug in the Women's Shift.'

Small shrugged, and was about to take a quick drink himself. Then catching the eye of William Daggett, who stood by with a frown, he stoppered the flask and tucked it away.

Louise walked off towards the stairs, but Betsy glanced at the scene-man, recalling her conversation with him a week ago in the empty theatre. Feeling her eyes upon him, Small met her gaze and quickly looked away. But in that moment she saw the man's nervousness, which she felt certain had little to do with the strain of an opening performance. Small, normally a phlegmatic man, was as jittery as a hare . . . as jittery, Betsy recalled suddenly, as Tom Cleeve had been that time, shortly before his death, only feet from where Small now stood. The memory troubled her more than she liked.

The performance rolled on, generating more restlessness in the theatre and more tension backstage. By the final act the cast was fighting off gloom. And more than once, scene-men were heard muttering that the play would have gone a deal better with a Betterton, a Rigg or even a George Beale in the leading male roles. Most disappointed of all, however, was Aveline Hale, on learning that neither the King nor the Duke of York had attended the performance.

'Once again, Mr Betterton assured me of a royal visit,' she said in an acid tone. 'Well, this time I intend to give free vent to my feelings on the matter!'

Mistress Hale, Betsy and Jane Rowe stood by the forestage watching Mary Betterton take a solitary bow. Their leader's wife had turned in a creditable performance as the Duchess, and her fame was such that she was applauded as of right. Whether the play itself merited such applause was another matter. Finally Mistress Betterton turned to walk off, and at once, as if relieved, the orchestra struck up with some lively, house-clearing music.

While the audience dispersed outside, the scene-room as always filled with people. But this time there was no jubilation, more the sense that the all-woman cast had survived the performance, and little more. So when Thomas Betterton appeared with a tense-looking Samuel Tripp, the company stood about in muted fashion. At sight of their master's expression, Silas Gunn and the Small brothers decided to busy themselves clearing the stage. Only William Daggett remained to hear what looked like bad news. Beside him, Downes the prompter stood with a sour expression.

'My good friends . . . ladies,' Betterton's eyes sought out the actresses, who were still in their costumes. 'You have done sterling work this afternoon. None could deny it!'

'None could deny the absence of the King either, sir.' Aveline Hale's voice rose from the centre of the little throng.

'May we talk of that later, Mistress Hale?' Betterton's glance strayed to his wife, who stood by in a dignified pose. In fact, it was only her presence which prevented Aveline from giving further rein to her frustration. Biting her lip, she lowered her gaze and fussed with her saffron yellow frock.

'Now hear me, all of you,' Betterton raised his voice. 'Contrary to rumour, the play will run a second night — that much I have decided. Whether it enjoys a third performance, that is, a benefit night for the author, remains to be seen.' He hesitated, looking about for Tripp, but the playmaker seemed to have disappeared.

'Whether that is the case or not,' Betterton went on, 'I urge you to put today's tiresome audience aside, and think of tomorrow. Until then.' He smiled and made a farewell gesture, before he and his wife moved off towards the Men's Shift. The rest of the company, seeing there would be no further announcement, began to disperse. At least, some murmured, closure had been staved off for another day; and who could say that the King might not come tomorrow?

The hirelings, eight or nine in number, had gone off to change. Betsy and Jane, followed by Louise, climbed the stairs to the Women's Shift where they sank down exhaustedly. Then, along with the loosening of uncomfortable, tight-boned bodices and the pulling off of breeches and periwigs, animated chatter broke out, helped along by the appearance of a bottle and several mugs. But a few minutes later there came a knock on the door, and the unsmiling face of John Downes appeared.

'Mistress Brand, Mr Betterton asks you to come down. At once, if you would.'

Half-undressed, Betsy was about to ask for a moment's grace. Then she met Downes's eye and read the urgency in his gaze. Without a word, she threw on a camelotte gown and went out.

The scene-room was deserted. Without explanation, Downes gestured to Betsy to follow him out on to the forestage. She did so, noticing that the pit was empty, and the musicians had gone. But there was a little group huddled about something at the far side of the stage, near the wings . . . and her heart jumped. With a growing sense of dread, she hurried towards the men, who made way for her. Then she looked down, and stifled a gasp.

Joshua Small lay in a crumpled heap where he had fallen. About him were Thomas Betterton, William Daggett, Silas Gunn and a couple of doormen, all staring down in dismay. And at once, Betsy knew what had happened.

A distraught Will Small was on his knees beside his older brother, shaking him by the shoulders and calling his name. As Downes and Betsy arrived, the young man looked up desperately.

'He just keeled over!' he cried. 'There was neither rhyme nor reason to it — he dropped like a stone!'

He called Joshua's name out, again and again, but received only a mumbled answer. After that he paid no heed to the others, as they stood in dumb silence about him. Finally Thomas Betterton placed a hand on the young man's shoulder, as his shoulders began to shake.

And all the group could do was watch the creeping paralysis that stole over Joshua Small, and the distant look that came into his eyes, as the Salamander's poison did its terrible work once again.

* * *

A short time later, the same group had gathered in the Men's Shift. Small's body had been taken away by his brother, and word sent to Doctor Tom Catlin. After speaking with the doormen, Betterton called together those who had witnessed the fellow's death: Daggett, Downes, Silas Gunn and Betsy. However, it was soon clear that he had done so not merely at his own behest but also that of his wife.

'This death must be kept secret!'

Mary Betterton, still in her Duchess costume, was at her most formidable when she used her full height. Now, shaken but remarkably resolute, she surveyed each of them in turn.

'The company cannot bear another catastrophe,' she went on. 'If Lord Caradoc hears of it he will close the theatre again — he would have little choice. And this time, it might never reopen. Dorset Gardens is already the subject of malicious rumour. They say we're jinxed, or haunted by some fey spirit.' She turned to her husband, who was looking very unhappy.

'I fail to see how we can keep His Lordship from hearing of the matter,' he said.

'We must!' Mary Betterton's eyes flashed. And those present, who knew her well, saw the familiar hardness in her gaze. 'You've settled it with the doormen,' she went on, to which her husband nodded. 'Then only those in this room know the truth of it.' She glanced round. 'And none of us, I am sure, wishes any further hurt to befall the company. Hence we must put it about that Joshua Small became ill, and was taken home by his brother after the performance. His brother, too, must be brought to our view of the matter . . . with a purse, if need be. Then later on, we may permit word to spread that the poor man died of some sickness.' She turned abruptly to Betsy. 'Mistress Brand, I know you have our best interests at heart. Will you speak of our predicament with Doctor Catlin, and see what might be done?'

The request was plain enough, and it made Betsy stiffen. Like Joseph Rigg's father, Mistress Mary wanted Catlin to attribute this death to natural causes.

'He'll examine Joshua's body, mistress,' she answered, meeting the other woman's eye. 'But I cannot ask him to lie.'

Mary Betterton's bosom heaved above her low neckline. 'He too would be rewarded for his discretion,' she said.

'Such arguments count for little with him,' Betsy replied. 'He often treats people for no payment.'

Betterton was frowning at his wife. 'May we speak of this later?' he asked, in a tone of distaste. 'For the moment, I would merely request that each of you,' he eyed Downes, Daggett and Silas Gunn in turn, 'that you each say nothing about what's happened, to anyone. When we know more about how Joshua died, we—' he broke off, as if irritated with his own words. Whereupon his wife spoke up quickly.

'Indeed! Meanwhile, we'll see Small's widow is helped.' She turned to William Daggett. 'Did the man have a wife?'

Daggett shook his head. 'She died in the Plague Year. His brother's the only family I know of.' He glanced at Downes, who remained tight-lipped, then at Gunn, who was looking like a tired, spent old man. It seemed to Betsy as if the three of them were only now taking in the import of what had happened: Tom Cleeve had died, as had Rigg, and James Prout too, supposedly at the hands of the one they had known as Julius Hill — who was also dead. But now, another scene-man had perished! What terrible force was at work? And who was safe?

Gunn spoke up anxiously. 'Who will work the scenes and the curtain tomorrow, sir?' he asked Betterton. 'Young Will's so torn up by what happened, I doubt he'll be back.'

But Daggett broke in. 'There are others I can call upon,' he answered. 'Otherwise, my old sparrow, you and I must fall to, and do our best.'

After a moment Gunn nodded, and now there seemed little more to be said. Looking relieved, Betterton thanked his backstage men and saw them out. But when Betsy started to follow, he put a hand on her arm.

'A moment if you please, Mistress Brand.'

The door closed upon Downes, the last to leave, who threw a suspicious look at Betsy as he went. Then, it was common knowledge that the man trusted no one . . . especially actresses. Betsy faced Betterton, and found both his and his wife's eyes upon her. Having an idea what was coming, she braced herself.

'Mistress Brand,' Mary Betterton said, 'we would ask your help.'

'I can only repeat what I said,' Betsy began, but Betterton raised a hand.

'You mistake us,' he said quickly, with a glance at Mary. 'What we ask is that you and Doctor Catlin — who know more of the terrible events of the past fortnight than anyone else — combine your resources, and try to find out what in God's name is going on!'

'I'm unsure of your meaning,' Betsy began, but the other interrupted.

'My meaning,' Betterton told her, 'is that despite the confession of Julius Hill, or whatever his real name was, someone appears bent on continuing his murderous work among the Duke's Company!' The man's voice had risen, as if only now was he able to vent his feelings. 'And more, none but another member of this company — player or sceneman, doormen or whoever it be — could've got close enough to Joshua Small to do what was done! Assuming, that is,' Betterton drew a breath. 'Assuming he died by the same poison Hill used, which seems more than likely.'

'I would swear to that readily enough,' Betsy said.

'Then let's face the truth!' Mary Betterton cried. 'And the truth is that there's a murderer in the company, who must be found, in the shortest possible time. So, Mistress Brand, if your pious Doctor Catlin won't show delicacy in naming the cause of Small's death, I pray he will at least help in uncovering who killed him!'

* * *

Will Small stood in the gloomy little parlour of his family home, beside the body of his brother. It was but a few hours since the man had expired on the forestage of the Duke's Theatre. Night had now drawn in, and the room was illuminated by a couple of smoky tallow candles. With the help of neighbours, Joshua Small had been laid out upon a bed raised on trestles, covered to his neck by a linen sheet. His handsome face was calm in death, his long hair unbound and combed out to his shoulders. Betsy and Tom Catlin, having offered a few words of comfort, were about to take their leave when Will turned to them.

'I knew something wasn't right,' he muttered. 'For a week or more, he'd been troubled. I never asked what it was.' The young man was close to tears. 'Now I wish to God I had!'

'It's been a dreadful ordeal for you,' Catlin began, but Will was not listening.

'Josh was never himself after Rigg died,' he went on, as if trying to make sense of things. 'It bothered him more than Tom Cleeve.' He frowned. 'Then, they went back a deal further — them and George Beale.'

'Beale . . . what was he to your brother, Will?' Betsy asked.

The young man shrugged. 'There was a few of them, used to drink in the Fleece.' He named the tavern on the corner of the Strand and Brydges Street, which had a bad reputation. 'Only after cockfighting and such,' he added. 'That was when Rigg and Beale were at the King's Playhouse. They'd go a bit wild, sometimes.' He gazed sadly at his brother's corpse. 'I hope he'll be able to enjoy a mug, where he's gone.'

Then he bowed his head. And without further word, Betsy and Catlin made their exit.

At Moorgate the two of them turned right to begin their homeward journey, skirting the city's north wall. In the distance, a watchman was crying the hour. For a while neither spoke. Then, unable to contain herself any longer, Betsy turned to Catlin. 'When you helped lay the body out, did you see—'

'Pinpricks? No, I did not.' Catlin kept his eyes on the darkened street. 'But I'm certain Small's death was caused by the same poison that the Salamander used. So the question is, how was it administered?'

But Betsy stopped, for the answer came at once. 'The drink — it could have been in his flask!'

Catlin stopped too. 'Where is it? Could you get it to me?'

'I'll try.' Betsy was thinking fast. 'Joshua often had a flask of strong water or Nantes in his pocket; it was no secret. If someone wanted to poison him, without having to get close, that is—'

'And not arouse suspicion?' Catlin started walking again, and Betsy fell in beside him. 'Then we seem to be back where we started,' the doctor added grimly. 'Only now we're looking for another link . . . not to the Salamander, but to those who work backstage at the Duke's.' He put on an exasperated look. 'Perhaps someone merely wants you out of business, in which case the chief suspect, to my mind, would be Mr Killigrew of the King's Company!'

But at that Betsy stopped again, so that Catlin carried on a pace, and was obliged to halt and turn. 'Let me guess, Mistress Rummager,' he said dryly. 'Inspiration has struck again, like a divine thunderbolt.'

'Not quite,' she answered. 'But perhaps you're close to the nub of things, after all,' s he frowned. 'I don't mean Killigrew . . . but you remember how suspicion fell upon Beale when Rigg died, and he'd wounded him with his stage dagger?'

'A superficial wound only,' Catlin reminded her.

'Nevertheless.' Despite the afternoon's unhappy outcome, Betsy felt a stirring of hope. Now, it seemed as if another avenue of investigation had opened. After a moment she took Catlin's arm, and the two of them walked on.

'Nevertheless, what?' the doctor asked.

'Beale,' Betsy replied. 'I should have talked to him sooner. Now, I need to find out where he lodges. It shouldn't be too difficult.'

CHAPTER FIFTEEN

George Beale lived above the shop of a gold-lace maker, whose sign — a peacock — seemed fitting enough for the abode of the haughty young actor. The shop was in Russell Street, a few doors from Wills's coffee-house. The morning after Joshua Small's death Betsy Brand arrived to be told that Mr Beale was indeed at home. In fact, the landlord added, he seldom appeared before midday. So having been directed, Betsy thanked the man and made her way to a stairway. But as she climbed the narrow steps there came a muffled oath from above, and a flurry of movement. Gingerly, she poked her head above the top floor, finding herself in a darkened chamber that stank of orange perfume, unwashed clothing and human sweat.

'Mr Beale?' she called. 'It's Betsy Brand.'

A figure loomed menacingly above her. Here was Beale in a greasy nightshirt and no periwig, gazing down. To her alarm, he was holding a dagger.

'God in heaven, Mistress — I came close to spiking you!' Relaxing somewhat, the man gestured to her to come up. As she did so he went to a cluttered table, dropped the dagger and fumbled with a tinderbox. He struck a flame and applied it to a candle, then sat down heavily on the bed. His shaved head gleamed in the flickering light.

'I confess you're one of the last people I expected to see,' he said, looking at her suspiciously. 'Do you bear a message from Betterton?'

Looking about, Betsy shook her head. After a moment Beale pointed to a chair piled with dirty linen. 'Throw that aside, and be seated,' he muttered. 'You'll have to forgive your surroundings.'

'In fact, I do have news,' Betsy said as she sat down. 'Sad tidings, I'm afraid: Joshua Small's dead.'

Beale's mouth fell open, but he made no reply.

'In the same, sudden manner as Tom Cleeve,' Betsy continued. When the man still stared, she added: 'Perhaps you've already heard of the deaths of James Prout, and of Julius Hill?'

'I heard about Prout,' Beale said shortly. 'As for Hill,' he swallowed. 'The ghastly tale's all over Covent Garden. But why do you carry it to me?'

Betsy gave a shrug. 'It was Small I came to talk to you about. I spoke with his brother. He told me about the time you and Joshua used to carouse together, in the Fleece.'

'What of it?' Beale's voice was sharp. 'It's a cheap tavern — many of the King's Company frequent it. And at that time, I was among them.'

As if wishing to occupy himself, the man rose suddenly and started looking about. 'I must dress,' he said. 'Had I known I was going to have female company I'd have put some breeks on . . . unless, that is . . .'

He stopped with a leer, which needed little interpretation. But reaching down, Betsy picked up a pair of wrinkled hose from the floor. 'Will these serve?' she asked, and threw them to Beale, who caught them awkwardly. 'I wouldn't want to raise your hopes.'

Beale sniffed as if to show it mattered not a jot and, sitting down on the bed, began to pull on his breeches.

'I can guess at your feelings towards Betterton,' Betsy resumed, 'after he dismissed you. Yet I would ask—'

'Dismissed me?' the other's voice was harsh. 'He all but called me a murderer before the entire company! He's lucky we weren't in the street — I'd have drawn my sword at the man!'

'You were there!' Beale went on, jabbing a finger at Betsy. 'You heard them turn on me — Betterton, that smooth-faced molly-man Prout — even the blasted tiring-maid shrieked at me! And I for one have never laid a hand on the girl!'

'The company had been badly shaken by Rigg's death,' Betsy said.

'As was I!' Beale retorted. 'I knew the man for years, since I first walked upon the stage as a youth . . .' he trailed off — and Betsy judged her moment.

'Rigg, and now Joshua Small,' she said, 'who was as nervous as a rabbit in his last days. Why do you think that was?'

'How in Christ's name should I know?' Beale countered, then drew breath, and gave Betsy a long look. 'Ah . . . now I begin to know your game, Brand. Then, you're Betterton's creature . . . you always were! You and Rowe, that blowsy little butcher's daughter . . . you never had to lift your skirts to get a role, did you? Unlike some!'

Betsy's temper rose, but she kept her voice low. 'You know Betterton has never abused his powers in that way,' she replied, 'and the actress he most admired, he married.'

'So, was it Mistress Mary who sent you?' the other asked, with a sneer. 'I'll bet a sovereign this scandal at the Duke's has made her piss her petticoats!' He gave a sour grin. 'Perhaps I'm well out of Dorset Gardens, after all.'

'You still haven't answered my question,' Betsy said flatly, as if to imply that she wasn't leaving until he did. 'Why do you think someone killed Rigg and Joshua Small, who had no connection to the Salamander or his grievances?'

This time Beale merely looked away, but Betsy sensed more than bitterness on his part. In fact, she now realized, he was more shaken than she had first thought.

'Could it be another matter of revenge?' she persisted. 'Like that of Hill — or Aanaarden, to use his real name — yet unrelated to it?'

'I've said I know naught of it,' Beale said in a sulky tone.

But now Betsy was certain he was hiding something. Deliberately she said: 'Whoever it is, they seem to have had no difficulty tracking down their victims. Rigg, for example: he wasn't Joseph Rigg then, was he? He was Joseph Griffiths.'

Beale frowned at her. 'What's that to me?' he demanded. 'Now, I'd like to dress, so if you've said all you came to say, mistress, I suggest you take your leave.'

But Betsy remained seated. 'I spoke with Small a week before he died. He was troubled . . . there seemed to be something on his conscience that went back years, to the Great Fire. That would be about the time you and he were carousing at the Fleece with Rigg, would it not?'

Abruptly Beale got to his feet. 'You're beginning to bore me, Betsy Brand,' he said, and gestured to the stairs. 'Forgive me if I don't show you out.'

Still Betsy did not move. 'What was it you did, in the Fire?' she asked quietly, sensing with some excitement that she was on the brink of a discovery. 'You, and your drinking and gaming friends?'

Beale stared at her — then for some reason, the fight seemed to go out of the fellow. With a heavy sigh he sat down again, and put his head in his hands. When he looked up, there was an emptiness in his gaze.

'A man was killed,' he said. 'There — is that meat enough for you, Mistress Scavenger?'

Betsy said nothing, but kept her eyes on Beale's. And to her surprise, as if relieved to unburden himself at last, the fellow began to talk.

'It began as a wager,' he said, with a distant look. 'A foolish bet, after an evening's debauch . . . we were half-distracted. In the west suburbs we watched the Fire draw closer by the hour . . . all of London ablaze, and none could stop it. After three days it seemed it would leap the walls and engulf us all. There seemed naught to do, but run or drink ourselves senseless. And that ranting fool Praise-God Palmer was on the streets, shouting of the Lord's wrath.' He hesitated. 'That was when Rigg — Griffiths — stood up and shouted: *The devil with your Lord. What of the French, or the Dutch?*'

Betsy's heart jolted, as Joshua Small's words in the empty theatre came back to her. 'So . . . you went hunting for scapegoats.'

'We went hunting for foreigners,' Beale told her. 'Others did the same . . . blaming them for starting the Fire. Dutchmen, Frenchmen, Irishmen, even Scots — a mob isn't particular. Especially when Rigg's leading it, fired up with brandy and patriotism, crying *God for Harry* or some other cant he'd got from Shakespeare.' He broke off, shaking his head. 'You remember it. Panic and mayhem everywhere . . . even the King was on the streets, they said. And what danger might he be in, if one of England's enemies came upon him?'

Now, the man seemed eager to excuse his actions. Keeping expression from her voice, Betsy prodded him gently. 'But instead, you and your party came upon one of them?'

Beale avoided her eye. 'A Frenchman . . . a wig-maker . . . in Wood Street near the Haberdasher's Hall. The fire was upon them already, and they were fleeing with what they could salvage.' He grimaced. 'I didn't take part!' he cried. 'I even tried to stop them, I'd swear that in any court in England! I was but a youth and I was caught up in the excitement, nothing more!'

Betsy waited, until at last the man looked up at her.

'Yes, I see the look on your face!' Beale clenched his fists. There was a wildness in his gaze now. 'I saw it on the face of the man's wife, when her husband was seized and bound . . . then she started screaming at us in French.' He screwed his eyes up at the memory. 'She didn't stop, even when his carcase was swinging from a beam.'

'You hanged him?' Betsy's mouth was dry. 'Because he was a foreigner?'

'*They* hanged him!' Beale threw back. 'I've told you, I took no part! Believe it or not, as you will . . . and though I wasn't alone in thinking that frightened little man no more set fires than the Lord Mayor did, there was naught I could do.' He lowered his eyes again.

'Think what you like,' he said after a moment. 'We've all paid, in one way or another: Rigg and Small, for they were like savages that day, bent on blaming others for their troubles. As for me,' he gave a bitter laugh. 'George Beale, late of the celebrated Duke's Company, is without a penny! Killigrew won't hire me at the King's. If someone's avenging the Frenchman after these years, then I say let him come. If he doesn't get me, my creditors will!'

Betsy got to her feet. She could find no words to say to George Beale, who remained seated.

'What will you do?' he asked suddenly.

She paused, struggling with her feelings. 'Do you know the name of the man you . . . who was hanged?' she asked.

'Colporteur,' the other replied. 'Jean Colporteur — it was on a sign outside his shop. I couldn't forget it if I tried.'

After taking a step towards the stairwell, Betsy stopped and turned to him. 'What did you think I would do,' she asked, 'inform on you?'

But the other made no reply, and she made her way downstairs. In a way, the man had been punished already. As she descended, she glanced back once towards Beale, who had not moved from the bed. He seemed to have forgotten her, and was staring vacantly at the floor.

* * *

From Covent Garden, Betsy walked back along the Strand to Fleet Street. The sun shone, but her mind was so busy that she barely noticed her surroundings. Only when she had crossed the Fleet bridge with Ludgate looming ahead did she stop, as the thought struck her that there was another person who might be able to shed light on the mystery: Sir Anthony

Griffiths, father of the man she had known as Joseph Rigg. And without stopping to ask herself whether she would be permitted to speak with the magistrate, she hurried through the busy gateway and turned to the right, towards the river. At Blackfriars Stairs she took a boat, and was soon scudding down the Thames.

She barely responded to the waterman's gruff attempts at conversation, and the fellow was quick to set her down at St Botolph's wharf, where she had once alighted in search of one who had sold a salamander to Julius Hill, though she did not know his identity then. Indeed, she reflected, there was no Julius Hill. Holding up her skirts, she climbed the slope towards Eastcheap. Then she was making her way through the dusty, half-rebuilt ruins of Fenchurch Street and Lime Street, to emerge by the church of St Andrew Undershaft. She had crossed the eastern border of the Fire's Reach where, thanks to the wind the north-east corner of the city, from Moorgate to the Tower, had escaped destruction. In Aldgate Street all was serene and orderly, the untouched houses tall and stark against the sky. And it was now but a matter of casual enquiry from passers-by, to find the home of Sir Anthony Griffiths.

It was a large house, protected by a crumbling brick wall overhung with trees. Betsy tried the gate and found it unlocked. Taking a breath, she marched up to the front door and knocked loudly. After some delay it was opened by a tall manservant who peered down at her in surprise. When Betsy explained that she was come to speak with Sir Anthony about his late son, the man looked startled. Quickly, she mentioned her association with Doctor Tom Catlin, who had taken care of the body. To all of this the servant listened in mounting discomfort. By the time she had finished he was frowning.

'Are you perhaps a . . . a woman of the theatre?' he asked in a voice of distaste.

Betsy admitted such, and gave her name.

'Sir Anthony disapproves strongly of the theatre,' he said. 'I've instructions to set the dogs on any actors who showed their faces.' He hesitated. 'Yet, I'm loth to do so. I'd say you're a bold one, mistress, to come here like this.'

Whereupon Betsy put on her most winning smile. 'I have news your master might wish to hear,' she said. 'Will you not tell him I'm come?'

'I will,' the man answered finally. 'But even if he agrees to see you,' he hesitated, 'you must pay no mind to his manner — nor will I permit you to stay long. Sir Anthony's not the man he was, since Mr Joseph's death.' He stood aside. 'Wait in the vestibule.'

Betsy entered the old house, finding herself in a dark hallway with a smell of damp. The manservant disappeared, but returned a minute later. Without further word, he conducted Betsy to a large room at the rear of the house, overlooking an untidy garden. Seated near the window was a figure in a black bombazine suit and long steel-grey periwig, who did not move. Smiling again, Betsy walked round to face him and made her curtsey — then saw her efforts were wasted. For the bent, crabbed old man slumped before her was blind.

'Mistress Brand,' the voice was cracked, as of one much older than the sixty years Betsy estimated. 'I'm told you bring news appertaining to my son.' His right hand gripped the knob of a cane, which he now waved as if to bid her speak.

Betsy took a breath, then under the watchful gaze of the manservant on the other side of the room, told Sir Anthony about the death of Joshua Small, and what she had since learned of his actions during the Great Fire. She did not mention Joseph Rigg's being the ringleader of a drunken mob which had hanged an innocent French wig-maker, but no sooner had she brought up George Beale's name, than her listener startled her by raising his stick and banging it on the floor.

'Enough! I'll not have their names spoken in this house! Beale, Small and the rest . . . villains all!' Griffiths was wheezing, and across the room Betsy saw the manservant look uneasy.

'Forgive me, sir,' she said. 'I merely wondered whether—'

'Did you, merely?' the old man echoed. 'And what, pray, is your interest in the matter? Do you want payment to keep silent, is that it?'

'I do not, sir,' Betsy answered. 'What I want is to solve a spate of murders, which threaten to ruin my company.'

To that the old man made no reply, so while she still had the chance Betsy ploughed on, until she had given Sir Anthony a truncated account of the grisly events of recent weeks, ending with her discovery of the killing of Jean Colporteur. But at mention of the Frenchman's name, Griffiths started.

'Good God, could you not have spared me that?' The old man sagged visibly; and now his manservant took a pace forward.

'Permit me to dismiss the woman, sir,' he said coolly. 'And forgive me for allowing her entry.'

'No! Wait.' Sir Anthony raised a pale hand to his forehead, and Betsy was dismayed at his expression of anguish.

'Leave us,' he said in a tired voice. And before the manservant could protest, he repeated the order. 'Leave us! What harm do you think this young woman could do me?'

The servant murmured in compliance and went out. As the door closed, the old man blinked and swivelled his vacant, white-filmed eyes in Betsy's direction.

'What do you know of Colporteur?' he asked.

'Very little,' she answered, but the other gave a grunt.

'So London's abuzz with it now, eh? After all this time.' He let out a short laugh. 'There's fitting retribution for me, then. All my efforts to paper over it are undone!'

'You need not spare my feelings,' he went on. 'For I know what my rogue of a son did. I'd already cast him from my house, forced him to change his name. Yet I would not see him hang for murder!'

Betsy started. 'But surely, in the mayhem of the fire, with hurt and destruction everywhere,' she began, 'who would even know the names of the culprits?'

'I would!' The old man stared fiercely at her with his sightless eyes. 'And when, after the Fire, my only son confessed to me in a fit of remorse what he had done, here in this room, I had to act.' He drew a wheezing breath. 'I gave her — Colporteur's widow — a sum in compensation.'

So he paid her off, Betsy thought, but at once the old man spoke up again. 'I gave her compensation,' he repeated. 'And despite her distress Madeleine Colporteur was a shrewd woman, with two children to care for. So in the end she took my blood money, and swore she would not identify her husband's murderers.'

'Two children?' Betsy's heart jumped.

'A son and a daughter,' the old man muttered. 'The son ran wild later, I heard, and caused her much grief.'

'And the daughter?'

But Griffiths was not listening. 'I could not let them starve!' he went on. 'Even though they're Catholics.' He gave a snort of contempt. 'They entertained such childish hopes, that our King would see the error of his ways and return to his mother's religion. One can't help but feel pity for them.'

Sir Anthony lapsed into silence. Pushing aside a sense of disappointment, Betsy thought to utter some words of thanks. But the old man interrupted her.

'Save your breath, mistress. Perhaps it's a kind of justice after all, that those men should perish . . . even my son.' His head sagged on to his chest. Betsy waited, then thinking she was dismissed, was about to make her way out. But once more, came the thud of the cane being banged down.

'Wait, for pity's sake.' Griffiths seemed to have difficulty finding the words. 'Tell me . . . how was my son regarded, in the . . . in the theatre?' he asked haltingly. 'As Joseph Rigg, I mean.'

In surprise, Betsy answered. 'With respect, and admiration,' she said. 'Like others, I learned a great deal from him. He was always kind to me, and many tears were shed when he died.'

There was a silence, before the old man spoke again. 'Then for that, I thank you,' he said.

There was time for a last question, perhaps, and Betsy seized it. 'Have you any idea what became of Madame Colporteur and her children?' she asked. 'Are they still in London?'

But the other shook his head. 'I do not know. I've had no dealing with the woman since that terrible time.' Then he turned away, and this time Betsy did not wait. With a brief farewell, she left the room, and was quickly shown out of the house.

* * *

That evening over supper, a tired Betsy told Tom Catlin all she had discovered. After listening in silence, the doctor looked up with raised eyebrows.

'So . . . you think the family of this Jean Colporteur have been wreaking vengeance on those who killed him?'

'It seems the likeliest explanation.'

'Do you know what age the man's children were when he died?'

'I suppose I should have asked Sir Anthony . . .' Betsy trailed off, thinking of the old man and his sadness.

'Well, it's only a few years ago. They may be children yet.' Catlin was looking for his tobacco. 'Or they may be young adults. Could you not have found out their names?'

'I've not really been very thorough, have I?' Betsy said, and managed a smile. 'I doubt I'd ever make a spy.'

Catlin shrugged, and changed the subject. 'If you could get me Small's flask, as I said yesterday, I could look for traces of poison . . .'

'Perhaps, but I still can't form a clear picture,' Betsy said tiredly. 'However the poison was administered, it was the same that killed Long Ned, and Cleeve, and Alderman Blake, so whoever killed Rigg and Small had access to it. And who could have given it to him, but the Salamander?'

She frowned. 'So it has to be another one of the company, after all.'

The doctor spoke up. 'Tomorrow's the Lord's day,' he said mildly. 'You should rest. The weather looks fair. Perhaps we can walk in Vauxhall Gardens, and see what entertainment's on offer.'

But Betsy gave a start. 'The pinpricks,' she exclaimed. 'Three or more of them, in Rigg's side, why was that? The toxin was so venomous, only one was needed.'

'Betsy, listen to me,' Catlin began with a frown — but to his alarm she sprang to her feet.

'What a buffle-head! How could I not have seen it?' She stared at him. 'In Banquo's murder scene when Rigg died, we first suspected the hirelings; then we suspected Beale with his vicious dagger thrust. What if it was none of them? What if the pin was in the costume?'

There was a moment, then Catlin too got to his feet. 'I suppose you won't rest until you've found out,' he muttered.

CHAPTER SIXTEEN

William Daggett was surprised, and not a little annoyed, at being disturbed after dark. Following the grim events of recent days the stage manager was enjoying a quiet evening at home, when Betsy Brand and Doctor Tom Catlin came knocking at his door. After hearing her request, the man's moustache began twitching at once.

'I've a key to the side door of the theatre,' he allowed. 'But I won't surrender it, even to one I trust, Mistress Brand.' Seeing the look on Betsy's face, he hesitated. 'Yet I see how determined you are. Is it truly as important as you claim?'

'I think I may be able to put an end to this whole terrible business,' Betsy said.

Daggett glanced at Catlin, who said nothing.

'Then I'd best come with you,' he said.

It was but a short walk from Daggett's house near Lincoln's Inn to Dorset Gardens. The lane was empty and dark, and the three did not waste time in finding a link-boy to light their way. Soon the stage manager was opening the street door of the Duke's Theatre and letting them into the deserted auditorium.

The place was eerily quiet, their footsteps echoing on the bare boards. There was no light, but having found a lantern and lit it, Daggett led them across the pit and up the forestage steps. Betsy started for the costume store, but the stage manager called her back.

'Rigg's clothes are still in the Men's Shift,' he said. 'No one's touched them since they were taken off his body.'

'That's fortunate indeed,' Tom Catlin murmured. 'Since they're the only evidence for what, I have to say, is still an unproven theory.'

On their way to Daggett's the doctor had begun to have his doubts, but Betsy would not hear them. Now, she turned quickly and headed for the steps. The two men followed.

The men's tiring-room was as she had seen it the day before, during that tense meeting with the Bettertons. Well, Mistress Mary would have to wait. As Daggett entered with the lantern, she began poking about the cluttered room, rifling through soiled shirts, hose and assorted bits of costume. After a while she looked round impatiently.

Below a shelf of wooden heads for men to put their periwigs on was a row of pegs hung with clothes. And here at last Betsy found what she sought: a padded doublet of russet-coloured taffeta, its sleeves slashed in the Elizabethan fashion to show the cream silk lining beneath. It was the costume that Joseph Rigg had worn in *Macbeth*, in his last role: that of the murdered Banquo.

'Be careful!' Betsy would have seized the doublet, had not Catlin grabbed her arm. 'Think what you do!' he cried. 'If it's doctored as you claim, you could die of a pinprick yourself!'

'Die of a pinprick?' Daggett looked blank. Raising the lantern, he gazed from Catlin to Betsy. 'I think it's time you two told me what you're about!'

But Betsy's excitement was such that the man could only listen. 'Do you know much about the previous century, Mr Daggett?' she asked. 'The time of Queen Elizabeth? Have you not heard how her life was often in danger, and how would-be assassins devised more and more cunning means by which to murder her? One scheme was to send her the gift of a gown treated with a deadly substance, so that when she put it on her skin rubbed against the poison.'

She pointed to the doublet. 'I believe this coat was the means by which Rigg was killed.'

Daggett swallowed, than a sceptical look came over his face. 'It can't be, else surely he would have died soon after he put it on . . . here, or down in the scene-room! Why did he not die until he was on the stage?'

But at that Catlin spoke. 'When I looked at the man's body I found three pinpricks in his side, just below his ribs,' he said. 'Perhaps, if the murderer was skilled in costume-making—'

'Precisely!' Betsy nodded. 'Now with your leave, I'll take the doublet by the collar and lay it on that table. Then we can examine it.'

But Catlin stayed her arm. 'Please, let me do it.'

And watched by Betsy and the flummoxed stage manager, the doctor picked up the object of their curiosity carefully by its neck. Holding it at arm's length, he carried it to the small table at which the actors often sat to take an after-performance drink, and laid it down. Then, with Daggett holding the lantern, the examination began.

Tentatively, Catlin unfolded the coat and ran his eyes across it, feeling the padding and running his thumb along the seams. But not until he had turned it inside out and commenced searching the lining did his efforts bear fruit. And then with a cry of triumph that startled both men, Betsy pointed.

'There! Hold the light closer!'

Daggett and Catlin craned forward, staring at the padding. At first they saw nothing. But following Betsy's gaze, Catlin peered at the garment's bottom edge, which had been stitched into a neat hem . . . and froze. In the lantern's gleam, several tiny spots of brown stain were visible, close together. Moreover, there was a small slit, no bigger than a buttonhole, but clearly cut by design. Gently Catlin lifted the edge of the doublet and poked his finger inside. Then he turned to Betsy, with his puzzling-out look firmly in place.

'So, Mistress Rummager — you were right!'

Moustache bristling, Daggett spoke in an agitated voice. 'Right about what?' he cried. 'In God's name, will one of you enlighten me?'

'A little spike was sewn into the coat,' Betsy told him. 'A sharpened hairpin, a needle, it matters not, and as I expected, it's been removed. What matters is the poison with which it was coated . . . and which left these stains.'

Daggett looked astonished. But with a glance at Catlin, Betsy lifted the edge of the doublet.

'Skilled with costume, you said. So skilled, she knew where to place the pin, so it did not prick the wearer too soon. In fact, it didn't prick him until he exerted himself and fell, during his death scene, when the murderers were upon him.' She met Daggett's gaze. 'And we all saw what happened after that.'

The man was beside himself. '*She*, you said,' he drew a long breath. 'You mean . . . ?'

'I do,' Betsy answered. 'Our little mouse of a tiring-maid . . . Louise.'

The man's face was haggard in the lantern's gleam. With a sigh, Betsy straightened up and gazed down at what was no longer an actor's stage costume, but a murder weapon.

'I'm fortunate in having an educated man for my landlord, Mr Daggett,' she said. 'For it was he who remembered what the word *colporteur* means. The one who provided her with the method by which she could take her revenge has a taste for nicknames. He merely translated the Dutch word *Aanaarden* for the English *hill*. Hence Louise took her cue from him, and did the same. *Colporteur*'s an old French word . . .' she looked at Catlin.

'It means a peddler,' he said. 'Or, if you like, a hawker.'

'Louise Hawker?' Daggett gazed at them both in dismay. 'Under our noses the whole time?' He swore an oath, then turned to Betsy. 'But in God's name,' he cried, 'why did she do it?!'

Whereupon Betsy told him of the death of Jean Colporteur, and of the daughter who had sought to avenge him.

* * *

Sunday morning dawned damp and misty. The din of London's bells was muffled, especially in the suburbs west of the city. But the small group of men, and one woman, who made their way across Holborn Bridge had not come from church. They had assembled an hour earlier at the house of Doctor Tom Catlin in Fire's Reach Court, then set out on foot for the north-western corner of the walls. Leading them was a heavy man in a brown coat: Gould, the constable of Farringdon Ward Without. It had been Thomas Betterton's wish that he be the one to arrest Louise Hawker, rather than the disgraced Quinn. Having been told late the night before of what Betsy and Catlin had discovered, a subdued Betterton had sent word to Gould among others, including Lord Caradoc. His Lordship, chastened by the news, chose to distance himself from the Duke's Company — at least, until the tiring-maid was taken into custody. Betterton, by contrast, had wanted to be a party to the arrest, until his wife persuaded him otherwise. So it was that, along with three under-constables chosen by Gould, the only member of the Duke's who, to the constable's irritation, refused to stay at home, was Mistress Betsy Brand. Once Doctor Tom Catlin agreed to be responsible for her, however, the man relented. Now Betsy and Catlin brought up the rear of the determined little party who, under the curious gazes of passers-by, skirted the fire-damaged walls of London as far as Aldersgate. Crossing the north boundary of the Fire's Reach, they marched up the street and halted at a corner.

When the matter had been turned about, late the previous night, it emerged that no one knew the precise address of Louise the tiring-maid; though it was believed she lived with her ageing mother. Beyond that, Betterton and Daggett had only an approximate knowledge of her whereabouts. However, the constable knew of a Frenchwoman named Madeleine Colporteur, a widow, who lived in a tumbledown house on the corner of Jewin Street, where they now stood. As the party gathered about the doorway Gould spoke briefly with his men, then banged hard upon the door.

There was no answer, whereupon the man knocked again. Finally the door squealed open on rusty hinges, to reveal the face of a woman in a frayed cap, who stepped back in alarm. To Gould's terse question, she responded in a voice of outrage.

'What d'you mean? Do I look like I'm French?' she demanded. 'If you seek the Cold Porters, they're up there!' She pointed a finger in the air, then shoved the door wide and walked off. Without further ado, Gould and his men pushed their way inside. Their footfalls thudded on the stairs, filling the house. Betsy and Catlin followed.

And almost at once there were voices from above . . . and a cry that was almost a scream. Betsy and Catlin exchanged looks, and quickened their pace. In a moment they had gained the upper floor, to emerge in an overfurnished parlour filled with bright colours. But Betsy had barely time to glance at the hangings, which were clearly fashioned from materials taken from the Duke's costume store. For there were more raised voices, and here were Gould's men in a half-circle about a small, wizened figure in black, her white hair tucked under a lace cap. At her side, the two women clinging to each other in fright, was the tiring-maid, whom she had known as Louise Hawker.

'Mistress Brand!' The girl started at the sight of Betsy, and seemed to fix upon her as a sign of hope. 'What in God's name is happening? My poor mother's terrified!'

But before Betsy could answer, Gould spoke up sternly. 'I'm ordered to arrest you, mistress,' he said. 'For the murder of Joseph Rigg and Joshua Small!'

A look of disbelief spread over Louise's face. 'This is madness,' she faltered. 'I wouldn't hurt a fly,' she looked anxiously at Betsy. 'Please . . . tell them!'

Betsy's mouth was dry. Face to face with the person she had been hunting for days, if not weeks, she now found herself torn. She remembered Louise on her first day at the Duke's Theatre: nervous as a kitten, but so anxious to please. In fact, she was such an innocent, yet so skilled and nimble-fingered, that even the most lecherous of the actors had for the most part refrained from pawing her. But now, in view of what she had learned, Betsy began to see Louise in a different light. Beside her, Tom Catlin was watching the girl carefully, as if waiting for some sign of guilt, yet there was none.

'*Je vous en prie, messieurs . . . expliquez-vous, car je suis foue de terreur!*' Madame Colporteur cried out in a voice that shook, and a stream of incomprehensible French tumbled from her mouth. But when Louise held her tightly and put a hand on her lips, the woman fell silent.

'My mother speaks little English,' she said, and faced the constable. 'Sir, I beg you to leave! I'll come with you to answer these charges. But they're false! I know nothing of . . . of what you speak.'

She looked desperately from Gould to Betsy. There was a silence, and the constables seemed to hesitate; it was indeed difficult to imagine this girl a murderer. But after some shuffling and staring down at boots, Gould gave a snort that made them all look up, and gestured to Betsy.

'Will you tell her what you found at the theatre, mistress?' he asked drily.

Betsy glanced at Catlin, who still remained silent. Louise and her mother watched her, the two of them visibly trembling.

'We examined Rigg's costume, Louise,' she said quietly. 'So I know how you killed him.'

Slowly, Louise shook her head.

'I too was threatened with that poison,' Betsy went on. 'Just a tiny amount is needed, is it not? Enough to cover a pin, or a needle,' and at last, she saw a look in the girl's eyes that was not fear. Emboldened, she raised her voice.

'How old were you when Rigg and his drunken friends seized your father and hanged him?' she asked.

The silence that fell was deadly. All eyes were upon Louise. But still the girl made no reply.

'I'd say you were but a child of twelve years,' Betsy persisted. 'Old enough to understand all that happened, yet too young to prevent it. A terrible thing was done to you and your mother . . . to your brother too.'

'My brother?' Louise spoke so softly, it was difficult to hear her. She had gone very still; now she removed her arms from about her mother, and straightened herself.

'I spoke with Sir Anthony Griffiths,' Betsy said. 'The father of the man we knew as Joseph Rigg. He told me about you and your family.'

Louise was no longer shaking. She merely held Betsy's gaze, as if daring her to continue.

'I know the whole tale,' Betsy went on. 'Save for one thing: how you learned Julius Hill's true identity, and how—'

But at that moment Madame Colporteur, who had been watching Betsy intently, gave a cry and wrung her hands in dismay.

'In the name of God . . . please, speak not of this!'

The men's heads snapped towards Louise's mother. Though her French accent was heavy, the words were clear enough.

Gould was quick to recover. 'So you do speak English!' he said harshly. 'I wondered about that, after all the years you've lived here.'

'Monsieur, I beg,' the old woman looked as if she would fall to her knees. 'My daughter is all I have — do not take her.'

'Enough!' The constable was unmoved. Turning to Louise, he made an impatient gesture. 'Speak!' he ordered. 'You're bound for Newgate whatever happens, but if you don't admit your crime, I'll take your mother too!'

'No.' Louise stepped forward, her hands at her sides. 'You will not.'

Her voice was ice cold, and along with the others Betsy regarded the girl in surprise. After a moment, Madame Colporteur moved to a nearby chair and sank down upon it.

'She knows naught of it!' Louise looked Gould in the eye, and now Betsy saw a spark of the rage that was within her. At once she was reminded of the look in the eyes of Julius Hill — the Salamander. Here indeed was his creature — his boast had not been idle, for she had continued his terrible work.

'You'll have your confession.' The girl stared at Gould with contempt. 'I've done what I could . . . what a good daughter should, to avenge her father!'

There came a choking sound, and Louise glanced at her mother, who burst into tears. But instead of going to her, the girl turned back to the others.

'You didn't know my father,' she said, 'which is your misfortune, for a kinder, gentler man never lived!'

She eyed Betsy, her delicate mouth flattening into a thin line. 'Of course I burned for revenge,' she said scornfully. 'Who would not, who suffered what I did? And when my brother proved unequal to the task, a weakling who drowned himself in drink like the rogues who rampaged through the streets that night, I knew it was my duty to see it done!' She glanced at her mother, but the old woman had buried her face in her hands.

'You think you're quite an intelligencer.' Louise threw Betsy a bitter look. 'It took you long enough to come to the nub of things, did it not?'

But Betsy did not flinch from the girl's hate-filled gaze. For now that she saw the true face of the tiring-maid, she felt little but relief. 'When did you learn it was Hill who killed Long Ned and Tom Cleeve?' she asked. 'Did he make himself known to you, or did—'

'He had no need!' Louise almost spat the words. 'You know nothing of me,' she said, her mouth curling into a sneer. 'I'm the one helps you in and out of your clothes, laces your stays, tucks your breasts into your bodice, fetches and carries for you — and you barely notice me! So with the men, who flaunt themselves at me in their undress, vying with each other to see who can make me blush . . . stinking of drink, their eyes on my neckline, hands at my skirts . . .' she broke off, and threw a scathing look at the constables.

'But he wasn't like that, was he?'

Betsy spoke calmly. Meeting Louise's gaze, she went on: 'Aanaarden — he was different from the others, was he not?'

'More than you'll ever know,' Louise said softly, and for the first time she lowered her eyes. 'So that I gave him the only precious gift I had, in return for his help.'

The girl's mother started, gazing at her in horror, then began weeping anew. But Betsy met Catlin's eye. Of course, Louise had been Hill's lover: what else had she, but her body, with which to tempt such a man?

'Jan Aannarden,' Louise spoke the name with such an accent that she had clearly been taught how to say it. 'He saw me not for the part I played . . . compliant little Louise, afraid of her own shadow . . . the timid girl you thought you knew! He saw me as he was himself: an avenging angel, come to bring justice!'

'Justice!' Gould had had enough. Lunging forward, he seized the girl's arm so sharply she winced in pain. 'You'll have your justice, at the end of the hangman's rope!' he cried. 'You and that murdering villain have sent half a dozen men to their graves between you. Avenging angel? Devil, more like!'

There was a moment, before something unexpected happened. Louise had remained still, staring at the constable with a look of defiance. Then her right foot shot out, connecting with the man's shin. As he grunted with pain, his grip loosened, which was all the girl needed. In a trice she had torn herself free of him and ducked aside, so suddenly that the under-constables were caught off guard. Cursing, one of them grabbed for the girl, but snatched only thin air. Like an eel, she darted between them, head low, and leaped for the stairwell, but Tom Catlin was quicker.

The doctor, who had been watching her intently, had moved a split second after Louise. As she was about to jump down the stairs, he caught her by her waist, his strong arms folding tightly about her. Then she was confined and, despite the writhing and kicking, the spitting and screeching, she was helpless, and she knew it. The constables hurried to take the girl from him, one seizing her legs, another her arms, while the third stumbled forward to take her waist. And clumsily she was transferred, so that at last Catlin was able to step back, somewhat red in the face, and recover his breath.

So at the final turn, Louise Hawker, who was named Louise Colporteur, knew she had lost. Her strength failed, she went limp, and finally slumped to the floor, surrounded absurdly by three burly men, each holding a part of her. Over her stood Gould, furious at how close he had come to losing her. But Betsy's eye had been caught by Madeleine Colporteur, who had risen from her chair. And as the men turned sharply, the old woman came forward, to peer down at her daughter with a tear-stained face.

The eyes of mother and daughter met, then Madeleine raised her hand and pointed. Betsy followed her outstretched arm, as did the others, to see a black crucifix hanging on the wall. And after crossing herself, in a shaky voice the woman spoke.

'*Mon dieu . . . pardonnez-moi, votre pauvre servante . . . j'ai donné naissance a une meurtrière!*'

Gould looked impatiently to Catlin. 'What did she say?'

'She asked God to forgive her,' the doctor said quietly, 'for giving birth to a murderess.'

CHAPTER SEVENTEEN

The night of the first of December brought a snowfall that covered London with a mantle of pure white. The day dawned sunny, however, which meant that the lanes would soon turn to slush; but for now Betsy Brand and Jane Rowe, walking down to Dorset Gardens in the morning, could admire the beauty of it. Before them the river sparkled in the sunlight, which was also reflected from the cupola above the Duke's Theatre.

'Let's hope that's a good sign,' Jane said, pulling her bertha about her. 'Not that I'm much of a one for omens,' she glanced round. 'Talking of that, it's quiet without old Palmer shouting at us, is it not?'

'So it is.' Betsy thought of the incorrigible ranter, recalling his wild stare. 'I heard he'd left the suburbs. Do you know where he's gone?'

'Taken up a new pitch by St Paul's,' Jane told her. 'Do you know they're going to blow up the ruins with gunpowder, and build it all anew? They're even talking about a monument, to mark where the Fire started,' she sighed. 'With all this rebuilding, I won't recognize the old place.'

Betsy took her arm, and together they walked to the theatre's side door. There were many footprints in the churned-up snow, showing that others had arrived ahead of them. But beside the doorway, a newly pasted sign stopped both women in their tracks.

'The Forced Marriage, or the Jealous Bridegroom.' Jane read the words out slowly. 'A tragicomedy by the celebrated poet, Mistress Aphra Behn.' She turned to Betsy.

'Do you know about this?'

Betsy shook her head. Without further word the two went indoors, to find a scene of cheerful disorder. At first Betsy assumed she had misjudged the time, and come late. But glancing up at the forestage, she saw no actors, only painters working busily on the screens. From behind the stage came the thud of carpenters' hammers. But here in the pit actors and hirelings were milling about, talking animatedly. Heads turned as the two women entered, though to Betsy many of the faces were unfamiliar. Then a figure emerged from the throng.

'Mistress Brand, and Mistress Rowe . . . how delightful!'

Aveline Hale looked radiant in a dress of indigo silk. The skirt was divided to reveal an embroidered underskirt of pale lilac, while the ruffled chemise sleeves were of fine lace. Her hair had been dressed in side-curls, and on her head was a net of little jewels.

To both women's surprise, Aveline offered her cheek. When they had kissed she stepped back with a smile, which was devoid of mockery. 'My dears, I'm come only to take farewell of the Duke's Company,' she gushed. 'For I shall not walk upon the stage . . . ever again!'

Jane threw a glance at Betsy. 'You mean—'

'I mean my life has turned in a more . . . a more fitting direction.' Mistress Hale looked at Betsy, and tapped her cheek with her small fan. 'I'll not elaborate just now — all will become clear!' And the woman moved off. Betsy turned to Jane with raised eyebrows, but there came a male voice from above her head.

'Mistress Brand!'

William Daggett was on the forestage, in his shirt sleeves. He hurried to the steps, descended, and came towards her.

'It cheers me to see you.' The man's moustache looked as fearsome as ever, but his smile was warm. Indeed, a deal of strain seemed to have been lifted from him since Betsy had last seen him, poring over the costume of the murdered Joseph Rigg. That was almost a fortnight ago, and it seemed even longer. In the intervening days, Louise Colporteur had been confined in Newgate, then hanged with little ceremony before the prison gate. It was said that a great crowd had gathered to see the event, but that at sight of the prisoner — a slip of a girl in white, wearing a silver crucifix — they fell strangely silent. By the following morning her body had disappeared. The rumour was that Madeleine Colporteur had also vanished, supposedly returning to France.

'I said, will you come and take a glass with me?' Daggett was standing before Betsy, who pulled herself out of her reverie. She summoned a smile and nodded.

'You too, mistress,' the man said to Jane. 'There's a bottle of sack in the scene-room. I've told the new men to keep their thieving hands off it.'

'New men?' Jane enquired.

'Will Small won't be coming back, which is no surprise after what happened,' Daggett paused, shaking his head. 'Silas Gunn's for a quiet life too, he'll only stay till Christmas. But by then the ones I've hired will be fit for their tasks. I've set the old man to teach them.'

He gestured to the two women to follow him to the scene-room. Outside, the din of conversation continued.

'What's this play, *The Forced Marriage*?' Jane Rowe asked him as they entered the comparative gloom. 'No one's said aught to me.'

Daggett found his bottle, and held out two mugs. 'Betterton will be here soon,' he answered as he poured out the sack. 'And Mistress Mary too. You'd best hear it from them. But I'll say this: it's the first time I've stage managed a play writ by a woman!'

Jane glanced at Betsy, who was looking thoughtful. 'I've heard of Mistress Behn,' she said after a moment. 'They say she's one of the cleverest women in London.'

Daggett's moustache twitched sharply. Fixing Betsy with a sober look, he said: 'Then you and she'll be well suited, mistress, and that's no flattery. For it was you, and the good Doctor Catlin, that solved those terrible crimes between you, maybe even delivered us from further catastrophe!'

'Oh, flap-sauce, Mr Daggett,' Betsy said, embarrassed. 'I think you exaggerate.'

'I don't.'

Jane was gazing at her. 'Now it's become clear who did what.' She raised her mug. 'You've earned the thanks of us all, Betsy dear. And I for one will make sure everyone knows it!'

So the two women clinked mugs with each other, and with William Daggett. And soon after, the stage manager was called away. They were about to leave the scene-room when there came footsteps from the direction of the Men's Shift. Turning, they saw a portly figure descending the stairs. Downes the prompter faltered when he saw who was there, then puffed himself up and strode across the bare boards.

'Are you well, Mistress Brand?' he asked gruffly. 'You know you're to take second billing, after Mistress Betterton?'

'Am I?' Betsy raised her eyebrows.

'So I understand.' Downes glanced at Jane, who gave him a sly look. 'You'll have to mind your manners then, Mr Downes,' she said with a smile. When the man bristled, she added: 'Since it seems the playmaker's a woman too. I'll bet a crown she's written a few good roles — for us harpies!'

Downes opened his mouth, then closed it abruptly. With a sniff, he moved off and disappeared by the forestage door.

Betsy and Jane looked at each other, and started to laugh: the day seemed to be getting better and better. And having drained their mugs, the two ventured into the pit to mingle with their fellows.

And it was indeed a day of new beginnings, one that enabled those of the Duke's Company who had lived through the terrible reign of the Salamander — and that of his lover, whom they had known as Louise Hawker — to turn their faces to the future. There were new actors now, hired by Betterton to take roles in *The Forced Marriage*. And with a lighter heart Betsy moved among them, offering greetings and gathering further news as she went. Mistress Behn, now talked of as one of the brightest new playmakers in London, would attend rehearsals, and she had indeed written some fine parts for the actresses. Betterton and his wife would have leading roles, Mistress Mary having been persuaded, with great reluctance, to take to the stage once again. Betsy heard this from Silas Gunn, who emerged from behind the stage to greet her.

'It's like a dark cloud has passed, Mistress,' the old man said, peering at her through rheumy eyes. 'Tom Cleeve and Josh Small, killed with poisoned pins — not to mention Mr Rigg. And poor Mr Prout stabbed to death — who could've imagined such?' Silas shook his white head. 'It's why I got to thinking, while I was sitting at home. I've been doing this long enough. I'm for the hop fields in Kent, where I grew up.' He gazed into the distance for a moment, then smiled.

'You'll wish me well, won't you mistress?'

'I will, Silas,' she replied. 'And I'll never forget how you were my protector that day, when we walked the length of Turnmill Street and the women mocked you for my *rum cull*.'

Silas searched her face for signs of mockery, but found none. Instead, Betsy startled the old man by taking his face in her hands and planting a kiss on his mouth. Then she walked off, leaving him speechless.

* * *

Thomas Betterton and his wife arrived soon after, and the company gathered about them. But it was soon clear that their leading player was not in a festive humour, and in her heart, Betsy was glad of it. For at last she knew that the storm was over, and the company could resume work with renewed strength. She stood near the forefront of the little crowd of actors, more than a score of them, and listened as her old mentor spoke of the tasks that lay ahead. Briskly, he introduced John Downes to the newcomers, and gave instructions as to how the parts for *The Forced Marriage* would be distributed. Betterton and Mistress Mary would play the principal couple, and rehearsals would begin at once. So without further ceremony, the man wished everyone success, and moved aside to speak with his wife. But Betsy was not entirely surprised when Mistress Mary caught her eye, indicating that she should join them.

Then having remembered something, Betterton turned back to the company and raised his hands for another announcement: the King himself, he said, had expressed interest in coming to see the new play!

In a mood of some excitement the actors drifted away, though some, like Betsy and Jane, exchanged wry looks. Betsy followed the Bettertons up the stairs. Together they climbed to a side box, where she was invited to sit.

'Well, my dear,' Mary Betterton put on a broad smile, 'with all the excitement there has been, I confess I've not had a moment to speak with you. Perhaps you've heard that Mistress Hale is quitting the Duke's Company?'

'I have, mistress,' Betsy answered. 'And it seems I'm to take second billing to you. I'm most honoured.'

Mary Betterton blinked, seemingly unsure whether or not sarcasm was intended. Quickly her husband changed the subject.

'Have you heard about Samuel Tripp?' he asked. 'It appears the man's luck has quite deserted him. Of course, it was through no fault of ours that we were unable to play *The Virtuous Bawd* again, and that as a result he never got his benefit night. But what happened thereafter is entirely of his own making!' The great man paused for dramatic effect, then went on: 'He was caught in a compromising position in the rooms of a certain Mistress Ann Roose, by St James's Park. Caught I should add, by a personage known to us all, who deputizes for the Master of the Revels.'

Betsy blinked. 'You mean, Mistress Roose was Lord Caradoc's—'

'Precisely so,' her mentor nodded. 'The result of this ill-tempered encounter being that Mr Tripp has wisely taken himself out of London, no doubt to seek an audience for his plays elsewhere. As for Mistress Roose, she was last seen with her maid, the two of them loaded down with baggage and, somewhat tearful, boarding a hackney coach in the Haymarket!'

'Thomas, that's quite enough tittle-tattle,' Mistress Mary said dryly. 'The matter is,' she said to Betsy, 'we both wanted you to know that we are not ungrateful for your efforts these past weeks. You and Doctor Catlin, I should say.'

'I can claim little of the credit, Mistress,' Betsy said mildly. 'Others, like Doctor Catlin's servant, did much.'

Below, voices and the din of carpenters' hammers drifted from backstage. In the pit, Downes was conferring importantly with Daggett. But Betsy's thoughts turned to those who had played a part, unwittingly or otherwise, in the terrible series of events: the villainous Dart, who paid with his life; the slippery Daniels, who had vanished without trace; and Peg, who had looked death in the face alongside Betsy. She glanced up, to see Mary Betterton was rising from her seat.

'We'll talk again,' the actress said shortly. 'Perhaps when we are called to practise our first scene together.' And with a nod, she made her way out of the box. As her muffled footsteps descended the stair, Betterton turned to Betsy.

'She only wants the best for the Duke's,' he said somewhat lamely. 'She always has.'

Only now did Betsy notice the carelines on the man's face. Of course, she should have realized how the Salamander's murderous spree must have distressed the man these past weeks. The deaths of Joseph Rigg and James Prout, not to mention Cleeve and Small . . .

'*The Forced Marriage* will be a great success,' she said, managing a smile. 'I'm certain of it!'

'It has to be,' Betterton sighed. 'Or we are finished.'

He looked away, but Betsy knew how to distract him. 'Now,' she said in a businesslike tone, 'might this be the moment to enquire whether my wages will rise, with my new status?'

The other frowned. 'Let's see how well the new play does, shall we?'

'Second billing!' Betsy wagged a finger at him. 'I think I should get twenty-five shillings.'

'What!' Betterton's jaw fell. 'That's preposterous!'

'And Mistress Rowe,' Betsy went on. 'Surely she deserves some reward for the loyalty she has shown to the company while the theatre was closed. Many would have taken their skills to Killigrew—'

'Enough!' Betterton exploded. 'You try me to the limits, Mistress Firebrand!'

Betsy smiled. 'Shall we say twenty shillings, then?'

In spite of himself, her mentor gave a sudden shout of laughter. 'I thank God for my periwig,' he said. 'For none can see how you've greyed my hair beneath it!'

Whereupon Betsy seized the moment. 'There's another matter that's been troubling me,' she began, causing the other to blow out his cheeks.

'Then you'd best broach it now,' he cried, 'before I throw myself down the gallery stairs!'

But Betsy was serious. 'Hannah Cleeve — Tom's widow — you remember you sent me with money for her. I was wondering—'

Betterton frowned. 'You think I should send her more?'

'Well, I'm sure it would be welcome, for she has children to keep,' Betsy told him. 'But it would be better if you could find her some work.'

'What sort of work?' the other enquired suspiciously.

'We need a new tiring-maid, don't we?'

'I suppose so,' Betterton allowed. 'But is the woman skilled with needle and thread?' Then before Betsy could answer, he added dryly: 'Not that it's the prime requisite! When I think upon the character of our previous maid, that cringing little sparrow whom we all misjudged so badly, perhaps a robust temperament's more apt. That and the ability not to be shocked by foul language, or troubled by the sight of men in their undress. Do you still think Mistress Cleeve will serve?'

'I'm certain she will,' Betsy answered, and favoured him with her sweetest smile yet.

* * *

At midday when rehearsals ceased, Lord Caradoc paid an unexpected visit to the theatre.

It was not a formal entrance. With a single manservant in attendance, His Lordship appeared at the side door and lingered there while the man went backstage, calling for Mr Betterton. Betsy and Jane, who were sitting on one of the pit benches sharing a pippin pie, rose to make their curtseys, to which Caradoc responded in perfunctory fashion. When Betterton appeared the two men went off for private conversation. A quarter of an hour later Betterton saw the other man to the door, but signalled to Betsy that His Lordship wished to see her. So with a glance at Jane, she got up and walked over. Caradoc gestured to her to follow him outside.

'Mistress Brand.' His smile was as winning as ever. Betsy stood blinking in the sunlight, all the brighter for being reflected off snow, then realized His Lordship was pointing. 'It's somewhat chilly for standing about,' he said. 'Would you care to step into my coach?'

Betsy looked at the magnificent coach which stood in the lane. Its four coal-black horses were blowing and stamping in the cold, their manes and tails tied up in red ribbon.

Caradoc's coachman was already holding the door open, whereupon Betsy turned to His Lordship with a questioning look. 'What is it you propose, my lord?' she asked. 'A journey, or something else?'

Caradoc raised an eyebrow. 'I wished merely to speak with you,' he answered. 'Yet if you prefer to go back indoors . . .'

After a moment, Betsy drew her whisk about her shoulders and walked to the coach.

The inside was warm, the cushioned seats soft. Caradoc followed her inside, pulling the door shut. He sat opposite Betsy, removed his plumed hat and threw it down.

'Well, my dear,' he gazed at her frankly. 'You've had quite an adventure, haven't you?'

When Betsy said nothing, he continued in a conversational tone: 'I thought you might care to hear some news about the Frenchwoman, Madame Colporteur. She has returned to France with the body of her daughter, so that she may be buried in the Catholic manner.'

'How do you know this, my lord?' Betsy asked in surprise.

'I'm well acquainted with Sir Anthony Griffiths,' His Lordship answered. 'When I learned the whole tale I sought him out, and the two of us came to an agreement. It was through Sir Anthony's good offices that the woman was able to leave.'

So, Sir Anthony had paid the woman off, once again. Betsy met Caradoc's eye. 'Well,' she said, 'now that all matters have been despatched, perhaps we may return to normality.'

'Indeed.' His Lordship smiled at her, — and Betsy was quickly on her guard. 'I would guess, my lord,' she murmured, 'that you haven't brought me here merely to tell me this.'

Caradoc's smile widened, and before Betsy knew what was happening, she found his hand upon her knee. 'My dear,' his voice was soft, 'you are wasted in the seething cauldron of the theatre. Surely you know that?'

'It's my life,' Betsy began, but an impatient look crossed the other's face.

'How much do you know of Mistress Behn?' he asked abruptly. 'Do you know, for example, that she was employed on intelligence work by His Majesty, during the last Dutch war?'

The coach windows were steaming up, Betsy noticed. Surprised, she merely shook her head.

'I tell you this in confidence,' Caradoc went on. 'Yet I'm sure you can see that the skills a woman of the theatre possesses may be turned to other uses?'

Betsy looked down at the man's hand, which still rested on her knee. After a moment he withdrew it, but his smile remained. 'I know you have ventured abroad in disguise, into environs dangerous to one of your sex,' he said. 'The Bermudas, for example, even the bagnio.'

Betsy chided herself for her naivety. Of course, there was little that happened about London and its suburbs that the wily Caradoc did not hear about.

'You're well informed, my lord,' she said.

'I have to be,' the other answered. 'Though for the present I fill the office of Master of the Revels, there are other calls upon my loyalty to my King, which is why I ask you now whether you might consider using your considerable skills in the service of your country.'

A dozen thoughts flew about in Betsy's head, but one soon took precedence: that still Caradoc wanted more from her. Then it dawned: the man had recently cast his mistress out of her rooms. Was he inviting Betsy to take the woman's place?

She drew a breath. 'You've given me much to think on, my lord,' she said. 'I ask you to give me time to consider . . .'

'Of course,' Caradoc was smiling again. 'But I pray you, don't take too long. The world moves on, Mistress, turn and turn about.' Suddenly he raised his hand and rubbed at the window with his lace cuff. Following his gaze, Betsy was startled to see a mass of indigo and lilac advancing towards the coach.

She turned to Caradoc. 'It's Mistress Hale,' she began, then broke off. For His Lordship had risen and was throwing open the coach door. The next moment he had jumped to the ground and was taking the hand of Aveline Hale, who smiled broadly at him . . . and at once Betsy understood.

'Buffle-head!' she called herself. Not only had she misread the man's intentions, but she had failed to guess what was afoot. She got up and alighted from the coach, so hastily she almost slipped over in the snow.

'Betsy Brand?' Aveline gazed at her in astonishment. 'What were you doing in there?' Then she looked sharply at Caradoc, who was wearing a sickly smile.

'I had some private theatre business with Mistress Brand, my dear,' he answered smoothly. 'We'll not detain her any longer.' He turned to Betsy, who read the warning look in his eye. 'I look forward to watching your performance, mistress,' he said. 'Now pray, return to your duties.'

There was an icy moment while Aveline Hale's eyes bored into Betsy's. Then with a flounce, the woman turned to Caradoc. 'Will you drive me to St James's now, sir?' she asked coolly. 'I yearn to see my new rooms.'

Still smiling, Caradoc took her hand and helped her into the coach. And he did not look round, as with a wry smile Betsy walked back into the theatre.

EPILOGUE

A few days later, after the most exhausting rehearsals the Duke's Company could remember, *The Forced Marriage* opened to a packed theatre. To the delight of every member of the company, from veterans to newcomers, it was a great success. It ran for six days, enabling the authoress Mistress Behn to garner the rare reward of not one benefit performance, but two. By the sixth and final afternoon there was an air of jubilation both on stage and off, as the company took their bows to enthusiastic applause. A talented new playmaker — who happened to be female — had arrived. She stood in the wings, a good-looking woman of about thirty years, acknowledging the cheers with a smile. Then, as the orchestra struck up, she moved out of sight to await the visitors who would surge backstage.

For Betsy Brand, weaving through the throng with a cup of claret in her hand, it was a time of relief rather than of euphoria. She had seen enough of Mistress Behn during rehearsals to form a good opinion of her, and to feel sure that the woman's relationship with the Bettertons boded well. Moreover, she had fashioned a play that poked fun at the custom of arranged marriage — and from a woman's viewpoint. No bad thing, Betsy mused; and in better heart than she had been for weeks she sought out Jane Rowe, the two of them retiring to a corner. But it was only now, having seen little of her friend since before the performance, that Betsy saw how low in spirits Jane was. And quickly she guessed the reason.

'I try not to think on him much, as a rule,' Jane told her. 'It's easier here, with all there is to do.' She gave a sigh, and drained her cup. 'But now and then it wells up and near knocks me flat. Five months now, Mr Cobus Hall — the rogue who stole my heart easy as he'd swipe an orange — has been clapped up in the Fleet. And he's no nearer to clearing his debts than he was when he went in!'

'Think on your new wage,' Betsy said, taking Jane's hand. 'And with mine increased, I could lend you a sum . . . perhaps Betterton would even advance you a little. Put all that together, and—'

'And it'd still fall short,' Jane broke in. She sighed again, letting her eye wander over the noisy press of actors, hangers-on and freeloaders here for the drink. 'My Cobus never did anything by halves,' she said. 'When he won at cards or dice, there'd be a new whisk for me or even a new dress, supper at Lockett's, and a coach home.' She sniffed, which was the closest she ever came to tears. 'And when he lost—'

'He lost in high style too,' Betsy finished. She looked away, trying to think how to help her friend. It was never easy to prise someone out of the debtor's prison, but surely some way could be found? Then all at once she stiffened, as her eyes fell on two new arrivals: Lord Caradoc, with Aveline Hale on his arm, was entering the scene-room. There was a brief lull in the chatter as heads turned, men bowed and women made their curtseys. Aveline's obvious pleasure in her new status caused more than one smirk before people resumed their conversations. But Betsy had had an idea.

'I'll leave you for a while, Jane dear,' she said. 'There's someone I should speak with.' And quickly she began making her way across the crowded scene-room towards His Lordship. A few minutes later she managed to catch the eye of the man, who was at once alert. He spoke briefly to Aveline, who was enjoying the attention of two or three young actors new to the company and, leaving her side, moved to join Betsy. But as he drew near, he startled her by bending to her ear.

'I hope you have an answer for me, Mistress,' he said. 'I'm not a man who likes being kept waiting.'

Maintaining a smile, Betsy addressed His Lordship through his immense golden periwig. 'It's not a matter to decide on lightly, my lord,' she whispered. 'Yet after further consideration, I believe I may soon be able to reach a decision.'

Caradoc struggled to conceal his annoyance. 'You mean you still haven't done so? Why in heaven's name not?'

'You press me too hard, sir,' Betsy countered. 'There's much to weigh up. Surely, when you ask a woman to risk her life, she may be permitted a period of reflection?'

'Oh, very well.' Caradoc sighed. 'Take longer if you will, then send word to me. A simple token will serve.'

'My lord,' widening her smile, Betsy seized her chance. 'First, there's a matter I must put before you. My dearest friend needs help, and I'm certain you're the man to provide it. Few others have your skills at diplomacy, not to mention your influence—'

'Flattery's a poor tool even in your hands, Mistress Brand,' the other answered dryly. 'Come to the point, if you please.'

So quickly Betsy outlined Jane Rowe's difficulty in a few sentences. When she had finished, she took a draught of claret and waited. But if Caradoc was irritated by the request he managed to conceal it. After a moment he turned to go, giving Betsy a moment's anxiety, as she knew he intended to. But before leaving, he bent his head to her once more.

'I'll promise nothing,' he muttered. 'Yet if you'll take my handling of this matter as proof of my good will, I'll assume I may in time count upon your gratitude in return. Do we have an understanding?'

'Of course, my lord.' Betsy allowed her gaze to drift towards Aveline Hale, who still held court across the room. 'And my discretion in your affairs, as always, remains undiminished. How is Lady Arabella, by the way?'

Caradoc's eyes flicked to Aveline. Then summoning a thin smile he moved away, to be swallowed up in the throng. Whereupon Betsy let out a long breath, and went to tell Jane the good news.

* * *

Night was drawing in when she returned home to Fire's Reach Court. There was a light in the window, and a warm feeling stole over her as she entered the hallway, closing the street door behind her. Tom Catlin's bag lay by the wall, and there was a promising smell of roast fowl from the kitchen. In the parlour, she found the doctor in his old bombazine coat, reading *The London Gazette*. He glanced up.

'I see that in spite of themselves, men of letters approve of Mistress Behn's play,' he said. 'Even the Poet Laureate.'

'I thought you gave a fine performance,' Catlin went on, as Betsy acknowledged the compliment. 'Assuming it was a performance.' He frowned. 'It's somewhat hard to know these days when you're acting and when you're not.'

Betsy looked blank. 'I wonder what you mean?'

'I speak not of your recent roles outside the theatre, Mistress Rummager,' he answered. 'Merely that you seem to inhabit the part of an indignant young woman so effortlessly, I felt it had been written especially for you.'

'Well, it wasn't,' Betsy told him peevishly, and sat down tiredly. She knew that Catlin had attended the performance at the Duke's: he had promised to, and he was a man who kept his promises.

'I'm glad you enjoyed the play,' she said. 'I wouldn't want you to feel you didn't get your money's worth. You could have had a free glass of claret too, if you'd troubled yourself to come to the scene-room afterwards.'

Catlin nodded soberly. 'I thought it best to accompany Peg home afterwards,' he replied. 'She was fretting about the supper. We've a couple of good capons, and some anchovies.'

Betsy's eyebrows went up. 'Peg came too?'

'She threatened to burn the supper for the rest of the week, if I didn't take her,' Catlin said. 'What was I to do?'

Now Betsy felt a smile coming on. 'That's not much of a threat,' she observed. 'More like an average week.'

Too late, she heard footsteps outside. The door flew back and there was Peg, hands on hips, hair sticking out like a poorly thatched roof. It struck Betsy then that Mistress Brazier might forge a career on the stage herself, in comic roles, perhaps.

'I'd moderate your voice if I were you,' Peg said acidly, 'when you insult folk behind their backs. Else they're likely to take it amiss!'

Catlin cleared his throat. 'We'll have supper, I think,' he said.

Peg sniffed. 'Burned or raw? I wouldn't want to disappoint.'

'Neither,' Catlin retorted. 'And those who eavesdrop behind doors hear what they deserve to hear!'

But Peg snapped her head towards Betsy — too late for her to remove her smile. The two women exchanged looks. But this time it was Peg whose face softened.

'You weren't bad in that role,' she said.

'I thank you,' Betsy replied. 'I wouldn't want to disappoint, either.'

She leaned back in her chair, stifling a yawn. Peg turned and stalked out, her footfalls receding towards the kitchen. Catlin picked up his paper.

The fire crackled, and Betsy found herself staring into it. Then she blinked: for a moment, she fancied that she saw a dark shape in the flames, spotted with livid orange, rising up as if it would leap out on to the hearth. Then gradually it shrank, and finally disappeared altogether.

She turned away, and watched Tom Catlin reading his paper. Then she closed her eyes, and fell asleep.

THE END

ALSO BY JOHN PILKINGTON

THE BETSY BRAND MYSTERIES
Book 1: AFTER THE FIRE
Book 2: THE JUDAS BLADE

Don't miss the latest John Pilkington release, join our mailing list:

www.joffebooks.com

Printed in Dunstable, United Kingdom

65192107R00122